THE CYCLIST

FRED NATH

FINGERPRESS LTD
LONDON

The Cyclist

ISBN (pbk): 978-0-9564925-1-7

Printed and bound in the United Kingdom by Fingerpress Ltd.
First Edition.

Production Editor: Matt Stephens
Production Manager: Michelle Stephens
Copy Editor: Madeleine Horobin
Editorial Assistant: Artica Ham

www.fingerpress.co.uk

For

Joanne Gillespie and my daughter Lara.

They both published before me.

Acknowledgement

Thanks to Ashley Stokes without whose help I would never have begun.

NOTE TO THE READER

I wrote *The Cyclist* as a tribute to the brave men and women of France who fought so valiantly to protect and preserve their culture and their homeland during the German occupation. We should never forget their courage, loyalty, and determination. It has never been my intention to be anti-German, only anti-Nazi in my character portrayals. The present population of that country, whom I know to be both kind and hospitable, have nothing to do with any characters portrayed here.

All characters and the physical resemblances to people in this book are entirely fictitious. In common with many writers of fiction, I have taken the liberty of tweaking both timelines and history to suit my story. If it offends, I humbly apologise.

I have based the geographical setting upon my own sojourns in the Dordogne Valley, a wonderful place, unsullied and green as it is. The references to various wines and their quality I stand by because they are genuine. Truly, France has the best wines in the world.

The main character represented to me a question that, despite the passage of time, remains unanswered, of how Christians could stand by, witnessing a Jewish genocide let alone collaborate with one. What did they feel? This is my answer to that question and I hope it will give enjoyment in the answering.

The premise? A search for absolution.

*Le Chant des Partisans

Ami, entends-tu le vol noir des corbeaux sur nos plaines?
Ami, entends-tu ces cris sourds du pays qu'on enchaîne?
Ohé partisans, ouvriers et paysans, c'est l'alarme!
Ce soir l'ennemi connaîtra le prix du sang et des larmes.

The Song of the Partisans

Friend, do you hear the crows' dark flight over our plains?
Friend, do you hear the muffled cries of the country being shackled?
Ahoy! Resistants, labourers and farmers, the alarm has sounded!
Tonight the enemy shall know the price of blood and tears.

PROLOGUE

London, 2010

Curtains opened and closed seeking furtive revelation from across the road. A driver slowed as he passed, staring at the BBC logo on the Ford Transit van standing parked at a slight angle to the kerb. An elusive sun slipped behind a white summer cloud as the crew brought up their equipment. They waited at the green front door of a semi-detached house in Blackheath while the presenter rang the doorbell.

An elderly woman, curly grey hair and sagging breasts, opened the door in response to the summons and without smiling, she stepped back to allow them entry. She proffered a liver-spotted hand and the leader of the crew shook it with both of his for a moment too long, as if to dominate, to accentuate his mastery.

'Mrs Ran-Davis? It is very kind of you to allow us to interview you —and in your own home too.'

'I told your producer it would be all right,' she said, her voice sounding cracked and tired already. 'Come this way.'

She led the way into a comfortable front room, lit by a bay window and separated from the dining room by glazed doors.

'Yes, I wonder if I could trouble you to sign the disclaimer. Only a formality, you understand.'

Her hand shook as she took the ballpoint from his hand. The signature was quivery and crenulated too when he examined it. She looked up at his face and he smiled the counterfeit smile of the media-man.

He glanced at the mantel, the photographs in their wooden frames, the china duck on the corner. The gas fire, black and cold, stared back at him like a guard dog, ready for action but quiescent now in the summer sunshine. Another story, another film. To him she was now a device, to be placed, positioned and nudged. Nudged into conversation, pushed into revelations and recorded, saved and archived. He possessed no particular feelings about her or her story but he knew where his money came from and it was enough. He had no time either. It was ten-thirty and there was a luncheon appointment with another war victim to consider. He felt as if he was drowning in victim-speak today. Time was short.

'Would you sit over there please?'

He guided her into a chair with both hands on her arms as if she might escape. There was a background now of plain pale-green wallpaper and he pictured how it would look on the screen. The telephone stood on a three-legged table next to the chair. It looked dusty, as if no one had used it for a long time, perhaps not since his producer telephoned and requested an interview. Next to the phone was a gilt metal cap-badge, worn and old, like the woman who sat beside the table.

Her voice tremulous, she said, 'This is for a documentary?'

'Yes. The BBC is interviewing a number of you French war survivors.'

'Before it's too late?'

'Of course not. We're not ghouls you know.' He chuckled then said, 'it's because we're making a documentary on the war and certain aspects of the German occupation and the Vichy French are of interest at the moment.'

'My husband always said I should have written it down, you know.'

'He did?'

'Yes, he said it was an heroic story.'

'Heroic?'

'Yes. My father...'

She seemed to stop then. A vacancy came over her grey eyes and she stared out through the window until a warm breeze took the net curtain and its gentle movement seemed to animate her. She was old, but felt no hint of bitterness, for there were memories stirring now, ones making her smile a wistful little smile. Her face was a mass of wrinkles, her teeth brown and stained and she wore an inappropriate flowery dress, like some young woman. It was her best and she wore it today in memory of someone she once loved as only a child can love but she would not tell these strangers that. They would not understand.

'Memories. Memories, you see,' she said.

'Stop there a moment would you? We need to get the camera set up. Would you look straight at the camera during the interview please?' he turned to the bearded cameraman, 'George darling, would you be ever so good and position it here. Jimmy, keep the mike up this time will you, we don't want a fluffy appearing at the top of the frame.'

He pointed to a place on the round, threadbare rug between the window and the object. The old woman sat with no trace of impatience, her hands folded in her lap.

'OK there is it?' he said. 'Right. We can start in a moment. I'll ask a few questions about the war and you look at the camera when you speak. Don't look at me.'

He turned and smiled at the cameraman. 'George, are you ready? We'll do the noddies later. No need to take up too much of this dear lady's time eh?'

Turning to his subject he said, 'You escaped from France during the war. What was your home country like in those days?'

'I didn't know much about the politics. I was only nine. I can tell you about my father though. In a way, it is his story. My mother told me many times. It was to keep his memory alive you understand.'

'Your father?'

'Yes, he was a policeman.'

'Vichy French?'

'Yes, but he was different.'

'Different?'

'Yes, he was a good man.'

'There are many who might disagree with that. The Vichy police collaborated with the Germans, didn't they?'

'Some did, no, most did. My father was not like them. He was naive at first, we all were. But we learned in time.'

'Carry on.'

'Do you think it is always like that? Clever, evil people lie and inveigle themselves and in the end, you don't know who is good and who is bad?'

'Well, it's your story, not mine. Start at the beginning. What was your first memory of the war?'

'No, I'll tell you about my father and you can judge. He was a good policeman. That was why they kept him on, the Germans I mean...'

CHAPTER ONE

Bergerac, February 1943

1

Dusk. Grey slats of cloud lay suspended above Bergerac's town square. Auguste Ran, Assistant Chief of Police, stood at the window of his office in the Prefecture; he was reminiscing. His thoughts made him frown as he looked out. He watched as the cold sunset shed its bloodshot light on the scene below. The waning rays of light filtered through the naked, brown elm branches around the square's periphery, weaving restless, lengthening patterns, seeming to deny the hope of a forthcoming spring.

A lone cyclist crossing below caught his attention. Auguste recognised the man with irritation because he should not have been there. The man bore the yellow Star of David sewn on the right arm of his coat, in testimony of his faith. Jews were subject to curfew after five o'clock and cycling past the Sub-Prefecture could only be a gesture of defiance. It must have been hard for the Jews now but he also knew they had it good before the First War and he at times half-believed the concept they were responsible for this second disastrous conflict, bringing down his country, perhaps even questioning his faith. Of course, he was not anti-Semitic, how could he be? His best friend as he grew up was a Jew. He understood how some of his countrymen reasoned, that was all.

For Auguste, the cyclist with his simple act of disobedience was symptomatic of the hopelessness and anger experienced now by everyone around him. He knew this man very well, but he would not have talked openly to him in the street. They had known each other since they were boys, yet somehow Auguste's life had changed so much, he could no longer greet some of his oldest friends out-of-doors even if he wished to. If an informer or soldier should see him, they might report it. If the occupying forces apprehended Pierre on his bicycle, Auguste knew it would mean internment for his friend and his friend's daughter Monique. Auguste had no appetite for more of the persecution his job seemed to be perpetrating on even his old friends. He had seen enough of it already, he reflected, as the cyclist disappeared from view.

The grey cobbles, dull and worn, seemed almost to stare back at Auguste, their emptiness taunting him with memories of happier days. Days of bustling markets in bright sunshine. Days of laughter and coffee in the open-air café next door. Duck breasts, pink, plump and succulent; foie gras, accordion music and clinking wineglasses—all gone now. In those days, before the Germans came, the farmers could afford grain to feed their ducks and geese. In those days, they had plenty to sell and there was always a sense of prosperity in the town. The elm-bordered market square, silent now, seemed to Auguste a dull mirror to these disconsolate feelings arising within him.

He was not a man to embrace the past from habit, but the events of the last few years forced him to look back at his pre-war life with a heartbreaking nostalgia. Auguste smiled, recalling a scene from those "old days". He was a young policeman then and as in all his memories of those times, the sun was shining. Off-duty, he sat in the café on the square under a bright red and blue striped parasol, he ate a salad with walnuts and duck gizzards, oil and vinegar. He could almost smell the balsamic odours, recall the taste of the Rosé and how it mingled with the flavours in his mouth. His superior pointed over his shoulder across the square and they shared a joke. What was it? Something to do with promotion? His memory seemed clouded, he was forgetting. It was a long time ago, a time of happiness and so details were out of mind.

He had worked in the City Police Force for over twenty years now, but in his early days, he was not ambitious and never sought promotion; it just happened. His precise police work and his tenacity investigating cases drew him to the attention of his superiors and so the elevation of rank came uninvited. It might have been that murder case when the murderer, a farmer, hid the body under a hay-stack. If Auguste had not brought his Scottie dog with him the seventh time he questioned the man, he might not have found it. It had been the dog's constant fascination with the yellow hay-pile alerting him, which led to his finding the body.

He did well out of the case; it was widely publicised. The town acknowledged his abilities too. Auguste knew he was a good investigator and experience now gave him an edge. He also knew he was too emotional for the job, as Odette, his wife, often told him. Auguste felt sorry for the murderer's wife at the time and her subsequent suicide shocked and depressed him. She was shunned and castigated by everyone but there was nothing he could do for her and he knew it. Those feelings blunted his triumph and made it all a hollow victory when they discovered her body hanging by the neck from a rafter in the barn.

The German occupation was changing his role and every aspect of his life changed with it. Auguste felt like a man on a treadmill who discovers he is only marking time but has long since ceased to care. His existence in the Vichy police was taking him nowhere now and he knew it. He was a second-class bureaucrat in the eyes of the German administration and nothing more. It was as if he spent the last ten years blinkered not seeing what was coming when it was obvious to everyone in the rest of Europe. At first, with the defeat, he felt shocked, threatened. Before it happened he trusted the Maginot line, he thought the Government knew how to defend the country. Disillusionment came when the Germans entered Paris and he wondered what would become of his wife and family; he feared for his life. The family felt tempted to flee like so many others all over France, but Paris was a long way away and salvation came for Auguste in the end. It was Pétain, hero of the last war, who seemed to save France, save him, Odette and little Zara. He thought then the President was right; the only way forward would be to work with the Germans and God knew, how as a policeman, he tried. Policing was his job and he continued to exist within its framework. He could no more buck those traces than he could leave his beloved France.

He was a short stocky man and he wore his brown hair close-cropped in a military style. Deep crow's feet were imprinted at the sides of his grey eyes, a relic of happier days when there was much to smile about. His black uniform, threadbare but neat, was sympto-matic of stringencies as well as his own personal quest for precision and tidiness in a time of upheaval.

A knock on his door drew him away from the window and he sat down behind his desk, trying to look occupied.

'Enter,' he said.

Édith, a short plump woman of middle years entered. She had worked at the Prefecture since long before the war started. She knew everyone in the town but Auguste felt her greatest asset was her experience and her knowledge of police procedure when there were difficulties. She showed him the ropes when they first promoted him; she kept him straight afterwards and he trusted her.

She smiled a sympathetic smile and presented him with a letter. Édith had a habit of wrinkling her small, up-turned nose, which supported the gold-rimmed, half-moon spectacles through which she peered down at him.

'This came from Lyon,' she said.

'Lyon? Late in the day for messages from Lyon.'

'Jean dropped it in. He said it came by special delivery—a

motorcyclist no less. It was to be in your hands immediately.'

He took the envelope but noticed his hand betrayed a faint tremble when he saw the Prefecture emblem. It had already been opened, he assumed by Édith.

'Something more?' he said.

'No, no.'

'Édith. It was addressed to me. Maybe you should have let me open this one.'

She walked to the door but turned back as if there was more to say.

'I assumed...'

Auguste shrugged and indicated the chair.

'You've read it, so you might as well sit down and tell me what's in it. Am I in trouble?'

The office door gave a quiet click as she shut it. She returned to sit in the chair in front of the desk and crossed her legs. Her worn black suit had seen better days but no one had money these days.

'No, nothing like that. It's more Jewish business.'

'And so urgent it has to be sent at the end of the day? No doubt, they think there is going to be a Jewish uprising, a declaration of independence. Perhaps every homosexual is carrying a gun as well.'

'It's from Tulard. A special directive.'

'More work, I suppose. He should, of all people, know I have enough on my hands enforcing all the new laws. I am used to prejudice against Jews, it's been common enough here, but the Germans seem to revel in it.'

'They want all Jews rounded up and interned in Drancy,' she said.

'All Jews?'

'Yes. Will you do it?'

'But of course I will do it. It's my job. We need to cooperate with the Germans or things may get much worse for everyone. They will replace the entire Civil Administration with German Military personnel. The work we do here protects the country and the people.'

'You really believe that? You don't sound so convinced.'

He was silent. She looked at the floor.

She said, 'I...'

'What do they want all the Jews for anyway? I know they use them to work in munitions factories, but how many people do you need for such a thing? They sent twenty thousand away at the end of last year.'

'Perhaps they die and need to be replaced.'

'Die? No, Brunner told me they have good, warm accommodation and they are well fed. No, the Germans are plotting something, mark my words.'

'Brunner is unreliable. You can't believe him. '

'He's *Sicherheitspolizei*. You might find him unpleasant but he can hardly be unreliable.'

'If he was just another SD officer it wouldn't matter. He has a bad reputation.'

'Keep your voice down Édith. You've told me already. I can't believe in rumours. I am a man who needs proof, you know that.'

'I understand, but all the same he makes my flesh crawl,' she said.

'Well, I have to work with him. He's not so bad once you get to know him. He's quite the Francophile you know.'

She was silent again. A gloomy atmosphere appeared between them now and Auguste wanted to end it. He read the memo.

'You can go now.'

'There was one more thing, Auguste.'

'Yes?'

'François Dufy.'

'Not him again? What's he done now?'

'Claude arrested him.'

'What for this time?'

She smiled and said, 'He caught some rabbits. He stood outside the prefecture and was shouting for people to buy them. He was drunk.'

'Well it's no crime unless he was selling at exorbitant prices.'

'No, he was shouting they were "as fat as Göring".'

'What?'

'As fat as Göring. Claude arrested him in case the Germans heard him. He's a fool.'

'Yes, always drunk. What did Claude charge him with?'

'Disturbing the peace.'

'Well at least it wasn't for sedition. He'd be deported for that.'

'Claude wondered if we could keep him in the cells for a week and then let him out. He's harmless you know.'

Édith stood.

'Yes, yes. I hope he learns his lesson.'

'I'm going home now. The keys are on my desk.'

She opened the door again.

'Édith?'

'Yes?'

'Thank you.'

She smiled and left. The click of the door as she shut it seemed to echo in his head. Had it not been for Édith, he would have felt an utter loneliness at work. He missed the time when he was a real policeman. A solver of crimes, a true detective. And now? All he did now was persecute people he had known or to whom he had once been close. The townspeople hated him for it. He felt as if he hated himself too at times.

Without Odette to come home to, he would have left the country long ago. She kept him sane. It was a sanity he needed, for he had begun to feel the world was mad. All sense of proportion had gone, its departure leaving behind an emptiness, a potent emptiness, consuming him, spilling over into everything he saw and did.

2

Auguste pulled the door shut behind him. He sighed, as he felt in his pocket out of habit. No cigarettes. He could do with a smoke. He wished Odette was less persuasive and he was still able to smoke, but she insisted. He pictured the packet of Gitanes in his hand and the light tap, tap as he knocked the tiny fragments of tobacco from the tip. He reached the stairs and in his mind he was lighting the cigarette as he stepped down.

His thoughts were interrupted by the telephone in his office. Damn, he thought. Should he leave it? The sound was insistent; intrusive. It might be important.

He relented then and re-entered his office crossing the floor-space fast.

'Yes?'

'Auguste.'

'Major Brunner.'

'I have bad news, my friend.'

'News?'

'Someone shot Meyer, right in front of our offices, from the shoe shop.'

'Yes, I know. My men are out searching the streets, making enquiries.'

'Shot in the face. What do you think?'

'Terrible.'

'I'm afraid there will have to be consequences. I have requested assistance from the Wehrmacht. They are sending troops and will be active north of the town. I expect the killer to be found, you hear?'

'I am doing everything I can. You said the shoe shop?'

'Yes, the murderer must have been there for days. He was a professional; it would have been a difficult shot even for a German soldier. The owner unfortunately was shot trying to escape or we would know more. Looks as if the killer escaped over the roof and ran or cycled away. No one saw a car.'

'That much, my men know already. There is nothing we can do now. In the morning…'

'We need to talk anyway. I will send a car tomorrow. You know poor Meyer had a wife and two daughters?'

'No, I didn't know him well. He and I never got on.'

'I have had a very distressing phone-call. She became hysterical.'

'I'm sorry.'

'He was a very valued comrade. I will ask the Mayor to erect a statue to him. It may comfort his family to know he is still remembered for his efforts by the loyal French here.'

'A very good idea. I'm sure it will be well-received,' Auguste lied. The thought of a statue to a German SD officer adorning the market square amused him. It was ironic. He had a vague feeling it was funny. He wondered if he was becoming hysterical.

'Tomorrow then?'

Auguste said, 'Yes, perhaps we will have more news then.'

The telephone clicked off and he replaced the receiver. He stood looking at the shiny black resin machine and cursed to himself. He wondered who Brunner would choose now to run errands for him. He had never like Meyer, the man picked on people and as happens to all bullies, someone must have borne a grudge. Not surprising in a world where reprisals for one German could mean twenty innocent farmers and villagers shot.

He tapped the desk with his fingers. He slowed his breathing. He had something to do now and although he recognised it was his duty, a trace of reluctance delayed him. He felt tired and as he left the office, he sighed. It seemed to him as if he trudged up a hill and each time he reached the summit another appeared before him. There was no end to this cycle of killings, reprisals and grief. Worse still, it dragged him and his men deeper and deeper into a mire of complicity with the Germans. He had to cooperate with them but he was finding it more difficult by the minute.

3

The rain came in sheets as Auguste left the Prefecture. He nodded to the desk sergeant as he closed the tall oak door behind him. The grey, stone steps echoed to the clack of his black boots as he descended and drops of rain pattered on his flat-topped hat. He crossed the square to his battered Citroën. Squatting, he checked under the vehicle.

Finding nothing attached beneath, he got in but did not start up. He sat a moment looking straight ahead. All registered Jews. It meant hundreds of people from Bergerac alone, a mammoth task. He knew he possessed the manpower. They were never short of recruits these days, since Vichy had come to power. President Pétain ensured funding for the police continued to escalate despite the German plundering.

Twenty francs to the deutsche-mark he was thinking. It was like downgrading everything in the land. You might as well give exports away, not that there was any food to export these days. Even if food was available, the food tickets limited the quantity to a mouthful.

He pressed the starter. Nothing happened. He swore. On the fourth attempt, the Citroën coughed then began chugging. It screeched as he put it into gear. He set off, double de-clutched into second, and turned left towards the bridge. Crossing above the swirling brown waters of the Dordogne, he turned left again and hit the main Sarlat road out of town. The windscreen wipers squeaked in the rain and he could only see a short distance ahead. He knew the way well enough: he had cycled here hundreds of times in his youth.

Passing through a gateway, he drew up outside a white-rendered farmhouse. It was a large building, wooden steps leading up to the porch, a pine rocking chair soaking in the rain on the left and a pile of logs on the right of the heavy wooden door. Raindrops dripped from a mature clematis plant, growing at the end of the porch and a dog barked somewhere inside. He knocked.

Presently, a man his own age opened the door. It creaked as it came ajar.

'Huh, it's you,' Pierre said.

'Can I come in?'

'Being discreet? You wouldn't want anyone to see you visiting a Jew would you?'

'No secret. My car is here. Everyone knows my Citroën even in the dark.'

'Yes, you're the only one who can afford gasoline.'

'Well?'

'Come in then.'

Auguste entered a large room, the floorboards creaking underfoot. An intricately designed Turkish rug quietened his footfall as he approached the middle of the room. Royal Danish china decorated the dresser on the opposite wall and some matching plates adorned the wall above. To the left was a French window, the door open a crack and Auguste could see the muddy green grass falling away to a stream a hundred yards from the doorstep. Memories of two boys fishing in summer sunshine came into his head.

No fire burned in the grate and the illumination depended upon a small oil lamp set on a low table in front of a chaise-longue. Portraits hung on the walls adding an air of family history to the room. He noticed little of this, for he was familiar with this room. The roots of half his childhood memories were here, after all.

'Wine?' Pierre said.

'You have wine?'

'Yes. No law against it, is there Inspector?'

'No Pierre, no law. I just wondered how you could afford it.'

'Homemade. Have you forgotten?'

'No not forgotten, just...'

'What do you want?'

'You broke the curfew this afternoon.'

Pierre frowned. He was a tall, dark-haired man, broad in the chest and muscular. His face seemed created around his nose, with wide-spaced eyes and a broad balding forehead. Auguste pictured him laughing and could almost hear the deep cavernous sound in his head. He had not heard it for years.

'Come to arrest me have you?'

'Don't be silly. I came to warn you, that's all.'

'Warn me? Like you warned me to register at the police station? Like you warned me to wear this?'

'The yellow star is as distasteful to me as it is to you. You know that.'

'No I don't know that. You've forced so many others to wear them they must be a favourite decoration for you and your German friends.'

'I didn't come for this.'

'And what did you come for then? To gloat?'

'What did you do it for? This cycling I mean.'

'A man has to have some courage. He has to fight sometimes, not just capitulate, cooperate and collaborate like you.'

'Pierre, however much you want to fight them, you can't. Think of Monique. If the Germans had taken you today, you would both be beaten and shut up in Drancy with wrong-doers and criminals.'

'This isn't why you came,' Pierre said, pouring a glass of dark red wine. He proffered it to Auguste who took it, sniffed and sipped.

'Nice,' he said.

'It's filthy stuff. All I have. I haven't tasted a good wine since the year Murielle died. What did you come here for?'

Auguste paused and stared into the half-empty glass. He felt abandoned. He felt like a man alone in a hospital bed, surrounded by strangers, and all of them wanted him to die but he was refusing. He was a stubborn man. Looking up, he saw the candlestick on the mantel, nine candles. The photograph of a young woman in its silver frame, smiled back at him. It tugged at his memory. All those years.

'Pierre, help me. What can I do? If I refuse an order, they will throw me out, maybe even try me for treason. Odette; my little girl.'

'You come here bleating for absolution. You come here because you want me to say, "Don't worry Auguste, we still love you! Don't worry Auguste, it will be all right". Well we don't love you. It won't be alright. The Germans plan to exterminate every Jew in Germany, Poland and France. And you? You close your eyes. You talk to me about workers' camps and good conditions. You're a fool.'

'Brunner told me...'

He knew it sounded lame. He knew telling his old friend an SD officer reassured him, was of itself, a kind of proof. It demonstrated the truth of what Pierre said and the emptiness returned.

Auguste said, 'Where is Monique?'

'I sent her to Murielle's mother in Beynac. I couldn't witness the treatment she receives here any longer.'

'And then you break the curfew?'

'What have I to lose? Will you arrest me?'

'Of course not. I came to warn you.'

'Very well, you've warned me. I won't do it again, Assistant Chief of Police.'

'No. Not that. I received a memo from Lyon today. It requires all Jews to be interned in Drancy.'

'So it has begun.'

'You knew?'

'You Nazis are all so predictable. Every Jew in France has known since last year when they rounded up the Paris Jews. What did they call it? The Vel'd'hiv round up? Thirteen thousand men, women and children. Where are they now?'

'I don't know. They were deported to work camps.'

'And now all Jews go to work camps. It'll get a bit crowded won't it?' What do you think they will do with all of us?'

'I came to warn you Pierre. Nothing more. You must take Monique and go. Switzerland maybe. You can make a life there, they are neutral.'

'With no papers? With a nine-year-old? You're mad.'

'The papers may not be a problem.'

'Not a problem? Maybe not for you…'

'I can get you papers. Letters of transit.'

'You would do that?'

'Yes, of course. We are old friends.'

'And the others you round up? Will you do it for them too? Maybe I should refuse?'

'Don't be a fool. I'm offering you life.'

'So you admit it then?

'What?'

'You admit the prospect of death for me and my child?'

'I have no proof.'

'Wake up Auguste. Can't you smell the blood on the wind? The stink of death, borne on a tide of hatred and prejudice.'

Auguste said nothing.

Pierre raised his glass to his lips; his brown, sharp eyes levelled at Auguste.

'That's all?'

Auguste said, 'I will return tomorrow. If I can get the papers, you must promise me you will go. First to Beynac and then avoid Sarlat, there is a garrison there. It may take you three weeks walking. Use the papers at the border. If you keep under cover, take plenty of food and hide your yellow star, you have a chance.'

'Suppose I choose to fight?'

'You will die. We're overrun with German soldiers and secret police. They have informers everywhere and there is no resistance. Be sensible. Think of your family.'

'And what about the families of all the others? These internment camps are like funnels—huge amounts go in but there is only space for a few. What do you think will happen to them if they don't fight?'

Auguste put down the glass. His fist clenched, his jaw tightened.

He said, 'Pierre, do you remember the day when those boys tried to take our fishing rods?'

'What?'

'Do you remember?'

'Yes.'

'There were six of them. Older than we were. You wanted to fight. I pulled you away. It is the same. The time for fighting is over. We have lost the war and the Germans occupy our country. We have to cooperate or die.'

'In my case cooperation is death.'

'Perhaps. I don't know if what you say is true but if it is, then what I'm suggesting must make sense to you.'

'I will consider it.'

Auguste smiled for the first time since entering the farmhouse. It was a thin transient smile but real enough.

'Tomorrow then?'

'Yes.'

'Pierre...'

'What? Forgotten your way out?'

'I just wish things could be different. Between us I mean.'

'As long as you serve those killers, how can it be?'

Auguste shivered as he descended the wooden stairs. He suspected Pierre was right. He was a police officer however and there was no proof. He spent his whole working life seeking proof. Without proof and evidence, life was nothing to him. It had been as basic as examination to a doctor or the law to a judge. But if his friend was right, there would be a thousand other men like Pierre out there and he would be responsible for their internment. Was it possible the German State wanted them all dead? Rational thought said no, but inside he wondered. The thought made him clench his jaw until it ached.

CHAPTER TWO

1

It was still dark when he awoke. He lay with his forearm under his head and his body wrapped around Odette. His left arm lay as if from habit, on her hip. He felt his erection and knew he needed to empty his bladder but he enjoyed the feeling of closeness and nuzzling into her, he stroked her hair and cheek. He did not intend to wake her but he felt gripped by a strange loneliness; he needed her. His drowsy mind kept replaying his talk with Pierre. The conversation droned on and on in his mind. He puzzled over the fate of his friend and his daughter. He wished he could change things, but like any man, he felt encumbered by his family, his responsibilities. He dared not take a risk, dared not gamble with their world; it was the world of the only people whom he loved, who would suffer if he did anything to cause official disapproval.

He looked at his watch. The glowing dial told him he was half an hour early. Sleep would not come back and he sighed, perhaps too loud.

'What time is it?' Odette said, her hair a sleepy mist on the pillow.

'Half past six. Go back to sleep.'

'How can I go back to sleep with you making such noise and

prodding me with that thing. Go to the toilet.'

'Sorry. I'm just worried.'

'Look, I have a busy day. I need to sleep,' she said.

'I saw Pierre last night.'

She turned, sleep dissipating.

'Pierre? Is he alright?'

'Yes. He's sent Monique to Beynac.'

'Well she's better off there. This place is getting worse.'

'He wants to fight the Germans, the police, even me.'

'Fight?'

'I don't know what he means. I'm going to try to get them papers.'

'Papers?'

'Yes, letters of transit. If I can get Brunner to sign them they will get Pierre and Monique across the border to Switzerland.'

'You realise how far it is? Are you giving him our car?'

'No. They will have to walk, sleep rough, avoid police. Lyon wants all the Jews interned in Drancy.'

She sat up. 'I give up. I can't sleep now. Drancy? All the Jews? What in the love of Christ for?'

'Pierre thinks it is so they can kill them. I don't believe it. It surely isn't possible?'

She said nothing. The first dull light of a February dawn began to bring the floor and walls back into their lives and Auguste got up. He felt dizzy as he stood up and he wrapped himself in his dressing gown to keep out the cold.

He heard a pattering of small feet and the door burst open. Framed in the faint early morning light, stood Zara, his little girl. With her auburn hair swirling about her shoulders and her nightdress flowing behind her, she ran towards him.

'Papa, I had a bad dream.'

Auguste gathered her up in his strong arms and smoothed her hair with his hand. He clutched her tight.

He said, 'Ma fleur, my little one. A bad dream. There, there.'

She was silent. He held on to her as a man might hold onto a lifebelt in a stormy sea. He felt the love within him, heavy, scary, laced with insecurity. He treasured it. It was as if without it, he would be nothing.

'There, there. It was only a dream. What was it about, my little flower?'

'I don't remember.'

'Then it has gone—pouf! No need now to be frightened. You get into bed with Maman, it is too cold to wander about without your gown.'

She smiled up at him, her face now visible in the breaking dawn light. Her brown eyes wide and clear, the freckles he could not see but knew were there. He put her down and she skipped to the big bed, slipping under the covers as if she had a right to be there and he had not.

Auguste smiled to himself as he found his way to the toilet. He wondered how long he could keep all of them happy. The police in Lyon, the Germans, his family. Now he had Pierre and Monique to think of too. He wished it would end. It was impossible to be of any help to the ones his men arrested and took to Drancy. It was his job to co-ordinate the uplift, not to stand in its way. Perhaps they would demote him if it went wrong, but there was nowhere for the Jews to go even if he disobeyed orders. They were all known and registered, curfewed and kept ignorant without even a radio or telephone. The consequences of his refusal to cooperate filled him with fear.

He knew the answers. The feeling of entrapment threatened to overwhelm him. He washed and began shaving. The act of running the razor over his face cleared his thoughts and he resolved to have the transit documents drawn up as soon as he reached work. Getting them signed and stamped remained a difficult and delicate matter but he had a good working relationship with Brunner, despite his dislike of the man and he was sure he could persuade the SD Major to sign the papers.

Breakfast was a meagre affair. They had bread but no eggs or milk. Coffee had long since been replaced by roasted chicory and even for a senior policeman, obtaining white sugar was an impossibility. If the foodstuffs did not exist, no influence would produce them. They had butter and a little buttermilk from a nearby farm and the honey was a rare treat. Nothing seemed to be available anymore. In Paris it was worse, shelves were empty and even bread was hard to find, according to his friends there.

Bergerac had been the main exporter of geese and ducks for many years but no one could afford to buy such things now. The German devaluation of the franc depressed the economy to rock bottom and the occupying German army took almost everything, paying either nothing or a pittance.

Zara smiled and drank the buttermilk. The bread and honey were a treat for her and she munched with an irrepressible smile as Auguste sipped his pseudo-coffee. He grimaced at the bitterness and put a hand out to stroke his daughter's hair.

'Ma fleur,' he said.

Odette said, 'You must get ready for school now, my little one. Let's get you washed and dressed and then we can do your hair.'

Odette glanced at Auguste but it was clear in her look there remained much unsaid. He knew what was coming. They needed to talk.

It was not until the neighbour whisked Zara away to school they were alone and Auguste began.

'Pierre has to leave. There is no other way,' he said.

'Monique told me she was leaving you know.'

'Yes?'

'She said the children at school picked on her because she had to wear that filthy yellow star.'

He said, 'Even her school friends? She's never done anything wrong.'

'Open your eyes Auguste. Our world has changed. You are no longer a police officer in a quiet town in the Dordogne. You have become an instrument of an evil political force. The SD arrests anyone they wish and they come back beaten. Some never return.'

'These are mainly communists and spies. Troublemakers, who cause damage to property and cause loss of innocent lives. Monique has done nothing, she's a child.'

'She is Jewish.'

'She and Pierre can only get into trouble by breaking the curfew or running away.'

She placed a hand on his cheek. 'Dear Auguste. There is an unstoppable force here threatening to devour us all. Now it is Jews. How long before it is Frenchmen? Orthodox Christians? You cannot work for them. It is not your nature.'

'How can I stop?'

'Please. You have to.'

'Perhaps I can pretend to be ill. Dr. Girard will sign me off sick perhaps.'

'Promise me you will try. We could leave the country.'

'If I am sick, how can I leave?'

'I don't know. I don't...'

She slapped a flat hand on the table and he saw tears forming in her clear blue eyes. He understood why he was still so attracted to her. Her face with its rounded cheeks, small nose and high cheekbones made her look ever youthful, child-like almost. Her figure sagged a little here and there but it was all since the birth of their daughter and he knew he loved every inch of her for it.

He crossed to the opposite side of the kitchen table and took her in his arms.

'Something will come up. If I am not here, they will replace me with another and who knows what injustices we would see? The SD might even put in one of their own men. At the moment, I have to stay. I am the law and even the Germans respect the law.'

She put her arms around his neck and said, 'You are a fool. Nothing you can do will make a difference. Don't you see?'

'I must go. I will be late as it is and I have those papers to organise.'

Their kiss was tender but brief. Auguste had to focus now on another day and there was much to do.

2

The night-rain left deep brown puddles straddling the road. The Citroën chugged its way through them, splashing showers onto the cobbled pavements in the Bergerac streets. The grey, uniform cloud above did nothing for Auguste's mood as he drove along the embankment towards the market square. He reflected there would be a market tomorrow and he needed to be early or the short food supplies would be gone. Of course, in the country, people often caught game and reared their own food but it did not stop the German garrisons plundering and taking anything they wanted, from wine and brandy to food or women. No wonder there were shortages.

He parked his car at the south end of the market square without thinking why, but he felt he wanted to walk despite the grey weather. Movement, any motion at all, meant he had less time to think, less time to understand what his life was becoming. His daily existence was now a mire from which escape seemed impossible or at least, dangerous.

His mind in turmoil, he turned to his beliefs as the only solid foundation he possessed, but he could not help but question where his Jesus was now, in this miserable world where he found himself. Where was his all-forgiving Lord in this travesty of human life? If the Nazis truly believed in God how could they consider killing Jews, any more than they would consider genocide aimed at Frenchmen? Odette was right, but what could he do about it? Nothing. He had to mark time, wait for an opportunity to escape. First, he had to ensure Pierre and his family would be safe.

He trudged toward the tall oak doors of the Prefecture. He was toiling to get there to begin another day of obedience. Another day chipping away at his soul, his beliefs and his will.

Still he could not reconcile his religious perspectives. Where was the Sacred Heart? Was his work really about death and assisting evil? The schism of his belief and his work puzzled him still. It was his job to believe in the things he could prove. Despite that, he still believed in Christ, in the Holy Trinity and an all-forgiving Father in heaven. These two facets of his life seemed such a contradiction, though he recognised it as the true meaning of faith. He bit his lip as his boots snapped and clicked on the flat paving stones but it brought no relief from the torture enveloping him.

Reality came soon enough. A black Mercedes crouched outside the Prefecture. Black was the colour of doom and death. He knew who had sent it. He knew too, it would be a summons. SD had no rules of etiquette or consideration. The swastika flags on the wings of the car told all. He even realised who they had come for. They had come for him.

He paused to look into the dead bakery window. The shop was closed, barren and desolate. Auguste stared at the empty shelves. No flour was available of course. Flour was an import and seemed a sad disappearing promise of a distant past – a time when apple tarts and croissants were available, cheap, pleasant and satisfying. Auguste felt a tightening in the throat and noticed his eyes were moist. Moist like a young girl's. Moist like a river, a river he realised now, soon would flow with Jewish blood.

He strolled now resigned. Level with the Prefecture, he waited outside long enough for a man to emerge from the black car.

The idiot who emerged began with a salute.

'Heil Hitler,' he said, raising his straight right arm.

He was a young man by SD standards. Auguste knew the uniform, it was SS. The SD used them and took them in and gave them new green uniforms, but they were all the same. A wisp of blond hair escaped in an errant journey from beneath the flat, black cap and the thin, bony face was one of meanness and corruption. Auguste knew the face, the thin lips, the pinkness of the cheeks, the blue eyes. He had seen it a hundred times before, a thousand perhaps. He recognised it for a face of anger and jealousy. If you do well in life, beware of such young men he thought. They will do anything to bring you down if you show ability.

'Major Brunner presents his compliments,' he said.

'Indeed,' Auguste said, 'is there a problem?'

'You will come with me.'

'Well, that's fine, but I have things to do this morning. Will you wait for twenty minutes?'

'My instructions are you should come now.'

'Well, tell Major Brunner, I have important matters to attend to and I will come in twenty minutes.'

'But he said...'

'You are?'

'Scharfürer Linz.'

The young man began to raise his right arm once more but Auguste had positioned himself close and there was no room for the gesture. The Frenchman looked, inches away, straight into the young German's eyes.

'When I say twenty minutes, I mean twenty minutes. You will wait, do you hear me Scharfürer?'

The young man seemed to have difficulties deciding who had senior rank. In the end, he decided to capitulate. He turned and went to his vehicle.

Auguste entered the Prefecture. He nodded to his sergeant and ascended the stairs, his mind turning over the events of the last day. He had done nothing even suspicious but the paranoia bred by the presence of the SD would make any man, even an innocent one, quake. He neared his office door and began to wonder what the word "innocent" meant in his own mind. Then he thought, 'am I guilty of nothing?' He knew he was responsible for rounding up and interning thousands of men and women, even children. Would they be slain by these Germans? He had no way of knowing, but his suspicions were enough to make him hate himself. Political duties had become a betrayal of its own and he felt like a drowning man, desperate to get to some surface to allow him air and time to breathe.

'Édith,' he called as he fumbled the lock of his office door. 'Édith.'

She came before he had even seated himself behind the pine desk.

'Auguste?' she said as she entered.

'I need some letters preparing immediately.'

'Letters?'

'Yes, letters of transit for Pierre Dreyfus and his daughter, Monique.'

'Where to?'

'Anywhere, everywhere, just out of this damned country.'

'Auguste, they will not be valid unless signed by you and countersigned by the German authorities,'

'If you type them now, I will ask Brunner to sign them. He has sent for me. I have fifteen minutes.'

'I will do it now then.'

'Good. Oh, by the way, get their names off the register.

'How?

'I don't care but get them off the bloody Jewish register or they can't get out.'

'I need to know the destination.'

'Destination? Well Switzerland will do, I suppose. Hurry.'

Auguste sat waiting. Édith was resourceful. If anyone possessed the ability to do as he asked, she did. He failed to understand why he felt nervous. He wondered if it was because it was the first time in his life, he had used his position to transgress the law. But what kind of law was it he flouted? This was not French law. It was a law of occupation and as a Frenchman, he could surely not feel pangs of conscience about breaking these foreign-forced laws?

He thrummed his fingers on the blotter amid the doodles and scribbled telephone numbers, and noticed he was sweating, although the office was cold. He thought perhaps he was contracting 'flu or something similar. He hoped Brunner would get it too, perhaps even pneumonia he thought.

He wrote a memo by hand. The orders for the internment were clear.

Presently, Édith came in. She held the documents in her hand. Auguste took them and began to read. He signed them and folded them with care, placing them in his pocket, before leaving the building.

Outside in the street, the black car waited.

3

They took over the Mairie within weeks of entering the town. They called it "requisitioning". The sad, old, building stood on a small square facing the cathedral. The cobbled surfaces between the buildings glittered wet and grey as Auguste stepped from the black Mercedes. He looked up at the double wooden doors, framed in their decorative archway. He felt like a man entering church having forgotten his clothes. They would all see him, point and laugh as he realised his mistake. He crossed the square to the doorway, thinking how he had been there many times before under happier circumstances. The invasion of the Mairie forced the Civic Council to shift all civil functions and procedures to an office block two streets way. The SD converted the eighteenth century building, with its lofty ceilings, its panelled walls and decorative ceiling plaster, for their purposes. Auguste saw it as an abuse of the building's former grandeur.

He had seen the cells in the basement, the new furniture and the busy secretaries, recording, typing and scurrying along the airy corridors. The once proud building became a hive of German activity and he often wondered what they did, these busy workers. He questioned too what there could make them so busy. Begerac was a quiet, friendly place; no one here caused trouble.

He had walked past shelf upon shelf of files, records of people, ways of tracking Jews, criminals, homosexuals. He had felt as if his own criminal records office had shrunk. Compared to the SD information system, he had nothing to compare. He often joked with Claude that the SD recorded every fart in Bergerac. He wondered now if perhaps he was right. The SD had no powers of arrest in official terms but depended upon Auguste to make the arrests for them. They still sent SS men to arrest and investigate anyone they wished, so Auguste had never understood why they needed French police officers to help.

Climbing the stone steps, he waited outside the frosted-glass door while Linz went in. Auguste could hear the clack of leather heels and the Reich salute. In moments, Linz opened the door and gestured for him to enter.

Major Brunner sat behind his desk; he did not get up when Auguste entered. The Major smiled. He was a man in his fifties, his hair a yellow-grey swept back from a round, white, balding forehead. Auguste reflected Brunner must have once been a good-looking young man, for traces of his handsomeness remained. Time however leeched it away and what remained of it was a ghost, vague and insubstantial. He had a furrowed forehead and bushy grey eyebrows. The nose was long, almost aquiline and pink, plump lips framed his wide mouth above a square chin.

Auguste was determined to control his inner feelings and work with this man. He smiled back, hiding his feelings and said, 'Helmut, enchanted to see you again.'

Auguste held out his hand and Brunner took it with a damp limp grip. The informality seemed clear to Linz who wrinkled his nose in distaste and left the room.

'I'm so pleased you could make it,' Brunner said.

'No uniform today Helmut? I thought SD Majors wore uniform all the time at work.'

'My rank as Standartenfürer is only equivalent to yours, you know, but it means I do not need to wear uniform except on formal occasions, like the last time we met, at the Mayor's party. Sit please'

Auguste sat in the seat opposite the desk.

'No, not there. Here, please.'

Brunner gestured to a chair at the side of the desk and Auguste was obliged to move closer. There was something distasteful in the correction, which made Auguste realise his position in the order of things. He wondered if it was some psychological technique to rob him of his confidence. To put him at his ease and then create tension and ensure he never relaxed. Brunner did not know him if he thought such techniques would be effective. Auguste was as experienced in interrogation as any senior policeman could be.

'So. We are no further forward with the investigation?'

'Investigation?'

'Into Meyer's death.'

'My men are still making enquiries but no, no further news. No one saw anything. The killer may have got clear away. He could be anyone in the town.'

'Well, the Wehrmacht have rounded up suspects in the north and they will pay the price. I am deeply sorry for your people, but lessons have to be taught. We have to demonstrate to Haupsturmfurer Barbie how we keep order here.'

Auguste said, 'You have my cooperation, as you know.'

'Yes, I know,' Brunner said, tapping the desk with his fingers. He paused and looked up at Auguste. It was as if there were dark background thoughts hidden behind the external veneer of efficient friendliness. He said, 'We need to discuss the mechanism for the internment of the Jews.'

'Helmut, can I ask you a question, off the record?'

'Off the record? Of course.'

'Why is your government so concerned with a few Jewish people? What do they want them for? Who cares what they do?'

Brunner looked at Auguste. He was silent.

Auguste said, 'I'm sorry, I hope I have not embarrassed myself.'

'Embarrassed? No, not that. You made me think. I am doing this because I have orders from Kaltebrunner himself to ensure all Jews are locked up. Ideology and political reasoning are not my duty. My duty is to the Fatherland. Do you question every law when you arrest a criminal? Do you think why is this illegal? No. I prefer to think of it as a means to an end. Germany has the means and the Jews come to an end.'

Brunner laughed aloud. Auguste, puzzled, stared at him. Brunner continued to laugh but it became mirthless. Auguste smiled but the look in his eyes held no tone of humour. He felt an involuntary anger stirring at the back of his mind and he could not understand why.

'Come to an end?' Auguste said.

He thought of Pierre. He saw Monique's face in his mind's eye.

'Figuratively speaking that is. They will trouble your country no more. They will not take Frenchmen's jobs. They will not be able to cheat honest men in the marketplace, with their deals and their intrigues. No, we will intern them and they will only be able to swindle each other. They will work with their hands. We have camps for them. Camps, which will keep them busy. They are not human in the way we understand the term. We are of a different race, a superior one. As a Catholic you can see, Christians will reap the rewards of our labours instead of passing them across to these killers of your Christ.'

By the time Brunner finished speaking, his eyes were shining. They were open wide and Auguste understood the madness in them. He wished he could get up and leave, run, escape and put himself far from this lunacy. But he needed Brunner in his job. There had been times when he thought the only way forward was to cooperate. Times when he had arrested people for Brunner who committed no crime he could acknowledge. He felt as if he was being pushed all the time towards a kind of rebellion. He had his limits; Brunner seemed to have none.

'Look Auguste,' Brunner said, 'I love this country. Not like my home of course, but the wine, the women, the countryside all beautiful. It is my love of your country which makes me want to preserve it. For you; for me. We have to carve out a race, pure and untainted from the mixture prevalent here now. The party is pure and a force for good. You even agreed with me the other night.'

'No, I merely said the aims of your party would have been laudable if they had been peaceful. People died to protect my country. There were always sympathisers on this side of the Rhine, were there not?'

'And you are one. I can hear that. It reassures me that you speak so frankly. You know, I hate the violence. I grew up in a more peaceful place, valleys with green landscapes, farmers and tradesmen plying their business quietly. And then came the Fürer. He showed us the way. The road to purity. He is a great man and anyone who hears him will follow his cause. Fatherland, race and party it is something you will understand one day.'

Auguste listened. He felt he was betraying, but he needed to play the game. He was forced to let Brunner rant on but he knew he could not be fooled. The Nazis were killers yet he still found it hard to believe this man was one of those whom Pierre described. An exterminator of Jews. He needed air. He wanted to change the subject before he exploded into rhetoric about the Church, his faith and his beliefs. It would have been such dangerous ground.

He said, 'Helmut, I have drawn up some preliminary plans and I have sent a memo to every police sub-office. We can begin in a month.'

'A month? No, it will need to begin here locally in the next week.'

'Can't be done. I don't have the infrastructure.'

'Then get it. You have enough men.'

'Yes, but not enough vehicles.'

'Cram them in. Who cares if they are comfortable? This is war. Like sardines.'

He smiled.

Auguste said, 'I still don't have enough vehicles. Can we requisition them? Your men will have to do it I suppose. It isn't within my jurisdiction.'

'Yes, yes, yes. Don't worry my little policeman,' he said.

'Linz. Linz,' he shouted.

Linz came to the door. He opened it and stood erect and serious in the doorway. This time he did not salute, which surprised Auguste.

'Sir?' Linz said. He had a look of puzzlement on his pale thin face. It was as if he had heard the laughter and assumed the atmosphere was one of informality.

Frowning, Brunner said, 'You will commandeer ten large covered vehicles for transportation of Jewish guests for a week's time.'

Auguste said, 'I cannot within reason begin until the end of the month. Please allow me to do it in my own time. My orders from Tulard were to begin this in six weeks.'

Brunner's smile melted away, as if Auguste had thrown a verbal bucket of water. The German's eyes narrowed a little. He turned to Auguste.

'You don't quite understand your position here, do you Auguste?'

'I beg your pardon?

'Well, your country is occupied by the Third Reich. We can do anything we wish. We wish to intern some sub-human beings who have inveigled themselves into French society like a cancer. They did the same in the Fatherland. We are helping you. Failure to comply might be interpreted as a form of resistance, I'm sure you understand?'

Auguste understood. Pierre and Monique had become a disease from which this man, a German, wished to cure him. The river, the house, the sunny days and the fishing were symptoms. His affection for his old friend was a lowering of his body's resistance. He needed the medication, the cure and the disease-free life offered by this man. All of it seemed so plain. Remove the Jews and the world would be clean and healthy.

But in Auguste's mind however, the question remained. What of the Germans? Auguste knew where he would classify them. If Pierre with his rotgut wine was a disease, these Nazis were an apocalypse. They were worse than disease, they were a filthy plague and one he was being forced to sub-serve. And why? If he did not comply, Odette and Zara would suffer. His family were now hostages to the occupying Germans and he began to feel helpless, impotent in the face of the implications Brunner voiced with such ease.

'Can we compromise?'

'Compromise?' Brunner said.

Auguste said, 'Is it not so, that in compromise, neither party is truly happy?'

Brunner said nothing.

Auguste continued, 'In four weeks, I will have the commandeered vehicles and all my men mobilised and the transfer can take place very quickly. Drancy is only an hour away from Bergerac. There will be no delays. I have registered every Jew in my catchment area and my men know who they are. Without me, it will be much more difficult. Compromise?'

Linz said, 'Standartenfürer, it may take some time to get the vehicles. Even if we mobilise military vehicles as well, the policeman is right.'

'You have an opinion, do you? Well that is a first. Since when do lowly SS officers become so bold as to offer opinions?'

His eyes were like steel as he gazed at his junior man.

Linz said nothing this time. The silence droned on like some oppressive mist between the three. Even Auguste felt uncomfortable.

Presently, Brunner said, 'Of course. Of course, there is no point in attempting the impossible. The end of February then.'

'I think you mean the second week of March, do you not?' Auguste said.

'Yes, yes, whatever. Linz you may go. Oh and by the way, get us some coffee.'

This time Linz saluted before he left. Silence descended upon the SD office. Brunner looked at Auguste. He opened his mouth to speak and a sudden explosive report sounded in the square outside. Both men jumped. Brunner got up, Auguste turned in his seat.

Peering out of the window, Brunner said, 'Only a car backfiring. Perhaps I'm getting paranoid in my old age. Now where were we?'

'Compromise.'

'Ah, yes. You may be right. Let us give some time. It can all happen overnight perhaps?'

'No. The various registered people are very widely distributed. This is a rural area. Leave it to me. It will require a good deal of planning and my men know the district.'

'Very well,' Brunner said.

'Oh there was something else,' Auguste said, reaching into his pocket. He produced the two letters of transit. 'I wonder if you would countersign these two letters of transit.'

'Passports? Who for?'

'You may understand I have some banking interests in Switzerland?'

'Yes, many of us have.'

'I have to send someone to make a small deposit. Clearly, with so much going on here, I cannot go myself, so I want to send an old friend. He is a widower and will take his daughter.'

'You think he will return?'

'Of course. He has relatives and he cares for them. He would not wish my disapproval.'

'Perhaps I should interview him first?'

'You don't trust me?'

'The quality of trust is stratified by nationality, Ran, is it not?'

'I had thought...'

Brunner paused but as if he had second thoughts. He took the documents and signed them.

'Linz and I are dining in La Bonne Auberge tonight; they have a good singer there. You will join us. Seven o'clock.'

Auguste knew it was no invitation. It was an order and he knew he would be there. He took the documents and replaced them in his pocket. When he left, he resolved to ring Odette if time allowed, to explain his absence but he knew what she would say.

4

Auguste sighed as he closed the front door; it had been a long day. His home was on the outskirts of town on a small street backed by woodland. He enjoyed the freedom of being able to walk into the woods where he and Pierre once played as children and he knew every tree stump, every gnarled root on the tiny traversing path. The wood was also where he had walked his Scottie-dog, Dedê, every day for ten years before she died. He thought of her often—he always considered her a kindred spirit, stubborn but faithful. He missed her company on a summer's morning when the sky was blue and the burgeoning day was fresh and green.

He wiped his feet on the brown horsehair mat and removed his shoes. He heard giggles and running feet upstairs and called, 'I'm home.'

Odette came from the kitchen. She smiled, but he knew her well enough to appreciate its hollowness.

'What's wrong?'

'Not here,' she said.

She turned and he followed into the warmth if the kitchen. The range on the far wall kept the room warm throughout the winter and it was the place in the house where they talked, laughed and ate.

'What's happened?'

'Pierre. He was here.'

'Pierre? I have the letters of transit. He wanted them?'

'No he didn't mention them at all. He came with Monique.'

'She's still here?'

'Yes.'

'I thought he was leaving her in Beynac with Maricelle.'

'He decided it wouldn't be safe after what you told him. He brought her here.'

'Well, when he comes back I can give him the letters. They may escape after all.'

'He isn't escaping. He's gone into hiding. He said something about joining a partisan group.'

'What?'

'He said he has some contacts and he wanted to fight for his country and his life.'

'Fight? Has he gone mad? What about Monique? He can't just leave her here. All the Jews have to...'

'I offered. I said we would take her in and hide her.'

'You did what?'

She was silent. She bit her lip.

Auguste sat down.

'Listen to them,' he said. 'Does it sound like something you can hide?'

The sound of laughter, pure, clear, childish laughter, drifted down the stairs. The sound of their feet provoked nothing but fear in Auguste.

'What have you done? I'm police. I have to arrange the internment. I cannot do this.'

'I gave my word. You've known that child since she was born. You've seen her almost every day of her life and now you think we can turn her over to an internment camp? What is happening to you Auguste?'

'I...'

A cataclysmic conflict raged within him. His whole life, his hopes, his fears twisted and turned within him. He thumped the tabletop with his fist. He took his head in his hands leaning on his elbows on the table. He could not shut out the reality and gravity of what was happening to him. He felt his life was in tatters.

'If you are the kind of man who would do that, then you are not a man I want to live with.'

'Odette. You will be risking all our lives with this.'

'What are our lives worth if we hand over a child alone to an internment camp. Pierre is certain the Germans plan to annihilate the Jews. Would you send Monique to her death to save your own life?'

'But it's impossible.'

'No one will question you. This is perhaps the only safe place in Bergerac for that little girl. She stays.'

'And if the SD come? Can we hide her? It may be for years? It will be no life for her anyway.'

'She stays. It is up to you whether you give me away with her or not.'

'Don't be stupid. I would never allow anything to happen to you or Zara.'

'Or Monique.'

He swallowed. She was stubborn, but it was her very intransigence he found convincing about her. He knew deep inside he had not the strength or perhaps weakness required to hand the girl over to his men.

'My God, Odette. Think of the risk. One tiny mistake and all is lost.'

'I will make no mistakes.'

'If anyone comes, she will have to hide in the wood. I can make a shelter, hidden, safe,' Auguste said.

'Then do it. Oh Auguste, thank you.'

She crossed the room to stand beside him. He stood up, strong arms proffered and they held on to each other for a long moment. Auguste realised he was shaking. She looked up at him.

'You will be doing a great thing. It is noble. Protecting a child.'

'No, not noble. It is you who does this. I am merely weak and complicit.'

'We will be strong, because we are together,' she said, looking up at him.

'What can I do with the letters of transit? They won't be needed now.'

'If you can get two more we can all get away.'

'I thought Brunner was suspicious when I asked him to sign. If I now ask for two more he will know.'

'I wasn't serious.'

'Does Monique know she is staying with us?'

'Yes, Pierre told her. He even told her why she is in danger. She is such a sensible child and she shows no distress. I suppose it will come later.'

'She perhaps measures it against Murielle's death. For a child, nothing could have been worse.'

'Perhaps. We should eat now.'

'I can't. I have to go out.'

'Out?'

'Yes, I'm dining with two SD officers tonight. If you answered the telephone you would know. I don't know how I can look them in the face without fear of their suspicion. One of them is Brunner.'

'They won't come here will they?'

'No my love. I've been told I have to go to the restaurant.'

'Be careful...'

A child's voice interrupted her.

'Uncle Auguste.'

Monique ran into the kitchen. She flung herself at Auguste. He gathered her up in his arms and hugged her, patting her back with a practiced gentleness.

'My little friend. How are you? It must be weeks.'

'Papa brought me. I'm to stay until the Germans are dead.'

'What?'

'Papa said he would chase them all away and when it was safe he would come for me. He said we won't have to wear the yellow star anymore then.'

'You know no one can know you are here?'

'Yes, Papa told me.'

'Papa! You are home,' Zara said from the doorway. She smiled. 'We were playing nurses.'

'My little flower. Is there a hug for your Papa?'

Zara ran to him and he hugged them both.

'Zara, you must always play quietly. I don't want anyone to know Monique is here. You understand?'

'We understand Papa,' she turned to her mother. 'We are very hungry. What's for dinner?'

'I must go,' Auguste said.

Odette looked at him. Her eyes betrayed helplessness. He thought she struggled with being unable to say what she wished in front of the two girls. Auguste left to the sound of the girls giggling. The sound made him shudder.

CHAPTER THREE

1

Auguste arrived early at the restaurant. His watch said nearly seven o'clock but he did not expect SD company so soon. He had to be there on time but the arrogance of the invitation made him sure they would be late. He began to wonder who he was in their eyes anyway. Had he become a traitor to France who they could manipulate and bend to their will? His father, a veteran of the first war would have thumped the table, his pipe in the corner of his mouth and accused him of betraying the Republic.

He felt shame. He felt passive, weak and then he thought of Monique. She was the same age as Zara but a different kind of child. Monique was serious. She seemed to have wisdom and she understood what was happening, though Zara had no concept at all of the dangers her parents were running. Auguste wondered if he had understood the danger too, when Odette presented him with it. He felt it was a fait accompli and there had been no going back, for her decision had sealed their fates, all of them. Her decision had also changed his life.

He entered the restaurant and made for the tiny semi-circular bar opposite the door. A sense of loneliness took him. Odette had pushed him into a dangerous situation but he was now in the wolves' den and alone. He felt he was facing the Germans without allies, without support. He it was, who ran the risk of them noticing some change in him. He wondered in a vague ponder, whether there could be some outward sign of the Jewish child hiding in his home. Some way they could detect her on him, on his clothes or even his demeanour. He knew it was nonsense and he discarded his thoughts as the ruminations of a frightened fool.

He sat on a stool and asked the barmaid for a Vichy water. He had no wish to come home drunk as if he had been carousing with these Nazis.

Seated next to him was a young girl. He knew her and he smiled to her when she looked round.

'Good evening, Bernadette,' he said.

'Good evening, Inspector Ran,' she replied.

Bernadette was short in stature but Auguste noticed her beauty as if it was a beacon on a dark night. It shone. She had curly blonde hair lashing her shoulders and a smile radiating warmth and friendliness. Her white teeth flashed in the lamplight when she smiled. She had blue almost iridescent eyes echoing her smile. He knew she was eighteen and like any man, he appreciated the gentle curves of her body and the relaxed way she moved. A young man would fall in love with her without any more difficulty than an old man would give her advice.

He compared her to Zara and knew his only feelings for this girl were paternal. He drank his drink, feeling good about the quality of his thoughts. He felt protective, he knew her after all.

'Bernadette? What are you doing here? Are you meeting a boy?'

'Inspector Ran. I am singing. Mother has been ill and so she cannot take in washing any longer. I study during the day and sing at night. What else can I do?'

'Nothing serious, I hope?'

'Well you know, since the accident she has trouble walking and...'

'This is not a good place to earn your money. It is full of men. They are not the kind of men you should be singing to.'

'I will finish at midnight. I never stay. Bernard makes sure no one molests me. Thank you for your concern.'

She turned away to leave him there. He had an urge to cling to her presence as one might to a lifebuoy in a dark sea. He had a feeling that if he could make her stay with him, the night would be less threatening, less suicidal.

'Bernadette, I will take you home. My car is outside.'

'But I am singing tonight.'

'No, I meant when you have finished.'

'Very kind of you. I do not get a police escort every night.'

Her smile lit up his life for a brief moment. He felt it was as though her presence would save him. Although he did not think of himself as a deeply religious man, it was almost like seeing some saint who had visited him in a time of distress. Beauty, he reflected could do such things to a man, it can uplift the spirits.

He looked into his glass as she began to sing. The words of the song were familiar. He wondered what regrets a child like Bernadette could have? She sang she had none, but she had not even sampled life. He was feeling older by the moment and worse still, he was aware of it.

He reflected on the first time he met Odette. At the time, she was a friend of Murielle's and Pierre had suggested they meet. She had charmed him, captured him and held him so he felt he was walking on air. They had talked and walked along the riverbank. By the end of the evening, they were holding hands. He had been eighteen. His inexperience helped him to love her immediately. Their marriage had changed things but the love remained. He knew in that moment of reflection there would never be another in his life.

2

Brunner's arrival interrupted his thoughts. A hard, bony hand descended upon his shoulder and he turned, looking up from his seat.

The pink lips, moist and repulsive to him, parted in the familiar smile.

'Ah, Auguste. I'm sorry to be late. We had some matters to clear up before we came. Have you met René Bousquet, my friend and associate? René has plans for reorganising all the French police, so you had better make a friend of him too. He might reorganise you out of a job and we couldn't have that could we?'

A tall angular fellow stood beside Brunner. Auguste thought his face looked as if someone once stretched it on the rack. Surmounting it was a head of greying black hair. The eyes were narrow and blue and gleamed in the lamplight like a man who is allergic to flowers. The lines on the man's face seemed to Auguste to be vertical and the man pursed his thin lips as if he was used to sucking lemons. He did not smile even though Brunner was laughing at his own joke.

Auguste stood and shook hands with them and though it was painful, he smiled.

'I thought you were bringing Linz. I did not understand.'

'Oh well, Linz couldn't come. He is questioning a prisoner. I will tell you all about it. Now we need to drink. The table nearest the entertainment I believe will be required. Garçon!'

Brunner turned and snapped his fingers. The Auberge's owner appeared as if by some conjuring trick, Brunner having summoned him from thin air. He was a short, balding man and he bowed his head in an obsequious gesture of capitulation. To witness how his compatriots made obeisance to the Germans evoked nothing but disgust in Auguste and he realised his whole thinking had changed in only two days.

The three men sat at a small table with a chequered tablecloth and a half-burned candle, perched somewhat askew in the end of an empty bottle of Chateau Malartic Lagraviére. Auguste wished it were full. Such wine was hard to come by these days. All of it was destined for German palates not French.

Bernadette sang behind him. He questioned what any passerby might have thought of the local police inspector, dining with a German wolf and a French giraffe. The description in his head made him smile. He thought it apt. His life was becoming a circus.

Brunner said, 'We are having champagne, then we can get to the more serious wines. I love this country. You have the best of everything. Wine, women, food and angels to sing for us too.'

Bousquet said, 'You are a man with excellent taste then, Helmut. Is he not Inspector?'

'Yes, excellent,' Auguste said.

Brunner leaned towards Auguste and said in confidential tones, 'That girl, the one singing, she has a wonderful voice.'

'Yes, her name is Bernadette. I have known her since she was a child. Her father died in a car accident and her mother cannot walk through the same disaster. She studies fine art at the Ecole des Beaux-Arts.'

'Then you must ask her to join us. She is beautiful. Such wonderful women you have here.'

Auguste said nothing. He could not imagine Bernadette would be anything but horrified.

They ate duck. Brunner had cassoulet of duck and the others had confit of duck leg. They ate in silence preferring to listen to the music. The wine was a local one, since any others were scarce. The label said it was a Bergerac but the best in the house and Auguste began to feel drunk. He was unused to alcohol nowadays and after sharing two bottles of champagne and two of red wine, he began to become incautious. He slapped Brunner on the shoulder

'Well isn't this a wonderful French meal. Better than sauerkraut eh?'

Brunner looked at him. The expression was one of distaste mixed, Auguste thought, with contempt.

'You think there is anything in your country matching mine? One German is worth ten Frenchmen any day of the week. We proved it when the Fürer took France almost with just a telephone call. The Vichy Government is his theatre and Pétain is his puppet. You would do well to recognise the fact. I can have anything in this room only for the asking. Can you?'

Auguste knew he could have said, 'I'm sorry, I did not mean to offend,' or he could have said, 'Of course you are right.'

He felt a sudden surge of anger. He controlled it but he realised his pride in his country and in himself too, was gripping him by the throat and it felt like it squeezed the life out of him with every moment he spent in Brunner's company. He had a sudden urge to shoot the man.

He said, 'I meant only the food.'

Brunner looked at him; his eyes cod-cold.

Bousquet said, 'I travelled to Germany before the war. I visited Bavaria. I found the food and hospitality second to none.'

Brunner said, 'My mother is from Bavaria.'

'Indeed? Such lovely people,' Bousquet said.

'Ah her cooking is wonderful, I miss home nowadays. Mutti makes a lamb stew with sauerkraut men would die for.'

Auguste looked at Bousquet with gratitude. He was uncertain where the conversation might have taken him and for the first time in his life realised he was slipping out of control. Whether it was the strain of what Odette had made him take on, or whether it was the question of the internments, he did not know; he had such a turmoil wheeling in his mind, the wine served only to confuse and bring these thoughts closer to the surface.

He was aware of Brunner and Bousquet conversing about the beauty of the German countryside but it took the proprietor's presence to bring him back to reality.

'Of course sir,' Bernhard said.

Jolted back to reality, Auguste said, 'Sorry, what was that? I can't eat another thing; your hospitality has been so generous.'

'Hospitality? You don't think SD officers pay for this type of lowly fare do you?'

'Oh,' Auguste said, 'I hadn't realised.'

'On the house man. On the house. The proprietor is pleased to have us as guests and that means you too Auguste.'

'What did you ask him for?'

'We are having some brandy. Armagnac of course. It is much favoured in Germany. I also invited the singer to join us.'

'I don't think she is that sort of a girl.'

'Nonsense man, all French women are at my disposal. See if they aren't.'

Brunner waved an expansive arm towards the rest of the tables. The wine seemed to have affected him too.

'I promised her mother she would be home shortly after midnight. I agreed to take her home. If I do not, I will have broken my word to a sick woman.'

Brunner was silent then. He stared into his glass and became serious.

'Let us see if she wishes to go with me. I am often persuasive. You'll see.'

Presently, the brandy arrived and Bernadette followed behind. She drew up a chair, her face pale, she looked as if she was about to be shot by a firing squad.

Brunner stood up and smiled a lascivious smile. He gestured for her to sit and the fool clacked his heels and bowed at the hips.

'I am delighted to meet you. You sing wonderfully. Like a bird of paradise. My compliments.'

She said, 'Thank you. You are very kind.'

Brunner sipped his Armagnac, never taking his eyes from her. Auguste thought the man was obsessed. He could see beads of sweat on Brunner's balding forehead and he knew what the German was thinking. He recognised the thought had in some form, been buried in his own head. The drink made his thoughts muddled but he recalled his fatherly feelings for the girl. He would not allow Brunner anywhere near her and he knew it then.

'Let me get you a drink,' Brunner said.

'No thank you. I don't take alcohol.'

'You don't? And you work in a place like this? Nonsense, I'll get you a brandy.'

He summoned the waiter and ordered more drinks. He grabbed the bottle from the waiter's tray and set it on the table. He waved the man away.

Auguste had not finished the first one and he did not intend to drink more with Brunner. He detested the man and this performance confirmed his hatred. It was not as simple as revulsion, Auguste pondered. It was to do with his pride in being French. This man was a German interloper. A beast from the forests troubling his country since Roman times. He also recognised he felt protective of Bernadette and he knew he needed to get her away from Brunner.

'Well it's getting late I'm afraid,' Auguste said, looking at his watch.

Brunner said, 'You entertain all these men with your mouth. Perhaps you would like to entertain me with it too? In private of course.'

Auguste looked at Brunner. The man was oblivious. It was now beyond his control, he had to leave. He stood up before Bernadette could reply.

'I'm sorry Helmut, but I have promised to take her home. I'm sure another occasion will present itself. I bid you a very good night and thank you for your gentlemanly company.'

He stressed the word "gentlemanly" too hard and he realised it. Perhaps it was the drink but there was something more in his mind. It was impossible for him to hide his contempt.

'But we have only just begun,' Brunner complained.

Auguste took Bernadette's hand and led her away. He glanced over his shoulder when he reached the door. Brunner was scowling and talking to Bousquet. He leaned forward. His elbow slipped and he almost hit the table with his face. Auguste realised the SD officer was very drunk. He hoped he had not caused a permanent breach in relations, because he needed Brunner in the long term. But some things, he reflected, were beyond any man's control.

The battered Citroën came to a halt in the narrow cobbled street. The lacklustre bonnet gleamed with a dull shine in the light of the overhanging streetlamp. Auguste turned to the girl seated beside him.

'Bernadette, you can never return there.'

'But I have no other way of earning money.'

'It doesn't matter. The man is evil. If you go back there he will cause you trouble. He is an SD officer. Secret police. Never go there again. I will speak to Jules, the baker and see if he can find you some night work in the bakery when it opens again. You can trust Jules, he is old enough to be my father let alone yours.'

She smiled.

'Will it be soon?'

'Yes, my little friend,' Auguste said. 'I will ask him tomorrow. Do as I say. I am the police after all.'

She opened the door and turned to Auguste. Her eyes shone and they reminded him of Odette in those days when their love was new.

'You are a good man, Inspector.'

Stung by the words, he said, 'I wish it were true. If I were a good man, I would not do the work I do. God will judge. I have much to make amends for, my child.'

She smiled.

'Te absolvo,' she said, grinning as she slammed the door shut. He watched her skip across the road, until she reached and opened the painted door to her mother's home.

Auguste drove home. He drove fast, the puddles scattering in shiny spray as his tyres hit them. For the first time in his life, he watched the rear view mirror at every turn, to check for following cars.

CHAPTER FOUR

1

Auguste expressed his impatience by tapping his foot on the linoleum. His office felt cold and he had promised Odette he would be home early. He levelled his gaze at the portly Gendarme Colonel in front of him.

'Colonel Arnaud, I have no choice in the matter,' he said.

Arnaud, an old man for his job, shrugged. He wore a grey moustache and his baldness seemed exposed as he fiddled with his cap. He shifted in his seat, as if he was sitting on something irregular. He was a relic. He was one of those left over from the old war, a German war and one still burning within him, as far as Auguste could see. Relics, he thought, should be locked up in museums, not administrating the Maréchaussée.

Colonel Arnaud said, 'Inspector. This is not a military matter, as I see it. This is political and so does not fall under my jurisdiction. If it had been a criminal matter in the countryside, of course we would be involved. We are always first in line when it comes to our duty, but rounding up Jewish people because of a change in policy, well...'

'This is a matter in which I need your help. I can send word to Lyon and you could be made to cooperate.'

The two men were silent for a full minute as they looked at each other, then the Colonel said, 'Very well. Two men to a truck. How many trucks will you have? I cannot supply any. It is hard enough to get fuel nowadays. I cannot waste the little we have on this kind of nonsense.'

'Brunner has instructed your men may not be armed.'

'What?' Arnaud said.

He leaned forward in his chair. It creaked. Auguste could smell the garlic on Arnaud's breath and he wrinkled his nose.

'Brunner will commandeer trucks and I have to supply the names and locations,' Auguste said.

'Tell me Inspector, what do you really think is going on here.'

'Well, one hears rumours...'

'Rumours?' Arnaud said.

'Yes, rumours. What have you heard?'

'I heard the internees will be deported to camps in Poland and Germany and they are places where they may not come out.'

'You mean death-camps?'

'I suppose you could say that,' Arnaud said.

'I have heard similar stories. I don't know what to make of it. I have lived here all my life. I know almost everyone in the town and the surrounding district. I know many Jewish people too.'

'Why don't you just say no? Let the invaders do their own dirty work. That was what I meant before, until you persuaded me.'

'Suppose they were warned?'

'How could that happen? They are not allowed radios or telephones. Your men saw to that, only last year.'

'You trust me?'

'We are both French. If the Vichy government chooses to collaborate with these invaders, then they can. I know to whom I owe my allegiance, and he is exiled in London'

'But he is not in France now. All we have is Pétain and God knows if de Gaulle will ever return. Some don't even think that is his real name. The Germans will defeat the Rosbifs and all of Europe will eat sauerkraut.'

'You are unwise to talk too loudly even here. They have spies everywhere. I realise now you are a good man though, Auguste. Of course, you might be working for them, for all I know. Life is a gamble after all—la bonne chance.'

'Someone else said that to me not so long ago. If it was true, I would not be sending all these innocent people to their deaths. Suppose the Gendarmerie were to have the list of internees and it got 'lost'?'

'Why, I would be furious with the man who lost it. I would have to kiss him upon both cheeks.'

Auguste smiled. Arnaud was turning into the first ally he had come across. He was glad he was not alone.

Arnaud stood up. 'I must go. Would you send me the records so I can go through them? I can then let my men know where they will be expected to go. Of course, some of them have great difficulty finding their way around in this neighbourhood. Some of them might get lost or go astray.'

'You appreciate the Germans will say we are incompetent?'

'Well, vive la différence, is all I can say. I must go.'

They shook hands and Auguste noticed the old man had a warm dry hand and a firm handshake. Arnaud had not found the conversation stressful. A spark of admiration grew within him and he smiled when the door made its soft click, as Arnaud closed it behind him.

Auguste could hear the old man whistling. It was a military tune, he recognised. He remembered his father singing it, after drinking wine. It was from the first war, to do with love triumphing over all and the importance of duty.

His admiration and nostalgia left him as fast as it had emerged; he felt sick. It was not the tune, it was his feeling of betraying his father, his country and his beliefs. He believed in God. God the Almighty, who gave ultimate forgiveness, ultimate absolution. Would his God —his Father, Son and Holy Ghost—forgive the internment and final murder of Jews because they had in some way, ancestrally, been instrumental in the Saviour's Passion? He knew it was not so, deep inside. It was not the God he believed in. His God was kind. His God was one who forgave. He had never believed in Mortal Sin, un-forgivable, eternal, final.

He had friends who had sinned, it was true. They had committed adultery. Did his God judge them so finally? Hell had no meaning to him for he could not believe it was eternal. He thought if his actions resulted in the death of some Jews, saving the ones he could, it would counterbalance the evil he committed for the sake of saving his child, his woman.

He realised his hand trembled, holding the pen. It was enough, he thought, to do what he could for the people to whom he had access. God would forgive him. Auguste would warn them. If they refused to run, refused to hide, then he could not help them at the expense of those whom he loved.

His thoughts this time, settled him. He had made up his mind and had a course of action ahead of him. He felt as if the tension of his indecisiveness had resolved itself and the calm came as a peace, a tranquillity he had sought for days. He wondered if it was always the same, whatever the mental conflicts. Decisiveness brings relief.

He stood and walked to the window. There was no Pierre, cycling in aggressive defiance. No marches, no protestations. The German occupation of his home, his country, had quietened them all, but he knew the fire raged, burned and consumed his countrymen. France would rise again; it had to. It was not a matter of God. It was a matter of justice. He had made up his mind and it felt good.

2

It was raining again as Auguste stepped from the car. For once, he did not care. He walked to his front door. A certain levity crept into his step, an elevation of his mood. He knew he was right and believed his God was there, helping him. He had never felt the presence of his God so strong, so emotive, before.

Odette greeted him in the hallway. She threw her arms about his neck and her lips sought his. It felt like a rekindling of their adolescent love. He was surprised, but his feelings for her made it an expression of pleasure. He thought there was nothing in his world like the embrace of the woman he loved.

'Auguste, I was so worried.'

'Why?'

'If anyone came to the house, what do I do with Monique? We have nowhere to hide her. All day it has been worrying me.'

'I have been thinking. It is no good using the woods. We need a place where she will be able to hide for hours at a time. The woods are no good. It is freezing. I need to make a place of safety here in the house.'

'But how?'

'Call the girls and we will discuss it.'

'The girls?'

'Of course. They are the instruments of the deception. They must know all about it.'

Within minutes, the four of them sat at the kitchen table to plan a hiding place.

Zara said, 'Papa, we can lift the floorboards and make a place there.'

'No ma fleur, it would be uncomfortable and Monique could not lie there for a long time. I think we should use the attic. We have a better chance then.'

'The attic?' Odette said.

'Yes the gable end would be a good hiding place. I can brick it up, a few feet from where it ends and no one would know.'

'And the bricks? Where would you get them?'

'I cannot buy them. It would be noticed. I can dismantle the outhouse. There must be enough bricks then.'

'If she hides there, will she not be stuck behind the wall? She could not live in such a way. If anything happens to us she might be left there.'

'Calm yourself,' Auguste said, 'I can make a door, faced with brick. Let's eat and then I will start work. Until it is done, the woods will have to do. We must be disciplined and strong.'

Odette looked at Auguste. She reached out and her hand descended upon his.

'Auguste, you are a good man.'

Something happened then. He felt a stab of pain. It was mental, not physical, as if some outside force had prodded his soul.

He said, 'I have no idea what goodness is. I know some men are good and it is obvious. There are others whom no one would recognise as anything but evil. Where I and my life fit into the scheme of things, I cannot tell. I want to be what you think I am, but my conscience is so weak. I have orders from an evil master, orders to cause the death and destruction of innocent people. I cannot save them all. I will try to do what I can, but death stalks me and I cannot stop it. I beg our Lord in Heaven to forgive me.'

Auguste looked from face to face around the table. The emotions tugging at his heart were so powerful he felt they threatened to overwhelm him. He noticed the tears forming in his eyes. He wiped his nose on his sleeve. He felt a breath cut short and realised he was sobbing.

'Papa, don't cry,' Zara said. She rose and came to him, and placed a gentle hand on his shoulder. He turned and embraced her and felt again the feeling he experienced in his heart after her nightmare. He reached for her not in body but in soul. His love overtook him then and he closed his eyes, feeling the depth of that love within him. Great fear and emotion seemed to Auguste, to be transformed to joy, as if love had converted everything to a bright white feeling arising out of the deep blackness of despair.

Monique said, 'Uncle, Are you frightened?'

Again, he wiped his face on his sleeve.

'Oh Monique. I am frightened for us all. I will protect you. We are all together here, a family. You are part of our family until Pierre returns. Frightened? Yes. But we will all together, make a place of safety upstairs and we will keep you safe.'

'Will the Germans catch me, Uncle?'

'No, my child. We will hide you and when this stupid war is finished, your father will come home. I am sorry if I make you scared. Are you frightened too?'

'No uncle, but I wish my Maman was here.'

He saw tears in her eyes and he realised expressing his own feelings to this child was wrong.

Odette reached for her and as he held onto his daughter, she held on to Monique.

She said, 'Monique, my darling girl, I loved your mother for many years. I will give you my love too. You are part of this family now. You belong with us and we will all love you.'

'Auntie,' Monique said, 'I need to say prayers sometimes. Father taught me to. I don't want to go to the church.'

Auguste, recovered now, said, 'Monique, you will do exactly as Pierre taught you. I cannot help you with it. On Sundays, we will go to church and you will remain here and say your prayers as you can remember them. It will be fine, don't worry. We will be like little bears in a den. One family.'

She looked at him and said nothing. Perhaps the enormity of the risk had finally come home to her too, or maybe, Auguste wondered, the absence of her only living parent insinuated itself in her mind, but she said, 'I am only nine years old Uncle, but Papa told me about it all. He said you would help me.'

'I am the one appointed to the task it seems, little one. We, as a family will not let you down, but you must learn to hide. It will be a kind of game for us to play. They will seek and we will hide, no? Now you two girls get off to bed and I will eat then start work on a hiding place to fool all those silly Germans.'

They sat for an hour after he ate, talking about the war and the dangers ahead until Auguste closed the back door behind him and strode through the icy drizzle to begin his task of demolishing his brick out-house.

CHAPTER FIVE

1

Auguste cursed the rain as he walked from his battered Citroën towards the Prefecture. Three hours sleep was all he had managed as he toiled into the small hours cleaning bricks and carrying them up into the loft. He drew his collar around his neck and pulled his hat forward as he passed the empty bakery window. He resolved to speak to Jules and find work for Bernadette. He was still scared but thinking about the work he embarked upon the previous night calmed him. At least he was doing something.

By the time he reached the desolate cafe, he noticed the crowd. They had gathered in front of the Prefecture and he recognised faces as the gathering grew. He wondered what the fuss was about and pushed his way to the front. Claude Desour, his second in command, was there and the desk sergeant, George, tried to press away the accumulating crowd.

Auguste pushed through the gathering of townsfolk and realised they were staring at something on the ground.

'Claude,' he said, 'What's...'

He stopped. A feeling of irritation struck him first. A naked body lay face down on the cobbles. No one could mistake the body of a young woman, shapely even in death, limbs twisted into the unnatural pose only the flight of mortality could imbue. He looked around and realised his men were clearing the area around the body and forcing the crowd to keep a respectful distance, despite their curiosity.

'All right, all right,' he said in loud tones and raising his arms to the crowd, 'please go home, we will care for her now.'

He turned to Claude and said, 'What has happened?'

Claude shrugged. He said, 'It is as you see. A man came in and called George, saying there was a body.'

'What time was that?'

'Ten minutes ago.'

'You've called the city pathologist?'

'I have called no one yet. I was keeping the crowd away.'

'Very good. Call the pathologist and we will have her taken to the mortuary. I'll have a look.'

Auguste knelt at the side of the body. He felt her neck first to ensure she was dead. The flesh felt warmer than he expected. He looked at the ground around the body looking for bloodstains and there were none. She had clearly not been killed here. He stared at the face.

Recognition began to come. Fear came too. He recognised her. He felt his heart beating, his breath came in rasps and he experienced a mounting and unreasonable anger. He knew her. He had spoken to her only hours before. It was Bernadette.

He sank to both knees and turned her over. The eyes were open and he tried to shut them. They would not stay closed and within moments he realised the gesture was pointless.

Auguste stood up in the drizzle and removed his overcoat. He draped the body with it and looked at the faces of the crowd. The faces had meant nothing to him moments before but now he felt an urge to explain. He had a desire to ask their forgiveness, he wanted to avoid their angry stares. Guilt took him.

She had gone home to her mother and he knew she had been safe on the night he took her back. How could she be here, naked, lifeless and forlorn?

Her feet peeped out from under his coat. Auguste noticed they were small, delicate and perfect in shape. Red-painted toenails stared at him, he thought, in anger. Red is the colour of hate, he thought. Had he failed her? Had this happened because he had discouraged her from her singing? Had she become a woman of the night, prostituting herself to earn a living and this had become the result?

No, he knew her. She was a decent girl and nothing would persuade him to the contrary. Why was the body here? No clothing lay nearby, he could see that. She had died elsewhere and her body left in the square hidden by the bushes. But why?

The noisy green van from the mortuary arrived. Two men in white uniforms emerged and after rummaging in the back, extracted a stretcher and a black body bag. Auguste wondered for a moment whether their white uniforms symbolised some kind of purity like the innocence of this girl's youth. He felt only anger and he swore to himself he would find out who had done this.

Bernadette, the beautiful singer, the child-like student of fine-art, the girl he had taken home, away from the leering, lecherous German that night in the Bonne Auberge.

Brunner. Had he done this? Would he do such a thing? He was a man of no conscience but this would be stupid even for him.

In his mind, he could hear Édith say Brunner had bad habits. Was this then, what Édith had meant?

The questions flew in his mind and he had no answers. He knew he should speak to Brunner but Bernadette's mother came first. If the German had done this, he would bring him to justice, to the guillotine.

Bernadette, so young, so beautiful. In death, her beauty had grown in his mind. Her vulnerability had been so clear and made him feel so protective of her. His thoughts wishing Zara would become like her, frightened him now rather than reassured him. Was this how it could end?

The two mortuary attendants stood nearby. They made no attempt to remove the body since the pathologist had not arrived yet.

It was some minutes before he did.

Claude returned and took a list of names from the crowd. Had they seen anything? Who was the man who had found the body? Auguste needed to talk to him.

Dr. Dubois arrived. He drew up his bicycle and leaned it against a tree. He waited to see if it would fall and satisfied, he turned to where Auguste stood, musing.

The doctor was a man who liked a drink but he did the post-mortems and prepared his reports with remarkable efficiency considering his wine consumption. Eight o'clock in the morning was of course a time of sobriety even for him so Auguste knew Dubois would be reliable.

'Good morning, Inspector,' Dubois said.

He was a small round man who reminded Auguste of an orange on cocktail-sticks. His globular body propped upon his thin short legs and his cherry-red cheeks belied a man of good intellect and Auguste knew this. He was after all, not a man who tolerated fools.

'Good morning Doctor,' he said.

'This is where the body was found?'

'Yes, I turned her over onto her back to make sure she was not alive.'

'Always you do this. You know you make more work for me my friend.'

'Sorry. I checked her pulse. Bernadette Leclerc. I knew her.'

His words seemed to have a hollow ring to them. He knew her. It was more than a simple acquaintance. He had known her a long time, since her father had died and her mother was crippled. And here she lay, cold in the drizzle of the morning air, her toenails the only sign of warmth or feelings. He hated his job now. Politics and now death. Death and then politics, it had all merged in his mind until he could not tell them apart. It was as if he faced a huge monster marching or crawling towards him, destroying all in its path, even young innocents. And she had been a young innocent, who had squeezed the last ounces of his desire to protect, from him. He had not been there for her and he hated himself for it.

'Auguste, there is hypostasis forming even now,' Dubois said.

'Yes, I realised. When do you think she died?'

'Auguste, please. You know, when the blood drains through the tissues into the lowermost part of the body at least two hours must have passed and the rigor mortis has only begun now which means about four hours.'

'You called it something else last time.'

'Eh?'

'Yes, you called it something else.'

'Livedo gravitatas?'

'Perhaps.'

'Auguste, my friend, please be patient. I will examine the body and you will get my report after the weekend.'

'After the weekend? Are you mad? I need to know the cause of death and the timing today.'

Dubois smiled.

'You are joking?' Auguste said.

'Of course. You are such an easy target my friend.'

Dubois slapped Auguste on the arm, 'I can do it this afternoon. I will have the written report in your hands tomorrow morning.'

'Can I come to the mortuary this evening?'

'Of course.'

'But you can't tell me how she died?'

'You don't know?'

'No.'

'You should have spectacles, my friend. You did not see the bruising around her throat?'

Auguste looked at the exposed throat, where Dubois had pulled down the overcoat.

'Yes, I see it now. Not very marked.'

'Ah, the laryngeal cartilages will be crushed, wait and see. Poor girl.'

Dubois raised his hand to his two porters and they came, black bag and stretcher. Auguste felt revulsion as they manhandled Bernadette into the bag and folded the edges. They were neat, practised in their work and it was another aspect of the matter filling him with revulsion. To be practised with death, to be used to handling dead bodies tugged at his feelings of disgust.

'I will see you later Auguste. Telephone at five and I will tell you if we have finished.'

'Thank you Jean.'

Auguste stood and watched as the mortuary attendants loaded the girl's body into the van. They departed, a green van disappearing around a corner, carrying with it the last remnants of his self-respect.

It had always been like this for Auguste. Every death was personal. Every one meant something to him. His teachers and seniors always taught him it was unprofessional to be too closely involved. A case is a case, they said.

Murders were unusual in Bergerac, where everyone knew everyone else. To Auguste, unpractised as he was in solving murders, each body was a person, a soul departed from its mortal shell. It was God's will but apprehending the killer was Auguste's will and he had never failed so far. He would find Bernadette's killer and bring him to justice. Good, honest, French justice.

He walked towards the door of the Prefecture and he swore by the soul of St Sacerdos of Sarlat, he would find whoever killed this child.

2

Auguste sat with his head in his hands. It tortured him. The Jews, Monique, the murder of the young woman. He felt as if he was a joist in a building and more and more weight bore down upon him. He wondered if he would crack. Three hours sleep and his mind was functioning at a level where he felt he was wandering in a mist. Basic functions of his working life seemed lost to him. Where to start? Brunner? Forensic pathology?

He began to panic. A crisis of confidence enveloped him. He felt he could not solve the crime. Too much was going on. His confidence sank. He had no faith now in his own ability.

And then it came to him. He saw his God. He envisioned his Lord on the cross and a warm feeling came. What had he himself ever suffered? What possible claim could he make to the Passion of Christ? Yet, there before him, he could envision how suffering could lead to justice for some or reclamation for others. And it was justice he wanted, no, needed. Justice for the loss of an innocent life, a child, in his eyes. He believed in the law. He led his entire professional life by it and now he felt compelled to further its inexorable path. And Bernadette? She was beyond justice, beyond the effects of revenge. Yet she or the concept of what she had been, depended on Auguste's actions now and he needed to have strength.

He wondered if his feelings for this girl were real or if they represented some ultimate peak of what he was going through. Perhaps it was not Bernadette's death but the addition of it to all the other risks and dangers driving him to this sad state of self-flagellation.

He took deep breaths and calmed himself. He knew it was lack of sleep, frustration and stress. Time. Let time pass and let him deal with each object in his path, one at a time. He had always reacted in this way to huge mounds of work, pressure, anger. One small piece at a time and endless patience.

He noticed he was breathing deeply and to his surprise, he noticed his eyes were moist. He was not tearful but his eyes were moist enough to make him wipe them.

The knock on his door made him panic.

Édith stood in the doorway. Her spectacles still on the end of her nose and her head up, as if they might fall if she leaned forward.

'Édith. Bernadette Leclerc has been murdered.'

'Murdered?' she said.

'Yes, strangled. The killer or killers dumped her body outside of the Prefecture.'

'Ah,' she said, 'it begins.'

'What?'

'It begins. It is symptomatic of the time in which we live, that's all. Who would do such a thing? I know her mother. She will die through this. Has anyone told her yet?'

'I'm going just now.'

She sat down opposite him.

He paused and looked her in the eye.

He said, 'I think Brunner did this.'

'Brunner?'

'Yes, she was singing in La Bonne Auberge the other night. He seemed interested in her.'

'Today, Bernadette Leclerc and tomorrow? You? Your family? Perhaps they will be kind enough to take me so I can be free?'

'Édith, what are you saying?'

'I don't know.'

He saw tears in her eyes and he understood as if for the first time, she was like him—tortured.

'Auguste, this place is becoming an entrance to hell, like Rosetti's gates. Jewish people interned for nothing more than their religious beliefs. Our children murdered in the street and those fat Nazi bastards sitting pretty, laughing at us. When will you do something? When do we fight?'

Auguste said nothing. The silence between them became a bond. No words were needed, their grief unspoken but vivid all the same. It was grief they shared. They grieved over the world in which they had grown up. It had gone; it had died.

Time passed and he knew he had to go.

'I will first go to her mother's house. Then I have to go to the Judge's chambers to report. Would you ask Claude to come up, I'll take him with me.'

'You can't trust Claude.'

'What?'

'He wants your job.'

'Of course he does. I know it. But how far would he go to get it?'

'He is capable of betraying you in any way in which he has the opportunity. I knew his father and he was the same.'

'Oh Édith. You see it all as black or white. There is a lot of grey too.'

'Not for the poor Leclerc girl.'

'No.'

He grabbed his coat, the smuts obvious where he had placed it on the ground earlier. As Édith left, he rubbed at them as if he needed to expunge the evidence of the contact with death. His tired mind steeled itself for what was to come. He hated bringing bad news and today, he knew he had to do so with gentleness. It had never been his forte and it filled him with fear.

CHAPTER SIX

1

A faint glimmer of sunshine peeped through the banks of grey cloud above as the Citroën drew to a halt in the little side street. The cobbles gave a weak reflection of it, making the browns grey and Auguste noted it had ceased raining. It caused him no optimism however. He pictured in his mind how Bernadette had mocked confession as she left his car. He remembered her girlish skip as she crossed the road. In his youth, he thought, he could have loved such a girl. No love had protected her last night and love was not here in this narrow cobbled alley.

It was like when he was a small child, going to see the headmaster at school, he reflected. He recalled the day when he had brought a mouth organ and played it during a lesson. Madame Velosovitch, his mathematics teacher, enraged, had sent him to receive discipline. He recalled the dampness of his palms and his heart thrumming against his ribs as he entered the dark panelled room; the look on the headmaster's face; the old man's eyebrows twitching as he administered the punishment. But this punishment was different. It would not be better in a few days. It would continue to smart in his mind. He wished he could refuse it, he wished, like his Saviour, he had a Father he could pray to—to escape the inevitable pain. He knew though, Jesus had capitulated to the fate assigned him and he must do it too.

He glanced at Claude, who stood beside him. The junior inspector was still wet behind the ears to Auguste's thinking. He had not chosen him after all. Claude was a Dubois. His father's cousin was the Judge, who pulled the strings for Claude's appointment. Auguste would rather have appointed his second in command himself, but politics was politics, he reflected.

Claude was tall and thin, lanky but strong. He had boxed at university and had done well obtaining a degree in history. His smart, brown side-parted hair reflected his neat and tidy ways so irritating to Auguste. Claude was a good police officer he had no doubt, but he disliked him all the same. Perhaps Édith was right.

Auguste reached forward to knock on the door. It swung open before them, even with his gentle tap. It was on the latch and Auguste called out.

'Madame Leclerc?'

No answer came, so they entered. A small entrance hall, dark and unforgiving, presented itself. Next to the stairs, stood a sad, brown wheelchair made of wood with a wicker seat. Auguste wondered who would push it now, now that Bernadette would never come home. A chandelier hung from the ceiling but no light reflected from its cheap glass facets. The stair-carpet was green and worn and the painted hospital-green walls sported family pictures, hung staggered as they ascended above the stairwell.

Claude and Auguste pushed past the hat-stand and Auguste put his head round the doorjamb looking for signs of life. The sitting room was empty and they looked in the kitchen too but Bernadette's mother seemed to be absent.

Auguste called again, but louder.

A weak feminine voice called down the stairs.

'One moment. One moment. I am coming.'

Auguste looked up the stairs and saw an indistinct figure there, at the top. She approached the stairs and he saw she wore a cardigan over a knee-length dress, flower-patterned and threadbare. She supported herself on two crutches, each jammed under her armpits and one hand held the stair-rail.

'Who is it?'

'It is Inspector Ran, Madame.'

'Police? What has happened?'

'If you could come downstairs, we can talk,' Claude said.

Auguste said, 'or we could come up if you wish.'

'What is wrong? Is it Bernadette? Has she done something wrong?'

The rounded shape began to descend the steep staircase and Auguste wondered if he should offer to help, but he knew better. Besides, he did not want to touch her, as if her pending grief might be contagious. The slow descent took minutes but Bernadette's mother knew how to do it and the two policemen felt forced to stand and watch, for conversation was not possible over her grunts of effort and discomfort. Her stiff legs swinging together between the crutches, she led them into the sitting room. The polished wood floor, the round brown rug shouted penury and the two men felt squashed together as they sat on the small couch, across a glass-topped table from the object of their mission.

Madame Leclerc lowered herself into a chair and sat silent, as if she knew what Auguste was about to say.

Her mouth drawn tight, her lips hard, she said, 'Something has happened, has it?'

She was older than Auguste remembered, perhaps five or ten years older than he was, though he felt very old today.

'Yes.'

'To Bernadette?'

'I'm afraid it is very bad news.'

The tight lips trembled. The hand holding the two vertical crutches shook. Auguste knew it was coming. He waited for an outburst.

'Bad?' her voice sounded angry, aggressive.

'Yes. I am very sorry...'

'Sorry?'

'I'm afraid she is... she is...'

His voice trailed away. He glanced up at her face but read nothing there apart from a trembling in the lips and a moistening of the eyes.

'How did it happen?' Madame Leclerc said.

'Her body was found in the market square this morning.'

'I see.'

Her voice was quiet now, relaxed. Her face had crumpled it seemed to Auguste, as if it was a paper, screwed up in someone's hand and then unwrapped. He also knew the wrinkling and furrows would never disappear now.

'We have some questions. Do you feel able to answer them?'

Silence.

'Madame?'

'The last time we spoke,' she said, 'you told me my husband was dead and you could not find out who the other driver was. I lay on that hospital bed and felt as if you were killing me. I have never walked without pain since that day. Bernadette was the only reason for my life to continue. Now you tell me she is dead. You are killing me again. Once more it is you.'

Auguste said nothing.

Claude said, 'Madame, we will need your help to find who did this.'

'Yes... yes,' she said, her voice trailing away.

Auguste said, 'Would you prefer we come back later?'

'No. I don't ever want you to come back here. I never want to see your face again.'

'When did you see her last?'

'Last night. I was upstairs and I heard her talking to someone. It was a man.'

'At what time was that?'

'I don't know. It was late evening. I was getting ready for bed.'

'And then?'

'She called up the stairs.'

She paused; a tear meandered down her tanned cheek and she said, 'She said she would be going out but would be back in a short time. I asked her who was there but she said nothing.'

Claude said, 'you're certain she said nothing more?'

'No. I mean yes, certain.'

'And she went out?'

'Yes. I heard the door bang shut. Is that all?'

'Was Bernadette seeing anyone? A young man perhaps?'

'No. She worked hard. She studied in the day and she sang at night. She told me she was finding another job because there were too many Germans at the restaurant.'

The policemen stood and Auguste said, 'Is there someone we can call? Is there anyone who can come and stay with you for... for a while?'

'No. I am used to being alone.'

'You will have to come to the mortuary to identify her. It is a formality but a necessary one. Claude here will ask you some more questions then, if you don't mind. I am sorry.'

'Yes.'

'I will send a car, later this afternoon.'

'Yes, you do that inspector. For your records. Your all-important records. But you don't have the name on those records.'

'The name?'

'The killer. The beast who robbed me of my little girl. Evil people. First Jean, now Bernadette. Who did this? Who?'

She struggled to her feet. She leaned forward on her crutches. She took hold of Auguste's coat lapels as if she could sense some contact with Bernadette, as if the last caress of the cloth on her naked body had left some trace of her and it attracted the crippled woman who stood there, desperate, wild-eyed and shocked.

'Madame,' Auguste said, 'we don't know, but we will find out and we will bring him to justice. I promise.'

'No. You speak of justice? Kill him. Please kill him. He must die for what he did to my daughter, my little one. She was only a young girl, don't you see?'

Her grip tightened and she pulled him to her despite the discrepancy in height and her instability.

'Promise me. Promise me you will get him. Promise, do you hear?'

'I promise. I will get him and he will face the guillotine.'

'Kill him. It is all such a travesty of a man deserves. Death in payment. Does it not say an eye for an eye in the Bible?'

'But it also says 'vengeance is mine, saith the Lord'. I will see Bernadette's killer gets what he deserves. Please, sit now. We know our way out.'

They found their way back to the street and Auguste felt relief for the first time since he parked the car. He turned to Claude and said, 'She's shocked. We won't get much out of her for a while.'

'No. I'll try her again when she identifies the body.'

'I want you to speak to the neighbours, maybe they saw something. Try to get a feel for the timing.'

'And you?'

'I will see the Judge Dubois. He will have to run the investigation.'

'How do I get back? My bicycle is back at the Prefecture.'

'Claude, my boy,' Auguste said, 'God gave you legs and he gave me a car. I want a written report on my desk by this afternoon.'

He sat in his car and watched as Claude began his questioning of the neighbours and he decided he would keep his promise. Whoever killed her would pay; he swore it. It began to rain again as he drove away.

'Poor Claude,' he muttered under his breath.

2

The stone stairs greeted each footfall with a resounding clack as Auguste climbed to the Judge's office. He thought about his report. He would describe where the passerby found the body and how it had attracted police attention. He needed to give some information on Bernadette's background and give some idea of cause of death. It was premature to speculate but if Doctor Dubois was right, she had been strangled around four in the morning.

Of course, a written report would be required but there had not been time so far. If he had returned to the Prefecture, he could have had Édith type his report before coming but he preferred to make these things factual and face-to-face. His life was based upon facts and it was his nature after all.

The oak door loomed ahead, closed and unassailable. His knuckles hurt when he rapped, for the door was solid, heavy, as if it was a more substantial bar to his further progression in the Police Force. He knew the obstacle was not Judge Dubois, but a more ethereal force and more subtle in its application. The German authorities would never allow a Frenchman like Auguste to hold an important position even though they owned the Vichy-French police like a farmer owns a duck.

He heard a faint acknowledgement greet his knocking, so he opened the door. The outer office was as large as his own was at the prefecture. A desk hovered next to the door of the inner office as if it was there to prevent entry, like some brooding, wooden guard-dog. Seated there was a woman, her hair up in a neat bun and her brown dress tidy and clean. A black metal typewriter stood on the desk and there was a small vase with flowers in as if to say the office was cheerful which he knew it never was. The constant visits by lawyers and criminals, criminals and lawyers in endless procession could never be anything but cheerless to Auguste and he wrinkled his nose at the thought.

'Well,' said the woman, 'what brings the Inspector of Police to these corridors?'

She smiled a cold, lacklustre smile.

He said, 'I need to see the Judge about a murder.'

'So my mother's favourite son needs his sister does he?'

'Juliette, she only had one son and I was never her favourite.'

'Now, now, Auguste. She spoke of you even in her dying breath. She never mentioned me.'

'So you say in your endless bitterness. I did not come here to argue about such things. My God, I am here on business and I need to see the Judge.'

Her lips tightened and she said, 'He is busy, Auguste.'

'This is important, a murder.'

'Well in that case, I will ask him.'

She stood. He stepped forward, close.

'Juliette, can't we stop all this? It is ten years since Maman died. Can't we have peace between us?'

'Stop what? I don't understand. I have no problems.'

'No problems? We haven't spoken outside this office since she died.'

'Why should I give you the satisfaction? She left it all to you. The house, the land, even her jewellery. And why?'

'But you were in Berlin. Maman had not seen you for ten years. She believed you were secure.'

'Secure? Married to a bankrupt? You turned her against me. Leaving it all to you was the final stroke. And when I came home? Nothing. I have nothing.'

'Juliette, please.'

'Wait there,' she said.

She strode to the door and knocked. She disappeared inside, closing it behind her. Auguste watched as the door closed. He felt inured to this scene, it had replayed in a monotonous eternity for years. He was tired of it and it was still painful.

Auguste felt exhausted and weary of conflict, tired of the war and most of all, he wanted peace in his soul and conscience. The events of the last few days were wearing him to a frazzle. This silly woman twittering on about her inheritance and Bernadette murdered, with no culprit in sight unless it was Brunner.

And Monique? What had he taken on? Odette and he were risking everything for one child. If he stayed in charge here, he could surely save many more lives. But he knew he could never hand her over. He knew he would protect Pierre's daughter. Whatever happened he would be there for her, though her father was not.

Presently, Juliette emerged.

She said, 'Judge Dubois will see you now, Auguste.'

Dubois sat still as Auguste entered. He looked up. The Judge was a small round man, like his brother the Pathologist; Auguste thought of him as globular. He was bald and his head sweated even in cool weather. His dark blue suit made him look official and his gold-rimmed spectacles, intellectual, as he would have put it. The beard was grey as if the hair on his head had slipped and resided now on his face, sliding across his sweaty brow and descending to its final position. No smile adorned his plump lips.

'Inspector?'

'Judge Dubois. I came to report a murder and to advise you of the investigation so far.'

'Yes, my brother telephoned me earlier.'

'He did?'

'Yes, he thought I should know.'

'But he was maybe premature. He hasn't done the post mortem yet.'

'Besides, I have the report from your office.'

'Report sir?' Auguste frowned.

'Yes, about the prostitute.

'What prostitute?'

'Found outside your office, was she not?'

'What report? I sent no report. I have just come from interviewing the only relative, the girl's mother.'

'Well, it is signed by Desour. You mean you didn't even read it?'

'Well, I...'

'Ran, you seem to be slipping. You don't even read the reports from your office, yet you come here in the middle of my constructing a judgement?'

'The girl was no prostitute. I knew her. She was a student and a singer. A decent family.'

'A singer? Opera?'

'No, popular songs. Piaf and the like. She was changing jobs, to work in a bakery before the murder happened.'

'She sang in bars? Not a prostitute? Seems a bit farfetched to me.'

'I can vouch for her character. Believe me, she was not a

prostitute. She was singing to earn money to support her mother who is crippled, and to pay for her studies.'

Auguste noticed his feelings of anger. He wanted to thump the desk and remonstrate, but he knew it was not the way to play this scene. Judge Dubois had the power here. Anger was neither relevant nor of value to him. This was a place of law and nothing more. Justice he thought was not the law. Law was a book with pages and justice was something less definable.

'I know she was murdered and her body was naked. This sounds to me to be the sordid murder of a prostitute. Desour says so in the report. Have you changed your mind?'

Auguste wanted to tell him about La Bonne Auberge. He wanted to clarify the girl's life, her purity, but nothing came now. It had been decided already. Bernadette, a voice like an angel and the body of a girl, had already been judged a harlot. He felt nauseated by the conceit, the arrogance of the man in front of him.

'The report was premature. She left her mother's home that evening and never returned.'

'So you have some leads?

'I think it may have been Brunner the SD Major.'

'You have proof? Evidence? Without it, there is no case and frankly, the chance of indicting a German SD Major is non-existent. Germany has defeated us. They hold the power and any attempt to dissent will be seen as treason and result in death.'

'He's a killer.'

'Prove it.'

'I will have to work on it. I am seeing your brother the pathologist, this afternoon.'

'Then do so. I want another full report in the morning. Until then you will pursue your investigation as you please.

Auguste made to leave,

'Oh by the way. Perhaps you should leave this case for a younger man to cut his teeth on.'

'Younger?'

'Yes, Claude could perhaps run the police case and you might wish to oversee him.

'Ridiculous.'

'Ridiculous?'

'I am the senior officer here. It is up to me.'

'No Inspector. It is up to me.

Auguste turned to leave.

'You had better find your killer. If you don't, perhaps Desour will need to be put in charge of the case.'

Their eyes met. Auguste detected the hostility and he knew there was no support here.

'Oh, by the way,' the Judge said, 'I think you have more important things to attend to.'

'Yes?'

'You need to begin transferring those Jews to Drancy.'

'It is going ahead early next month.'

'Has it never occurred to you they might be right?'

'In what respect?'

'About the Jews taking our jobs and cheating us with high prices?'

'They are people. They may have been too clever for the dull Germans to tolerate but the discrimination and degradation is not French. France has always had tolerance and treated everyone equally.'

'You sound like a communist, Inspector.'

'Liberty, equality and brotherhood. We have lost the first and last, have we lost the middle one too?'

'As I said, you have more important things to attend to. Make sure you do. We have new masters and they do not tolerate bungling.'

For a moment, their eyes met. Dubois' eyes held steel. Auguste looked away but he wondered as he left the office whether he should have defended Bernadette in stronger tones. She deserved better from her compatriots than to be labelled and discarded. It seemed to Auguste it was symptomatic of the capitulation of his country. They had lost respect for each other as if defeat brings with it a form of intolerance directed at anyone who was weaker.

As he drove back to the Prefecture, he found himself in a

whirlpool of anger, hatred and injustice. He was determined to swim and not sink. He had family who needed him, depended upon him and he would no more succumb to these pressures now, than he would give in to his urge to flee. He felt he was there to stay and he would do the best he could as a Christian, a Catholic.

CHAPTER SEVEN

1

To Auguste the world began to change. His secure base of work now seemed to have foundations of sand. He still clung to his morals, his beliefs and his conviction that justice was everything, like a man would cling to a crucifix when facing death. He did not intend to allow the Jewish internment to go as planned. He would enlist the help of the old Colonel and ensure the Jews knew what the government intended. How they might escape was another matter and not one with which he could help them. His biggest problem was he had no contacts in the resistance, the Maquis, or the Communists. Every one of them whom he had known, languished in some prison or was dead.

He stood with his hand on the door-handle of his office as if he felt reluctant to enter. He heard his stomach complain and realised he had not eaten since breakfast and began to feel hungry.

'Auguste,' Édith said behind him.

'Édith, I need to get a message to Colonel Arnaud. Can you...'

Édith stood with her extended index pressed to her lips. He frowned in ignorance.

She said, 'We have had visitors. The SD were here with some SS soldiers.'

Auguste said nothing.

'They came to check the building. Linz said they had confession evidence a bomb had been planted.'

'They searched everywhere?'

'Yes. They made the most thorough search of your office and spent a long time in there.'

'I understand. There was no bomb then?'

'No Auguste,' she said.

She handed him a note.

He read:

> They were in your office for half an hour and the door was closed.

'I am glad our German friends are so efficient. It makes me feel secure.'

Auguste wrote as he spoke.

> See if you can get a message to Arnaud. I can meet him in the square outside at 3pm. I want a copy of the Jewish file too.

'Yes, Auguste we are most secure.'

Édith smiled and turned to go.

'I need to see Dubois this afternoon. He will have news of the post-mortem. I also have to write a memo to my men but it is, under no circumstances, to be circulated until the night before the uplift. Oh and is there a chance of something to eat?'

'As you wish Auguste. There were some brioche left over from this morning. I will make some coffee. By the way, can François Dufy be released?'

He smiled and said, 'I don't see why not. He's had enough meals at the state's expense.'

Édith brought a copy of the file containing the names and

addresses of the Jewish families in his catchment area. It was on a tray under the coffee and bread rolls. He ate as he studied the list. Most of the addresses were in St Cyprien and Beynac et Cazenac east of Bergerac. He made up his mind to go there before the end of the month and try to get a message to any who would listen. He was uncertain how he might achieve this, but he believed not only in God, he believed in luck and he hoped an answer would present itself.

2

It was not often Auguste slept at work. On this day however, he sat at his desk, reading some reports and as his eyes blurred and his breathing calmed, his eyelids began to droop. He shook his head, he got up from the desk and paced for a few minutes, but as soon as he resumed reading, his eyes insisted on letting him down.

He awoke with a start. He realised he was drooling on the report he was reading and he wiped his mouth on his sleeve with an involuntary movement. A knock on the door made him start. He felt dizzy and forced himself to awaken fully. He glanced at his watch and realised he must have slept for two hours.

'Come,' he said.

It was Claude.

'I thought you might have had someone in here.'

'Oh?'

'Yes, I was waiting for minutes at the door.'

'You got back easily?'

'Yes, a friend gave me a lift. He was just passing and he stopped, thank you.'

'You have friends who can afford gasoline?'

'Yes. I have written a report on the case, reflecting our progress so far.'

'Not your first from what I hear.'

'Excuse me?' Claude said.

'Judge Dubois, your cousin more correctly, received a report from you before I ever reached his office.'

'It was only a preliminary report to warn him of the case. I thought it was the right thing to do.'

'Without showing it to me?'

'Oh, sorry.'

'Sorry? You bungled it. You described Bernadette Leclerc as a prostitute. It was incorrect.'

'Well it seemed to me...'

'As police officers we are not here to engage in supposition. We deal in facts. Facts. We have no facts and that is all you could put into a report. As for going behind my back, well...'

Claude switched his weight from foot to foot, he was beginning to look uncomfortable and it gave Auguste a feeling of satisfaction.

'That will be all,' Auguste said with an air of finality.

Claude said, 'May I come with you to the post-mortem? I have only been to ten or so.'

'There is no need. I'm sure you will have many opportunities to see young dead girls cut up in the future. I don't need you. Shut the door on the way out.'

The scowl on Claude's face made Auguste smile. He did not intend for an ambitious young man to upstage him, whether everyone important in the town was a relation of his or not.

He glanced at his watch and grabbed his coat. On the way out, he smiled at Édith. She was clever that one. What he would do without her he could not imagine. Who else would have known Brunner's trickery? He felt hamstrung however by the loss of privacy in the office but felt relief that he knew. He could perhaps use it to his advantage if he needed to impart disinformation to the SD. It could work in his favour.

CHAPTER EIGHT

1

He parked his battered car outside the hospital. A tall stone building, it loomed above the wide street, peering down at him. A man on crutches hobbled to the steps through the wide archway of the main entrance and hearing Auguste's footsteps he looked up. He stumbled and fell; a heap of pain and flailing limbs. Auguste rushed to his assistance but the injured man pushed him away. It was then Auguste noticed the yellow star on the man's right arm.

'Please let me help you.'

'You,' the man said looking up with narrowed brown eyes, 'you've helped me enough you bastard.'

Auguste stepped back and watched as the man struggled to his feet. He was maybe forty years of age, with black greying hair and a tattered grey jacket. His beret had fallen and Auguste picked it up.

'Do I know you?'

'No but maybe you should.'

'I should?'

'Your men took my wife and son away and left me here in Bergerac to rot.'

'I don't understand.'

'I was knocked down by a German car. The driver got out and pulled me into the gutter. When he got back into his car, my wife hammered on the windscreen. She begged for help. I can hear her crying and begging for help even now. The driver got out and took her name. Next day, your men came and took her and my son away. I was in hospital; my son was fourteen. Give me my hat.'

'I... I... I'm sorry.'

The man stared at him, the hatred in his glance made Auguste shudder.

'Give me your name and I will try to find out where they are.'

'For what? So you can send your men for me too?'

'No,' Auguste said his voice low almost muttering.

'Vichy-French. All the same.'

The man spat on the step. The glob of spittle sat there between them, small enough to step over, yet to Auguste as wide and deep as a lake—a lake of utter bitterness. Auguste reflected it was not the quantity of it but the venom with which it was delivered.

'I will find out where your wife is and she will be returned to you. My men acted under orders, it's not their fault.'

'Orders? Orders? A good excuse. If they ordered you to kill us all, would you do it? Would God forgive you? Do we not both believe in the same God? Yahweh? Jehovah? Whatever you want to call Him, is He not our common Lord?'

Auguste was silent. He felt as if the man had thrust a massive weight upon his shoulders and he could feel how they sagged. He wanted to be somewhere else. It was easy to sign an arrest warrant. He was not used to facing the human result of his actions and it came home to him how easy it was to be passive. It was a few simple strokes of the pen. The Germans had told him to arrest these people. They were French, his brothers and sisters, yet he acted against them. He knew now the passivity to which he had become inured made him as guilty of the crimes to come as if he had committed them himself. He was ashamed. The injured Jew had shown him the truth.

He turned away and walked inside, head down, the feeling

threatening to overwhelm him. He knew he could do nothing for this man and worse, he should never have offered. It was fruitless. Soon the man would join his family not in a work camp, but in death.

A wide corridor stretched to left and right. The high arched ceiling rose above him and on the walls were paintings, hung in long rows on each side. Auguste turned left and he glanced at a picture. It was a print of a Swedish picture he recognised. Inappropriate as it was, he stopped to look. In the foreground and facing away, stood a naked boy, fists clenched, shivery and intense, poised to jump into a river. Water dripped from the boy's wet, glistening hair and a sense of excitement leapt from the picture. For Auguste, it was almost as if he was there. Either side of the boy were others watching. He knew its name. It was entitled 'A Great Place to Bathe'.

Had it not been for the Jew on the stairs he would have smiled. The picture brought back childhood memories of long, hot summers when Pierre and he bathed in the Dordogne, leaping headlong from the rickety wooden platform near Pierre's parent's home. He bit his lip and turned, trudging down the corridor towards the mortuary.

At the end of the corridor, opening a heavy wooden door, he descended the stone steps and crossed a small courtyard to the square brick building ahead.

He knocked but there was no answer so he pushed the door open and entered. It was cold inside and he shuddered again but this time with the cold. His boots clacked on a stone floor and pushing open another door, he entered the mortuary theatre.

It was a large airy room. Lecture seats lined the walls and in the centre stood the plinth topped by a porcelain slab. On it lay the butchered remains of the girl he had heard singing—her angelic voice silenced now, her very substance exposed by a cruel cut from chin to pubic bone. As ever, for Auguste, the intolerable aspect of the place was the smell. It had the stench of death and the odour always clung to the nostrils long after leaving. It was a smell of bowels and chemicals; it clung to his clothes, his hair and his soul. He felt like retching but swallowed hard and it passed.

Her abdomen and chest were empty, recalling the flesh and ribs exposed in abattoirs and butcher's shops but this was human. Human and sacred. A girl. Bernadette. The singer. The student; opened, exposed and examined. Auguste hovered on the edge of running away. It was like some macabre horror story, yet it was his job and the dread of it simply strengthened his resolve to find who had killed her.

Doctor Dubois was there. He stood with his back to Auguste dressed in a long green apron. He turned when he heard the footsteps behind him and Auguste noticed the blood and semisolid material adhering to the doctor's apron.

'Ah Auguste, my friend,' Dubos said. 'You are just in time. I have more information for you. Are you unwell?'

'Unwell?'

'You look a little green.'

Auguste swallowed. He could taste the bitter and sour flavour of his long since swallowed pseudo-coffee.

Dubois chuckled. He said, 'I suppose you do not come here very often. For me it is an everyday horror. One becomes used to it.'

'You have more news?'

'Yes, the girl was killed at around three or four in the morning. She had been raped and strangled. There was semen in the vagina. I may be able to get a blood group from it, but I'm short of chemicals this month. The larynx had been crushed. That in itself is not unusual but there were marks on her buttocks.'

'Marks?'

'Yes. Burns. I think whoever did this tortured her before killing her. The burns are a design.'

'May I see?'

'It would mean turning the body over and my mortuary assistant has gone home. I can draw it for you.'

Auguste felt dizziness overtaking him. Dubois reached out and held his arm, guiding him to a chair, which stood in the corner.

'Perhaps we can talk in my office, away from...' he waved his left arm like showing off the mortuary to a group of students, 'You will get the report late tomorrow morning.'

Unsteady, Auguste allowed the doctor to support him to the pathologist's office. The door shut, the smell became attenuated enough for Auguste to feel he was surfacing.

Dubois sat down at his desk and Auguste sat opposite. The doctor found a pen and began drawing. The desk was an old carved affair with a leather top and a telephone stood, black and ancient, on the left corner. He looked at the walls, adorned by charts and anatomical pictures. A bookcase stood gathering dust, propped against the left-hand wall. In a glass case stood specimens, preserved in some cloudy fluid and to Auguste's relief, the opacity of the fluid obscured the outlines.

'There,' said the doctor. He handed his sketch to Auguste who felt as if he was taking some strange and mystical cipher scrawled on a secret parchment.

'I think you will understand what it means.'

Auguste looked at the symbol. It was a circle with a cross inside.

'No.'

'It is a sun-cross.'

'Well?'

'You haven't heard of it?'

'No.'

'It dates back to prehistory. Neolithic peoples used this as an emblem and it was used even in the Greek civilisation as a sign of the sun.'

'So we are no further forward.'

Auguste made to stand.

'We are, I'm afraid.'

'How so? She was tortured by an ancient civilisation?'

'No. It is the original basis of the swastika. It derives from this sign. It appears in far-eastern cultures but the Nazis have adopted it as theirs.'

'I understand now. We are looking for a Nazi.'

'Well, probably. It is not a swastika, but a sun-cross; perhaps intended to tease or confuse. It could be anyone wanting to throw blame on the Germans.'

'They cut this into her flesh?'

'Yes, it looks like burns. There are also ligature marks on her ankles and wrists and a rag was stuffed into her mouth.'

Auguste stood up. This time he was sure he could escape. He had learned enough for the moment.

'Undertakers?

'They are coming the day after tomorrow. I have to put her back together again first and it's getting late. It won't matter to her if I do it tomorrow.'

'Oh yes, I wondered why you telephoned your brother before the post mortem examination.'

'Telephone? No. I telephoned no one.'

'Judge Dubois said you telephoned him and told him of the murder.'

'No, why would I do that?'

'Oh, it doesn't matter. If you find anything else, will you let me know?'

'Tonight, I will find nothing else but a glass of good Bergerac and a glass or two of Calvados. At least the Germans don't have a taste for it yet.'

They shook hands and Auguste could not recall whether the pathologist had washed his hands or not. It was no use sniffing his fingers since he was unable to rid his nostrils of the mortuary-death-formalin smell.

He would be late getting home and he was tired and hungry. He had to work on the attic wall and he had promised himself a glass of wine before then.

He pondered what he had learned from Dubois. The rape and the strangulation he had known. The sun-cross burn was something else. It could be a red herring but equally it could be a sadistic joke from the killer and he still thought Brunner was involved. He had not read Claude's report to see whether the neighbours had seen anything.

Tomorrow would do. As Dubois had said, it made no difference to poor Bernadette and he had pressures to preserve the living rather than worry about the dead. He was seeing Arnaud, but he had no idea how he could avoid arresting the members of the Jewish community and he patted the list of names and addresses in his pocket. The Lord would reveal a plan to him. He was sure.

2

The farmhouse kitchen in which Auguste sat was his favourite room in the house. It recalled his memories of his mother Marie. At times, he could almost see her bustling, cooking, baking and squatting to the low oven of the black-lead range. She had never cursed; only remonstrated in gentle tones when she bumped into the garlic hanging from the rack above the kitchen table, the one the copper pans hung from, the ones she spent hours shining. Her ghost haunted the place still he reflected, but he knew these were fanciful thoughts and best kept to himself.

'Sometimes, Odette, I think I married you for your cassoulet,' Auguste said.

'Well you're lucky there was any left; those two girls could eat for France.'

He spooned more into his mouth and swallowing, he said, 'Not much meat though.'

'Ha. Try getting meat now. Everything has gone up in price. I paid a lot for this rabbit. One rabbit for four people.'

'Where did you get it?'

'François Dufy. He was selling them near the Prefecture in the market square. He was drunk but he is such a nice man even so.'

'He was in the cells most of this week. His game will be well hung by now.'

'When will you be finished in the attic?'

'I have a joist to move then I can start the brickwork. I will make the door too small for an adult; that way, even if they suspect, they cannot get in.'

'Why would they search the home of the assistant chief of police?'

'Well maybe not for Jews, but they have already put microphones in my office. Brunner and his men. They pretended it was a security check, looking for a bomb. Édith warned me.'

'She can be trusted?'

'I've known Édith since I started work at the Prefecture. What, twenty years? I trust her.'

'I don't understand what is happening in our world nowadays. You can't trust anyone anymore.'

Auguste reached for her hand across the kitchen table, the tabletop scored and scratched from long years of use. He smiled.

'I trust you and it is all that counts,' she said.

'Yes. We live in a confused world. A world where young women are murdered and their bodies discarded in the street, and foreign soldiers walk our streets as if they own the place, own us. And worse, we are fettered and bound watching cruelty and injustice everywhere. It is not what I joined the police force for, it is not what I've led my life for. And I am partly to blame.'

'You are not to blame Auguste. It isn't your fault.'

'Doing nothing, signing arrest warrants for the Germans, sending my men out to intern innocent people makes me culpable. You know it.'

'Then make amends. Fight. Do what you can to retrieve your soul Auguste. Is it not so? You cannot spend your life looking back. In any case you did not know.'

'I could have worked it out. I just didn't want to believe it.'

She sighed. He stood to leave, but she crossed from the other side of the table and placed her arms around his neck. He kissed her cheek, impatient, wanting to go.

'I love you still and I know you will fight.'

He looked at her and shrugged. In silence, he left her there. He ascended the stairs and heard the chink of plates and cups as Odette cleared away the remains of their meal.

'Not enough meat,' he said to himself.

3

An oil lamp illuminated the attic as Auguste worked. He realised he needed to strengthen the side of the house where he was laying bricks. Removing stones around a joist-end over the main part of the house, he chipped away at the mortar. He rigged ropes to support the joist and using a crowbar, he dislodged the ancient oak baulk.

It was awkward work; there was no flooring so he had to balance on the crossbeams to prevent himself from putting his foot through the lathe and plaster ceiling beneath. He thought he had done enough damage already by loosening the joist and a foot-hole would add nothing to the appearance of his daughter's bedroom.

He lifted the beam end and pushed it, so it swung in gentle pendular movements from the supporting ropes. He looked at the beam. He noticed he was hot and sweating. He removed his shirt and mopped his brow with it, then prepared to shift the joist towards the other end of the roof-void.

A candle's light flickered in the loft opening.

'Auguste, how is it going?'

'Odette, I thought you went to bed long ago. What time is it?'

'Three o'clock. I thought you might want some water. I crushed some blackcurrants into it.'

He crossed the attic towards her.

'Are you not cold?'

'No. The work warms me up.'

'I like you warmed up.'

'The drink may cool me.'

'Then perhaps you shouldn't drink it.'

'It won't cool me down overmuch.'

She reached out as he drank and touched his sweating chest. She teased the hair around his nipples and he coughed, almost choking.

'What are you doing?'

'Wondered if you might want to have a little rest?'

'I'm all sweat and filth.'

'I know.'

He smiled. He felt the beginnings of a gentle tumescence adjacent to his groin.

'I'll have to come back and finish this.'

'I know.'

'The girls?'

'They sleep.'

He reached for her. Their lips met, her soft moist kiss arousing him further. She smelled of a familiar perfume whose name he did not know. In his mind, he associated it with happy times of love and youthful passion. He was tempted to take her there and then, but she turned away from him and holding his belt buckle, she laughed and tugged him away, her feet nimble on the cross-beams.

Descending, he followed her into the bedroom. She stopped and they collided in the darkness. She giggled and her childish laugh aroused him even more. She guided him to the bed, laughing, playing. Moments later, naked, they lay, pleasuring each other with their mouths.

He sensed her orgasm in her breathing, the way she tensed her body, arched her back. Her fingers caressed his hair, pulling him deeper towards her. In waves it came, he felt it, as if she struggled up some steep and arduous slope, stopping now and again for long seconds and then on, on until the summit came.

'God,' she called from that pinnacle.

'My God,' she cried, as if desperate and alone.

She shuddered, breathing fast. With gentle pressure, she eased his head away.

In the dark, he sensed her smile and turned, facing her, he entered her, thrusting soft and gentle, slow at first but rising in his own rhythm, as his pleasure escalated.

He fought to keep his day from entering his mind. He struggled to keep the visions of Bernadette's body from insinuating themselves in his mind. Glimpses of the Jew on the steps flashed in front of his eyes and all the time he stroked and caressed Odette wanting her to take it away, cure him; rescue him. He touched her breast as he made love to her and she held onto him with a desperation he could feel in the strength of her grip, as if she understood. She called out again and began to breathe with him. Faster, ever faster. Ever deeper.

Then he finished. The deepest thrust of all and for one brief moment in time, all his troubles went. At this glorious moment, nothing interfered or stood between them and he shuddered as she had done, as her hands slipped on the sweat on his back.

They kissed, long and deep, feeling they were alone in the world, as if all war-torn Aquitaine had gone forever to trouble them no more. The moment lasted minutes then was gone like a breath on the wind, dissipated, dispersed.

Auguste rolled away breathing hard and she lay on her side facing him, her head on his shoulder. Her hand played with the hair on his chest and his right arm encircled her. He moved his head to escape the tickling of her hair on his face.

'I must get back to work.'

'Not yet, Auguste. Please. We have so little time together.'

'The joist won't position itself. And besides the concrete will set before I use it.'

'Can I help?'

'No. This is for me to do and some of it is heavy. Besides we need to have one of us available in case anyone comes.'

He dressed fumbling in the dark for his clothes. He swore when he fell over trying to put on his trousers. Odette giggled, hand over mouth. In poor temper, Auguste stomped up the stairs to the attic. He knew it would be a long night.

CHAPTER NINE

1

Brunner. Auguste was sure of his implication in the murder, even if he was not the perpetrator. He had little to go on, but the expression in the man's eyes when he looked at Bernadette that night in the restaurant was enough to convince.

And her body? Cut apart by the pathologist, lying in pieces—it was unthinkable. He walked up the steps of the Mairie, now the SD headquarters, and he sighed. He wished he were not alone but he knew there was no one he could trust. Claude had already betrayed him with his 'preliminary' report. He could almost hear Édith warning him not to trust the man. Yet, we judge others by our own standards and Auguste was not a man who would ever betray another; at least, not knowing he did so.

Brunner. Auguste resolved to interview him but he had no plan. He supposed he would enquire about his movements, but what was the point?

The Major needed only to say it was none of his business and question what right Auguste had to ask and it would all be over. No. He had to be more subtle. He had to try to trap the swine in some way. He hoped it would come to him in a flash of divine inspiration though he was losing his faith in the concept of God's intervention in the pursuit of justice.

It was his second night of sleep deprivation. His usual night's sleep was seven hours and he wondered how he would be able to keep going at this rate. He pictured the little room he had constructed.

He had placed a cot and a table with a chair into the room before bricking it up. The space was big enough for Monique to crawl through and he had shown her how to draw the false door into the tiny opening. When she had done it to his satisfaction, they had laughed.

He recalled how in the attic, Zara stood behind watching him with Monique and he wondered if she was jealous or if the danger of it all was making her withdraw into herself. He knew also, he should pay more attention to the girls. He made up his mind to make more effort.

Auguste waited in the anteroom by the secretary's desk for Brunner to allow him into his office. He felt like a fisherman baiting a hook not knowing what creature he might pull out of the deep.

The secretary came out. He was a tall man who towered above Auguste, his black hair tousled but clean. He had bushy eyebrows perched above his eyes like crows' nests and his black SS uniform reinforced the idea in Auguste's mind. He looked like a crow.

'Please go in,' he said.

No smile disturbed the long face. Auguste wondered what kind of people they awarded smiles to in this hellhole of interrogation and torture. He entered the office.

Brunner had changed the furniture and the wall hangings. The desk was an antique, eighteenth century, Auguste reflected. On the floor was a rug he imagined was Turkish, stolen from somewhere, the previous owners interned or killed. On the far wall was an oil painting Auguste recognised with shock. It was a watercolour by Renoir. Renoir was his namesake and he knew all of his paintings. It was detailed, showing a countryside boating scene, similar in style to a Monet but more elaborate. Auguste wondered if the artist had used a smaller brush than Monet, though it might have been the converse. A smiling Brunner, who held out his hand in an informal greeting, ripped him away from his thoughts.

Auguste took Brunner's damp hand and realised the German was sweating. He wondered why. He had no power over this man. Brunner had the SD rank of Major but this was equivalent to a full Colonel in the SS. He was immune, inviolable and he knew it. It showed in the smile drawing his pink, sickly lips across his face and in his eyes, from the steel of his gaze.

'Auguste,' Brunner said, 'how nice to see you.'

'My pleasure too, Helmut,' Auguste said.

'And what brings you here to see me?'

'We need to discuss the mechanism of the internments.'

'The internments?'

'Yes, I have a promise of one or two members of the gendarmerie to go with the trucks but if they are unarmed, then they will be of no more use than my men. Can we modify the orders?'

'None of this concerns me. I am content to leave it up to you. I trust you, Auguste. Your men carry guns so there is no objection from the SD whether the gendarmes do as well. I don't really care if they appear naked for that matter.'

The smile again. What was he hiding?

'Have you been in a fight?'

'Excuse me?'

'The scratch on your cheek,' Auguste said indicating a diagonal cut on the Major's left cheek below the cheekbone extending to the corner of his mouth.

Brunner touched his face. He said, 'this? Oh, it is nothing.'

'Looks painful.'

'Yes, yes. I fell into a hedge, please don't tell anyone. A little too much of your French Armagnac, a little too much wine. You understand.'

'Of course,' Auguste said.

'You French have such wonderful wine and brandy it is hard to be moderate.'

Brunner spoke in a slow rhythm, blinking his eyes and avoiding eye contact. Auguste thought he would have to be stupid not to realise Brunner was lying.

'Who has a need to be moderate in such things? Why when we were in La Bonne Auberge, we drank so much wine and brandy...'

'Yes, yes, I remember tumbling into bed and wondering what we had been up to.'

'And the entertainment. Such a beautiful girl Bernadette. What a shame?'

'A shame?'

Again traces of moisture on Brunner's brow. It made no sense. Brunner was impenetrable.

'Yes.' Auguste said, 'It seems you were right about her moral fibre and her clothing fibre.'

'Fibre?'

Auguste feigned a laugh.

'Yes, sorry it was a forensic joke. No, she was murdered the night before last. She must have been plying her trade in the streets and someone killed her. Pity, don't you think?'

'Terrible, such a young flower of French womanhood.'

The look in Brunner's eyes changed to one of confidence now.

'I am surprised. Did no one tell you? I thought the SD knew every little thing happening in Bergerac, every tiny event.'

'I am sure there will be a report about it somewhere. I just haven't seen it. You said fibres?'

'Yes, forgive me, it was a joke. The murderer left fibres of his clothing and some hair on the body. It will take no time to find out his clothing and a great deal of where he may have come from.'

'How astute.'

'Yes, I thought you were police, like me.'

'No. I am a security policeman, we do not pursue criminals.'

'Of course not. You will understand, I do. I am also very, very good at it.'

'No doubt. Was there anything else? I have to read some reports you understand, my friend.'

'Of course, Helmut. I have learned all I needed to learn. You are very kind to give me the time.'

Auguste rose. He made for the door.

Brunner said, 'Will you find her killer?'

'I never fail. Don't worry my friend, you will be safe enough to fall into your hedges without molestation once I have caught him, and I will.'

They smiled their insincere smiles to each other and Auguste left.

He made for his car and realised it was the only comfortable place where he could now rely on privacy. So Brunner had a scratch. Bernadette had fought back. Good for her. Like a Frenchwoman, she fought and did not go quietly. A hedge? Who did Brunner think he was fooling? Bernadette had fought for her life. It gave him an idea. He touched the ignition and smiled again with satisfaction. It was the first time in months the little tin-pot car had started first time and Auguste, like any superstitious man, thought it meant something.

2

By the time he knocked on the door of the pathologist's office, it was late morning. The tap of his knuckles on the scratched and worn surface gave a hollow tone. Auguste reflected it was worn so by countless undertakers and relatives of the dead. The smell was more of formaldehyde than bowels this time, he noted with relief. The mortuary was one of the least pleasant places in the realm of his police work.

'Come,' commanded the voice through the door.

'Dr. Dubois,' Auguste said.

'Very formal today Auguste? Come in.'

'I'm here on formal business, I suppose.'

'Oh?'

'I wondered if you examined her fingernails. Took scrapings and the like.'

'Well, I looked at her hands, but took no samples. I have to be economical with my materials these days. I can't get hold of anything, so the little I have is precious.'

'The body is still here?'

'Naturally.'

'Can we have a look?'

'Yes, of course. Don't be ill this time.'

'No,' Auguste said.

He followed Dubois into the mortuary and to Auguste's relief the Pathologist had reassembled poor Bernadette's body. He knew from experience, they would have replaced her internal organs and closed the incision. They had wrapped the body in a white sheet. Dubois unwrapped her body enough to pull her hands out and looked with care at the fingers using a magnifying glass.

'Hm, here maybe,' he said, indicating the right middle finger. 'Under the nail. Maybe just dirt, but we will see.'

He took a small blade from the sink top and obtained a scraping from beneath the darkened nail. Auguste watched as the doctor smeared it onto a glass slide and he followed as Dubois shuffled back to his office.

Placing a thin glass cover slip on top of the sample the doctor popped the slide under his microscope and began to hum to himself. Time passed and Auguste grew impatient.

'Do you see anything?'

'What? Oh yes, naturally. There are some cells here that could be blood, some that could be skin cells, but it is hard to be sure.'

'But why hard? I thought you could see the difference.'

'One has to fix and stain the sample. Then it needs to be incubated in the stain for a while, to tell what cells are visible. The nucleus stains dark blue and the cytoplasm...'

'If it is blood you can test it for blood groups?'

'No, no, no, my friend. Impossible with such a small sample. I would need a much bigger specimen. And stop interrupting me.'

'But you're sure it is blood?'

'You police are all so impatient. This is not like surgery. Pathology is an art. One has to take care in preparing a masterpiece. Well, look,

I'll have to stain it. I don't have any eosin and just a little haematoxylin.'

'What?'

'Never mind. They are stains we doctors use to examine the cells. I may have a little giemsa. I made it up before the war. It can be used for blood I suppose, though you may know, it's better for white blood cells. A pity. I cannot now get the reagents. No one accords priority to pathology these days. It's almost as if with so many dying or being killed pathological or forensic examination counts for nothing.'

'How long before you can give me an idea?'

'Auguste, I'm sorry but it will be at least tomorrow morning. The stains take twelve hours to light this path for me, I'm afraid. Come back in the morning.'

'If I told you I met a man whom I suspect of this murder and he had a cut on his face, on the left side as if she had defended herself, what would you say?'

'I would say, don't count on my evidence. You cannot prove the injury was caused by that girl.'

'The murderer does not know that. If anyone asks you, it would be a great help if you suggested you could tell.'

Dubois smiled.

'Of course Auguste. If a murderer telephones me and asks, I will say we are jointly solving the case and an arrest is imminent.'

'I wouldn't go that far; just say we've identified fibres of clothing and blood samples. It may be enough.'

He took his leave and returned to his office. The worn desk-chair creaked as he moved in his discomfort. After half an hour, he looked at the desktop. He realised he had been sitting there, staring straight ahead, pondering only the crime and how he could prove who was the guilty party. He wondered whom he could trust. Claude had become so ambitious Auguste felt he could not trust him. Judge Dubois seemed unusually hostile which seemed strange to Auguste. As far as he was aware he had done nothing to irritate him but Auguste was no politician and was not known for his tact, so he could easily have said or done something unwise at some time. He still wondered who had telephoned the Judge about the murder if it was not the pathologist. He did trust Doctor Dubois to a certain extent he decided, and if the doctor had told the truth, then perhaps Brunner had contacted the Judge. Auguste felt he was on the verge of grasping something vital but the plaintive ring of the telephone interrupted his line of thought.

'Yes?'

'I have Commissioner Tulard on the line.'

'Put him through, please Édith.'

The receiver buzzed in an unusual way for a few moments in his ear.

'Ran?' It was a high-pitched voice for a man, but Auguste recognised the Commissioner of Police, based in Lyon. He heard a distinct echo and knew he was not alone with his senior.

'Yes sir,' he said.

'Ran, I've had a request to host a meeting, seminar, you know what I mean.'

'Request?'

'Yes, it comes from high up. One of the German General Staff will be visiting tomorrow and he wants all senior Security Police and Gendarmes to be there so he can address them.'

'I'm very busy at the moment sir. Can I send a deputy perhaps?'

'Ran, your position as Assistant Chief has been called into question. Failure to attend might be a cause of serious disapproval. Not from me of course, I know you, but all the same...'

'Called into question? Who do you mean?'

'Oh I'm not at liberty to divulge. You will be there.'

'Where exactly?'

'At the University. The Medical College.'

'Tomorrow?'

'Yes, afternoon, two o'clock.'

'I wonder if I could mention another matter, sir?'

'Is it urgent? I really don't have much time, I need to ring Arnaud.'

'It's about a murder enquiry.'

'Murder? I'm too busy to deal with that sort of thing. I leave it to people like you. Now if you've finished?'

'No, sir. A decent local, young woman was raped, tortured and murdered.'

'Well?'

'Would you back me, whoever was responsible?'

'Back you? Well naturally I would back you.'

'Even against a German senior officer?' Auguste could feel how he enjoyed saying this. He felt alive for once. He said, 'The forensic evidence is quite strong and I may have to arrest the man.'

'Well… er… I can't cause a political scandal can I? Things here are delicate. It would be easy to cause such a mess even Petain's Government could fall and we would be ruled by the Germans directly. It simply wouldn't do. No. You can't go chasing the Germans. It would look as if we trumped up charges. Wouldn't do. If the case goes in such a direction, I'm afraid you will have to drop it.'

'But…'

'No, my last word on it. Be careful. You wouldn't want to lose your job over something so trivial, would you?'

'Trivial?'

'Compared to the Government of France, a single death is trivial. Nothing else?'

'No sir.'

'Good. Tomorrow then. I won't be there, but I'm sure they will look after you. Remember you are representing the department won't you?' The line clicked and echoed then died.

He knew he had Brunner rattled. Why else would the man be listening in on his telephone conversations? It had to be him. But proof was another thing. He had to get him to confess, on purpose or not.

CHAPTER TEN

1

Auguste had no desire to go to Lyon. It would take all morning and he had fears that anything could happen at the Prefecture while he was away. He had lost trust in all of them except Édith, but of course, she was unable to prevent political manoeuvring behind his back. He also hated leaving in the middle of the murder enquiry. He believed such things were best served hot and he had no desire for the trail to dissipate. He was fishing. He was dangling a line in the river and he had baited the hook. He waited only for Brunner to try to take some kind of action against him to bring it all out into the open.

'Why do you have to go?' Odette said.

She cleared away plates and cups and Monique and Zara sat at the table with Auguste.

'But I have no choice. What can I do?'

'Who is this great German General? All the Generals are fighting a war. Why do they want to lecture? You are not one of their soldiers anyway.'

'Whatever it is, they will probably need my men to carry it out. It must be big. Tulard said he was informing everyone, including the

Gendarmerie.'

'It won't be for anything good, I can tell you Auguste.'

'Papa,' Zara said.

'Yes ma fleur.'

'When do wars stop?'

'Well, I suppose it is when one side wins and the other gives in.'

Monique said, 'If the Germans win, what will happen to me?'

Auguste felt his heart sink. He had no answers. Neither Odette nor he had considered what would happen if the Germans took all of Europe. There might then be nowhere for Jews to escape to, unless it was Israel and there was no actual country there anyway.

'My dear little one,' he said, 'you will be with us. We will see you safe whatever happens. Even if we have to smuggle you out in a suitcase, like a pair of shoes.'

He reached forward and placed his big hands over hers. He smiled and then caressed her cheek.

'You are scared?'

He saw the tear in her eye almost as it formed and he brushed it away with the back of his hand. 'Come, my little one. I can't take it away but I can always spare a cuddle for a little girl. He took her onto his knee and she wept into his shoulder. Odette watched, she placed a hand upon Zara's shoulder.

'How long does she have to stay? I want my Papa back.'

Zara's stool clattered on the stone floor as it tipped over behind her. She ran from the room pursued by her parent's calls.

'Zara, ma fleur. Zara,' Auguste said, reaching towards the stairs with one hand, grasping the empty air as if by doing so, he could mend the hole Odette and he had made in her life.

And it was a hole. She had been an only child and the centre of her parents' universe. In one moment, they had swept it all away. Now there were two little girls and no matter what Auguste or Odette could say, Zara felt pushed aside. No, it was not true; it was the way Auguste supposed a child of nine would see events. Both of her parents knew it now. It was as if they had ignored the obvious, living in another bubble of ignorance. Auguste sat and studied the face of the little girl still sitting on his lap. Her dark eyes and her high forehead, so like but so unlike his own daughter. Her nose, longer than Zara's, her smile, short, small and lingering did not match his daughter's, yet Auguste understood one thing if nothing else in the world he moved in was true. He loved this little girl as if she was his own and he would die for her. His reservations, when Odette had broken the news to him, had passed away long ago now. Like a dead swan floating on the Dordogne, like a vanished memory, they had gone, replaced by a certainty lingering on, cast iron, palpable and true. Auguste had no second thoughts any longer. He would protect this child but he had to make amends to Zara. Zara was after all, his flesh and blood and he knew it was she who mattered most to him, but he also knew he had a duty to do.

It was another schism stabbing at his soul, but one he took on happily to help his friend's daughter. Monique, a child he had known all her life, like a favourite niece or a child of his own. Blood runs thicker they say but for Auguste it made no difference.

One night before Monique came into the world came to mind, how the four of them sat around this very kitchen table and argued over a bottle of wine what Pierre's daughter should be named. When Pierre had suggested Monique, Auguste had laughed and said it was the name of a grape used in Italian wine. Pierre had risen and threatened to leave and had not Murielle dissuaded him, he might have done so. They argued more but Pierre was intransigent as ever and although they parted friends, he reminded Auguste of the incident many times in the following years.

He knew he should have pursued his daughter upstairs, told her how much he loved her, reassured her nothing would change, but somehow he felt he had to be there in the kitchen, embracing Pierre's daughter and he could not do both at once. He glanced at Odette and it was as if she understood his dilemma. She ran up the stairs and he could imagine the scene. She would take Zara in her arms and hug her, stroke her hair, reassure her and absolve him of this strange infidelity, one which circumstance thrust upon him.

'Monique.'

'Yes, uncle?'

'Do you and Zara fight?'

'Yes,' she said, 'sometimes.'

'You must love each other. There are hard times coming and we must all stick together. If we do not, then we will all fail and maybe die. Do you understand?'

'I think so Uncle, but sometimes I don't.'

'No?'

'Why does Zara seem so cross?'

'It is because she worries that if Odette and I love you, perhaps we are taking some love away from her.'

'But it's not true is it?'

'No my child. One can love many children whether they are your own flesh and blood or not. Love is love; it is the same wherever you spend it. Remember that.'

'I don't understand.'

'No. One day you will. All I ask is you remember.'

'Yes, Uncle.'

Auguste regarded the child and felt emotions stirring in his mind. He wiped his eye and pulled her close. He heard raised voices from upstairs but had no need to hear what was said.

'We will have to learn to live together for a time. Your Papa will come back one day and everything will be fine. You'll see.'

He had no hopes of that happening and he was aware he lied. He had always believed one should never lie to a child and it was a principle he had stuck to so far with Zara. It pricked his conscience but he could see no other way to remain positive. He thought it was merely another nail in the casket of his morals and it slid off him as water slips from glass when he compared it to the rest of his burdens.

The sound of a car drawing up outside drew him back to reality and he realised Monique had to hide. She ran up the stairs and Auguste called in as quiet a voice as he could to Odette to get her into the attic.

2

A knock on the door made Auguste jump. He heard it as though it were the sound of gun-butts hammering, though he knew his nerves were on edge. Odette did not respond but he had to open the door. He stood in the vestibule and could see a uniformed figure looming dark on the other side of the windowed door. His hand trembled as he drew the bolt and grasped the handle.

'Auguste. Were you busy? You seemed to take such a long time.'

It was Brunner. He stood with his hands behind his back. Auguste wondered whether he held a gun.

'Busy, why no Helmut. Not busy at all. As a matter of fact, I was just leaving to go to Lyon. I have been ordered to go there to hear a talk by one of your Generals no less.'

'But of course, it is why I'm here.'

'Really?'

'Yes, I thought it would be only fair to give you a ride to Lyon. No sense in both of us wasting gasoline.'

'Wasting?'

'Yes, in travelling separately.'

'I... I was planning on leaving as early as possible. I am in the middle of the murder investigation, you know.'

'Do not concern yourself. I too wish to leave as soon as I can. I have a list of suspects I must pursue and you have your killer to find. We both cannot spare too much time, but I think... Can I come in? It is very cold out here, draughty.'

'I... er... Odette isn't dressed and I was just...'

'Is there something you don't want me to see?'

'See? Of course not. Come in. Don't stand there in the cold. How foolish of me. Please come in.'

Auguste gestured for Brunner to enter, which he did, his black boots leaving mud trails on the polished wood floor. Oblivious to the mess, Brunner said, 'And who is this young lady? I heard you had a beautiful daughter.'

Auguste looked. He looked back at Brunner. He wanted to vomit. Monique stood at the foot of the stairs. She had come back down.

'This is Zara. She is nine. Zara, go back upstairs and get your Maman.'

'Not so fast, Auguste,' Brunner said.

Auguste wondered if he might be able to kill Brunner where he stood but he had not donned his firearm and it was six feet to the hall-table where it lay in its holster, ready for him to go. He still imagined Brunner had a gun behind his back.

'No?' Auguste said.

Brunner stepped forward towards Monique. He bowed slightly at the hips and his heels clicked together.

'You father has not introduced me young lady. I am Helmut Brunner. I am a policeman like your father. I am pleased to make your acquaintance.'

Monique drew away, she said, 'My Papa isn't a ...'

Brunner drew his hands from behind his back. His hands held no firearm but a doll. It was a life-like doll, the face of white smooth wood and the body covered in a frilly gown. It looked antique. He reached forward with the toy and Monique accepted it with a curtsey. The German took off a black leather glove and extended his hand.

'A man who lets me talk to strangers, she should have said,' Auguste said, 'Zara is a little shy of people she doesn't know. I have taught her to be careful.'

Brunner turned to Auguste and smiled.

'A very wise thing to do. This doll is a traditional Kammer & Reinhardt. It belonged to my mother. I am honoured to present it to your daughter.'

'You are very kind, Helmut,' Auguste said. He had a feeling he wished to throw the doll on the floor and stamp on it.

'Your daughter, Zara was it? Looks quite different from you. Her hair is darker. One would scarcely know you were related.'

'Her mother's father had black hair. We sometimes joke she is a throwback.'

'The long nose is... Oh well, no matter. Now where were we?'

'Lyon.'

'Yes, Auguste, you will enjoy the talk. It is called "the final solution" and is of great relevance to you and your people.'

'Solution to what?'

'Well, I won't spoil it for you. If I tell you all about it there would be no point in you going.'

'But if you know all about it why are you going?'

'Ha. Very clever, you have caught me out. Me and my silly mouth. I will have to be careful what I say around you Auguste.' Brunner wagged a finger at Auguste. He said, 'I confess.'

'You ... you do?'

'Yes Auguste,' Brunner said as their eyes met for one moment in a serious almost combative stare. 'I have an ulterior motive. The speaker is Heinrich Himmler himself. You will have heard of him?'

'Naturally.'

'He is very successful in his work. The Führer trusts him and so does Goebbels. I had hoped to meet him. He may be helpful in my career.'

'Oh? Just meeting him won't get you far, will it? Don't you have to do something to impress him?'

'Ah, Auguste, I am about to do many things to impress him. Last night we apprehended a member of the terrorist group calling themselves "the Maquis". You know about them.'

'Of course.'

'I'll tell you all about what we learned on the way to Lyon. Come, we must not be late.'

Auguste turned to Monique. The girl stood staring up at Brunner and he had to turn her around and guide her to the stairs. 'Now you go and find Maman and get her to do your hair so you won't be late for school.'

He patted her back as she ascended. Satisfied she was going, he grabbed his pistol and fastened it around his shoulder and waist. Coat in hand, he tramped down the stairs, shutting the door behind him.

Auguste wondered now what possible way there was to prevent Brunner from finding out the truth. As he got into the black Mercedes he realised if he and Odette went to church without their daughter, everyone in the town would realise. He felt sweat on his brow despite the cold and his heart beat a military tattoo on the inside of his ribs. How to survive? How to run? When to get away? These questions burned in his mind but with them was the question of Bernadette's tortured body. He had to stay long enough to settle the matter. Tomorrow was Sunday. He would have to hope Brunner was not going to become a regular churchgoer. Auguste was relieved Brunner was no Catholic. If he had been, the Ran family's days would have been numbered.

CHAPTER ELEVEN

1

It seemed to Auguste, Lyon was a huge city. Having ridden past the beautiful wine country, past chateaux and fields, he felt impatient to arrive. The morning cloud cleared and a cheerful sun at last, peeped out, casting shadows behind the black car. He could never understand why people would want to live on top of each other in the way they did in big cities. The main city thoroughfares extended from north to south and several bridges crossed both the rivers Rhône and Saône, which met forming a sort of island where the medical college stood with many other grand buildings.

'Make sure your daughter looks after that doll. It is very old. I don't know why my mother packed it in my things.'

'It was your mother's?'

'Yes. She packed my suitcase. Poor Mutti, she was distraught at the thought of me being so far away.'

'Oh. You are married?'

'No. There was someone once, but no matter. Mutti means mother in German. She is a dear soul, my Mutti.'

'You live alone then?'

'My mother lives with me. She keeps house since I am away a lot.'

'It was very kind of you to give Mon... Zara the doll. I will ensure she gives it all the care it deserves.'

They were silent then. Auguste stared out of the window thinking that a bonfire would be the best treatment for the German doll.

They crossed the Saone Bridge close to the confluence of the rivers and the sleek, black Mercedes glided to a halt outside an old, grey stone-built building. Auguste looked up feeling bored. He wondered how he would be able to sit through some tedious lecture and he had no illusions about the importance of it. Whatever this final solution might be it would not involve police work, it would be political and therefore of no interest to him.

'So, we are here at last,' Brunner said.

'Yes. You still haven't told me what all the fuss is about.'

'Fuss? No fuss my French policeman. It is simply the answer to the Jewish problem.'

He had emphasised the word 'problem' and Auguste knew from what had gone before how the Nazi Major felt about it.

'I am not a political policeman you know. I have not been trained for these things. Bernadette's murder is the kind of thing I can pursue, not interning a lot of innocent Jews.'

'Innocent? I don't know what you mean. They are not strictly human you know. Goebbels has shown they are a sub-human order and not worthy of co-existing with us.'

'Sub-human?'

'Yes, of course. You will understand when Himmler has spoken. I will not spoil it for you. We are expecting great things from you, Auguste.'

'I will do my duty to France.'

'No, not France. The Fatherland, the new Third Reich. You are part of it now.'

'Of course, how silly of me Helmut. There is so much politics to consider these days. How can a simple policeman be expected to remember?'

The look in Brunner's eyes was as if he was a man who had come home to something familiar, a place of comfort and Auguste knew what it was. Brunner was returning to the fold of his own philosophy, his stamping ground in policy terms. The whole thing was a way to control Auguste, a way to make him believe in their cause and a way of convincing him. The foreknowledge protected him. Knowing about evil prepared him, but it added to the flames of his hatred as well and he knew he had to get the warning out to the Jewish families in his catchment area. He made up his mind he could no longer do the job the Nazis inflicted on him. Meanwhile, he smiled sweetly. Brunner did not reply.

The Medical College was a part of the history of the city and its architecture emphasised the fact. A grand entrance-hall revealed itself as soon as they entered through the Renaissance archway. Beyond it, a generous stone staircase climbed to a galleried landing. Auguste had visited Lyon before but not since his first interview for his current job. He had never visited the College. It was a place revered for its teaching of fresh new doctors and they had learned their trade here for centuries. Auguste wondered if all of them had now been re-educated and become vassals of the Third Reich.

A red carpet decorated the stairs as if royalty were about to arrive. He walked up the stairs without misgivings. He knew whatever he heard today would make no difference to him. He envisaged Monique's face, Zara's face and he knew. He was certain, in the eyes of his Lord, everyone was equal and if he chose to protect Monique his God would be with him.

The lecture hall loomed across the landing from the stairwell and Auguste noted the threadbare floor-covering stretched across the long stone-floored landing, crossed by the crimson, new-laid carpet. He glanced to his right and the paintings of past professors and surgeons lining the walls confirmed his impression of the grandiosity of the medical profession. He wondered why the Germans had picked a medical college. It seemed as if it was because they fed the medical hunger for blood and body parts. Apart from Dubois, the pathologist, he trusted none of them.

The lecture room was vast. It seated perhaps two hundred without difficulty and it was semi-circular in shape. Tiered seats surr-ounded a table and a lectern and he could hear even whispers from the front row without straining, although he was at the back and highest up in the room.

Brunner did not sit with him. The SD Major joined a group of men in uniforms like his own and they were shaking hands and slapping each other on the back. They laughed as if there was a common, shared joke and soon everyone in France would appreciate it, but for the moment, it was their secret, their singular knowledge.

A hand descended upon his shoulder and he looked up wondering if his thoughts had been overheard. Arnaud looked down at him and the old face smiled a wrinkled smile under its grey moustache.

'So they have brought you here too?' Arnaud said.

'Yes, I have been instructed to hear a speech or lecture on a final solution to the Jewish problem.'

'I think we will learn very little new.'

'Perhaps. It may be a way to confirm what we suspect.'

'But of course, my friend. I think...'

Auguste put his index to his lips.

'The acoustics in here are marvellous, don't you think? Why, one can hear everything being said.'

Arnaud sat down beside him.

He whispered, 'You know who Himmler is?'

'He is Hitler's right hand man. A rising star of the Third Reich according to Brunner.'

'Ah. We are no doubt honoured then.'

'Yes, honoured.'

Their eyes met expressing a common understanding. Auguste had a feeling they were both rats in a trap and perhaps Brunner would denounce them both as traitors. It would make sense. Brunner would be able to escape justice and Auguste and his only ally would be removed from the scene with the Rising Star looking down upon them from some German firmament above. He noticed he was sweating as the SD, SS and uniformed Gestapo assembled in the room. They must have numbered more than a hundred men. Arnaud and he were the only Frenchmen in the place. Auguste wished he had a bomb. It was the only final solution he desired.

A short man entered, wearing a Senior SD uniform. Auguste did not know what rank he proclaimed; he had always found the German system confusing.

Arnaud whispered in his ear, 'Klaus Barbie. He became the SD leader here in Lyon last November. Even his own men are afraid of him.'

Auguste studied the man's face. He felt disappointment; he had expected a more impressive figure. Barbie was short and singular because he was ordinary looking; one would have walked past him without noticing him at all. His back hair rose to a spiral above his square-jawed face and it made him look to Auguste, like a black-topped turnip. Barbie glanced towards Auguste as he surveyed the room. It was then Auguste understood who and what this man was. The dark eyes burned with a cold flame. They were the cruellest, most unfeeling eyes he had ever seen. It was like looking into a coalmine. They absorbed everything and expressed nothing but disinterest.

Barbie held a gavel and he banged it on the lectern for silence.

'Gentlemen, when the General arrives, I want you all to stand and salute. I do not want him to return to Berlin with the impression his visit is greeted with anything but the highest respect.'

The silence continued. It was as if a cold satanic presence had descended upon Auguste and he felt a faint shudder at the change of atmosphere.

2

The man who entered was short and fat. He had a round face, his nose long and aquiline. Receding fair hair swept back from a broad forehead and slit-like eyes characterised the face, which was pale and smooth. He wore round, gold-rimmed spectacles adding roundness to his already rotund features. Auguste did not feel the same about Himmler as he had about his minion, Barbie. The man possessed a charisma and an attractiveness Barbie lacked. When Himmler smiled his eyes seemed to soften. Could this be the man who had ascended the Nazi ranks? The risen star of the Third Reich?

He wore the black uniform of the SS with full General's flashes and he clutched his peaked hat in his plump fingers as he entered. The silence continued and Barbie called the assembly to attention. Every man rose to his feet. As one, they raised their right arms.

'Sieg Heil.'

The salute reverberated in Auguste's ears and he was uncertain whether or not he should raise his right arm as well. He made a faint gesture and out of the corner of his eye, he could see Arnaud struggle with the same reluctance, one borne of fidelity to France. It made them both unwilling to give all to the conquerors of their home country. In truth, Auguste was frightened someone might notice his hesitation and he hid behind the man in front as best he could.

Himmler positioned himself behind the lectern. He began to speak. His German was accented and sounded strange to Auguste.

'He's from north Germany. It's hard to understand.'

'What's he saying?' Auguste said.

'Just that we Aryans are a great people and superior to anyone else.'

Auguste struggled; German language was not his forte, though he had a smattering. Brunner always spoke French when they conversed. He understood enough. The words '*Juden*,' '*Die Endlosung*' and finally he heard, '*Er hat den Juden prophezeit, daß, wenn sie noch einmal einen Weltkrieg herbeiführen würden, sie dabei ihre Vernichtung erleben würden.*'

Arnaud leaned towards him and said, 'They are all mad.'

'Yes,' Auguste whispered. 'They think the Jews caused the First World War and they have caused this one too. We must talk. I can do this no more.'

He understood more of what Himmler said but he was too emotional to listen well. He heard that elimination and concentration were planned and how the Jews would be shipped away to the east where the eastern authorities would be directed to carry out the 'final solution', an extermination.

Auguste found his balance upset, he wanted to leave, felt nauseated. He closed his eyes and thought of his God. He pictured the sacred heart, the crucifixion and resurrection. He had always been a more lax Catholic than many but now he used his faith to give himself strength. Evil. He knew it when he saw it and he was an ally to these demons, the Nazis, the killers. How could he have been so blind as to think they wanted him as a policeman? He had become, by the strength of his passivity, a lackey of the Devil himself and where could he lay the blame? He could accuse no one but himself. He had gone along with the yellow stars. He had persuaded people to register their Judaism. Now he was supposed to round them all up for the Nazis to ship them to the east to be killed. It went deep. It penetrated his very soul and he knew there could be no redemption if he capitulated.

'Arnaud,' he said, his voice a hoarse whisper. 'It is possible? Can we fight?'

Arnaud smiled, 'I have nothing to lose but my soul and I shall keep that untarnished, along with my honour. What will you do?'

'I have a family, but we will have to get out.'

'Then if you value your soul, wait until we have warned the Jews.'

Auguste took heart from the face of the Gendarme. The old man

winked and they leaned away from each other in case they were seen
to be talking. Himmler's speech seemed to captivate his audience
however and Auguste felt certain no one had noticed or overheard
them.

He took in little else. Anyone could have been speaking, even
Hitler himself. His mind worked with a desperate velocity, thinking,
planning. He felt dizzy. It would be hard, but he thought he could
find enough people to carry the message to the Jews if he worked
hard at it. The new laws had forbidden them radios or telephones
and even their letters were censored. He needed someone to contact
the Maquis. He needed a contact of his own, but who? No one
remained. He had already arrested all known suspects, handed them
over to Brunner and heard no more. He hated himself now for it. Of
course, he had heard no more about the fate of the men he arrested.
The SD were torturers and killers and he had ignored it, thinking he
had served his country in his way. But had he now become part of
their machine? He was a collaborator and he knew it. His shame
tortured him.

He wanted to leave. His desperation to be away from the lecture
room rose in his stomach. He felt suffocated, nauseated once more.
His heart beat a rapid rhythm against his ribs and then it happened.

He vomited. He re-visited his breakfast and then bitter green bile
and as if in a dream, he saw it spray over an SD officer seated in
front. His head swam and he felt barely conscious but was aware of
strong hands gripping his arms.

3

The sharp, intense smell of ammonia, pungent and stimulating made
Auguste shake his head. They had dragged him away to the upper
landing and Arnaud and Brunner stood looking down at him. He
realised he was lying on the floor. He could smell vomit on his

clothing and he struggled to stand.

Arnaud pressed him down with a hand on his shoulder.

'Take some deep breaths and wait until you feel better,' he said.

Auguste obeyed and his head began to clear.

'I am so sorry. I don't know what came over me,' he said.

Brunner laughed.

'No but my colleague who you deposited your breakfast over, certainly knows.'

He laughed again. Auguste saw no mirth in his eyes and realised what a fool he must have made of himself.

'I am so sorry,' he mumbled.

'No matter,' Brunner said, 'he was not a friend of mine.'

Arnaud said, 'Can you sit up, Auguste?'

He reached towards Auguste's arm and helped him to his feet. Arnaud smiled. He seemed to think the situation was droll. He said, 'The lecture finished abruptly. There were no fond farewells.'

'I... I...'

Brunner said, 'Once you have cleaned up we will go. I hope to be back before it is too dark to see the road. You French need to learn how to build proper roads like those we have at home. We Germans will teach you. Our engineers are the best in the world.'

He turned around and walked away. Arnaud escorted Auguste to the toilet along the corridor. The door closed behind him and Auguste found reassurance in the room's emptiness. He cleaned off some small dribbles of vomit without difficulty and he wondered with vague interest where the rest of his stomach contents had lodged and who would be unlucky enough to clean it up.

He had never fainted before and he still felt dizzy. He inspected his face in the mirror. The gaunt features stared back at him and he ran some water into the sink. Leaning forward he washed his face using both hands and when he was done, he dried himself with a towel. On re-inspection, the bags under his eyes looked the same and the afternoon stubble had not changed but in his eyes, there was something. It was guilt. He could not define it at first but then he realised he had learned much about himself in the short time since he entered the Medical College.

He had sinned. He had committed the worst sin possible—the sin of ignorant indifference. He wondered if God forgave mortal sins in a sinner who cared but he knew with certainty such a man could never be granted forgiveness if he was unconcerned. The change in his eyes, he felt, reflected the fact it all mattered to him now and the burden was expressed there. He cared more deeply about what would become of the Jews he had registered than he cared for his own safety—his own life. It was a delicate balance whether his family mattered more than the Jews did. He hoped the cup would never be offered to him and he had no conception of which way he would jump if it came to it. He did know his soul dangled by an unravelling thread, suspended over a bitter sea of eternal punishment.

The silence cracked like a mirror with a knock on the door and Arnaud entered.

'I told Brunner I would take you home. He was impatient to leave.'

'It is very kind of you André. You must think I am a fool.'

'We can talk on the way home. Ready?'

'Yes, thank you.'

They descended the two flights of stairs and as they entered the hall, Auguste noticed Brunner was still there. He was talking to Himmler and Barbie. They were smiling as if they were discussing a football match or a holiday. When the two Frenchmen attempted to pass, Brunner said, 'There you are. General, let me present Colonel Arnaud of the Aquitaine Gendarmerie and Auguste Ran of the Bergerac Police.'

Himmler turned. The smile never left his lips but his eyes narrowed. The Frenchmen gave the expected Hitler salute.

Himmler said, 'Which one of you was it brought my lecture to a close then?'

'I do apologise, Herr General. It was involuntary,' Auguste said.

'Indeed,' Himmler said, 'I do not mind, I have had a sore throat today and was in two minds whether to finish early anyway. I said what I needed and I presume you understood.'

'Yes, General. I am glad it did not cause inconvenience.'

'The man you doused with vomit may not see it that way,' Barbie said.

'Please offer him my respectful apologies and I will be pleased to pay for any damage to his uniform,' Auguste said.

Barbie, face crimson, stepped forward and Auguste realised the man was a head smaller than he was.

Looking up, Barbie said, 'You stupid shit-eating farmer. You think I am your errand boy?'

Himmler placed a hand on Barbie's shoulder.

'Klaus, Klaus, that is no way to speak to one of our noble allies. Soon we will have to depend upon the services these men provide, and it would not do to insult them.'

Barbie stepped back, scowling. Himmler apologised to Auguste and wished him a speedy recovery. Auguste could see Brunner behind the General. He wore a bored expression and looked up at the ceiling.

When the two Frenchmen were finally on the road, Arnaud said, 'I must congratulate you.'

'Congratulate me? It was embarrassing.'

'Well if only you had done it on purpose it would have been the first time we French have prevented the German General staff from anything since the beginning of the war.'

He began to laugh. The laughter became a guffaw and presently, Auguste could not stop himself from joining in. The chuckles continued for minutes until Auguste said, 'I suppose it emphasises the respect we both feel for these men.'

'Yes.'

They were silent then for twenty miles.

'We have to do something,' Auguste said.

'You know anyone in the Maquis?'

'No, no one.'

'I may know someone but I have not seen him for a week.'

'I will research it. My secretary may be able to tell me.'

'We only have three weeks and the clock ticks, my friend.'

'Then if we both work at it, we may see success.'

Arnaud produced a voluminous hip flask. He took a long swallow from it and offered it to Auguste.

'It will settle your stomach,' the Colonel said.

Auguste took a pull of the flask. The eau-de-vie burned his throat but he could feel warmth spreading through him as if it had ignited a fire inside his bloodstream. He took another gulp and handed the flask back. Dusk turned to stygian, starless night and the headlights cut a thin beam ahead of them. They shared the flask in silence, each lost in their own ruminations.

It was eight o'clock by the time Arnaud stopped outside Auguste's house. Arnaud refused to come in and as the military jeep pulled away, Auguste wondered how he could find the Maquis. The tiny red dots of Arnaud's taillights faded and still he did not move. He still felt shocked he supposed, after the events of the day and he turned to his home, drenched in the hope Odette and the children were safe. His greatest fear now was whether one day he would return and find them gone.

CHAPTER TWELVE

1

Auguste awoke in a sweat. He knew he must have been dreaming but had no recall of it. He rubbed his face with his hands and swung his legs out of bed. It was still dark but he had no idea what time it was. He sat for a moment on the edge of the bed, staring ahead, wishing for a way out.

'Auguste, are you all right?'

He felt Odette's hand on his naked back, gentle and reassuring.

'Yes.'

'It's two o'clock,' she said.

'Really?'

'Come, you need your sleep. What's troubling you my husband? Is it Monique?'

'No, it's everything. Everywhere, I see danger. I see hate, death.'

'What do you want to do?'

'I don't know. Maybe flee.'

'Where to? We would have no life away from Bergerac.'

'It is all so dangerous. What do we do about church tomorrow?

Brunner thinks Monique is my daughter. If we are seen with a different child, he will know. If we take Monique with us, Zara will become even more jealous.'

'We go to church with our daughter. If Brunner is there checking up, we say it is our niece and Zara is ill.'

'He will know. He is SD. They have ways of finding out.'

'Nonsense, Auguste. Have faith. Love will bring us through this.'

'You know I love you.'

'Yes.'

'Love won't protect us from Brunner. We have to get out. When the rounding up of the Jews becomes a debacle, Brunner will know about that too. He already knows I am aware of his guilt.'

'Guilt?'

'Yes, he raped, tortured and killed Bernadette, I'm sure of it.'

'Then you must convict him.'

'I have to prove it.'

'Will they let you? Brunner is a big fish. Do you really think you can indict him?'

'Not me. The Judge.'

'Then ask Judge Dubois about it. Come back to bed.'

'I need a drink.'

Auguste found his shoes and his dressing gown.

Padding downstairs with sleepy footsteps, he saw a light outside. Curious, he went to the dining room window and peered out. A dim light flickered near the remains of his outhouse. A shiver ran down his spine and he wondered if he should investigate. He thought better of it and stood for long moments watching. The light, he was sure came from a torch and he saw it hover then extinguish. It did not reappear.

He heard a crunch on the gravel in front of the house. He still saw no one. It was cold and he wrapped his gown around him but saw nothing more.

Was it Brunner's men, investigating? Even a simple burglar would have been welcome to Auguste then. At least the prospect of robbery was better than the alternatives if it was not a burglar. He crossed to the hall table and grabbed his gun from its holster. He waited.

The crunch of the footfalls became fainter and faded altogether. He noticed he felt relief. His breathing slowed and with gentle tread, he entered the kitchen. Peering out of the window, he scanned the view of the ruined outhouse. Nothing.

A sound behind him. He turned. He levelled his weapon.

'Auguste?'

'Odette. I could have shot you.'

'What?'

'I...'

'What are you doing wandering around the house with that thing? You could have shot one of the children. Are you mad?'

'I'm sorry. I heard a noise outside.'

'A noise?'

'Yes. And I saw a light by the outhouse.'

'Really?'

'Yes.'

'Who? Who could it be?'

'I don't know, but I'm not going back to sleep. If I hear them again, I'll phone for help.'

'I won't sleep without you. Coffee?'

'Chicory you mean.'

'Yes, but we can pretend.'

They pretended. They toasted each other and Auguste told her about his day and about Himmler and his plans. He even explained why the meeting broke up. All the time, he listened and glanced out of the window, insecurity still gripping him. He fingered the pistol.

'You vomited on a SD official?'

'Yes, it was an accident.'

He listened. Nothing. He kept his eyes on his wife but his attention was elsewhere.

In the candlelight, he saw her smile. He sipped his drink still listening. Then he searched in the drawer of the kitchen table.

'What?'

'Cigarettes.'

'You stopped.'

'I had some here, I'm sure of it.'

'In the drawer by the range Auguste. I hid them away.'

Auguste smiled and his stool screeched behind him as he pushed it back. His bare feet slapped on the cold stone floor though it was not cold in the kitchen. He stared out of the window but all he saw was the dark misty wood. His hand groped in the dark and finding what he sought, he turned, still smiling.

He dropped the cigarettes. He had left his gun on the table and he stepped forward, groping towards it.

'Not a wise move, my friend.'

The voice was deep and local. All Auguste could see was a silhouette, faint and dark in the doorway. What stopped him in his tracks was the outline of the rifle in the man's hand. Odette turned.

'Pierre?'

'Is it safe?' Pierre said.

'Safe?' was all Auguste could manage.

'Would you shoot an old friend? Have you slipped so far into the Nazi life?'

'Shoot you? Of course not. Don't be stupid.'

'Can I trust you?'

Odette stood up; she walked to Pierre and put her arms around his neck. She hugged him as only a close friend could. When the embrace broke, Pierre stepped forward reassured.

'What are you doing here?' Auguste said, 'have you come to take Monique?'

'No. I just wanted... wanted...'

Odette said, 'I understand. I'll get her.'

'No. Wait,' Pierre said.

'I needed news of her. Don't wake her. It will break her heart.'

Auguste said, 'Haven't you done that already, you fool. I got the letters of transit. I had them for you. An adult and a child. You could have gone to Switzerland. Where have you been?'

Pierre said, 'Been? I've been where you and every other self-respecting Frenchman should have been. I've been with the Maquis, the real soldiers. The ones who will drive these swine from our country.'

He pulled the beret from his head and sat. His long brown hair dangled about his ears and his full beard.

Auguste said, 'Pierre. I was a fool. I never believed they wanted to exterminate all your people, until today that is. I heard it from the lips of Himmler himself. I'm sorry.'

Pierre slammed a fist on to the table.

'Sorry. Sorry? You help these murderers from hell and you now say you are sorry. You Catholics! You are all the same. You give your confession and they absolve you, then you can sin all over again even if it means the deaths of thousands.'

'I need to get a message to the Jewish families. I have their names and addresses. They must be warned and given a chance to escape. Can your new friends help them?'

No one spoke.

'I need their names and details.'

'I have a list upstairs in my jacket. I will get it when you go. Pierre. I was wrong. I believed there could be no human being who would want to destroy a whole nation. I never understood.'

His voice broke. He felt tears forming in his eyes and he drew a deep breath to prevent it.

'Pierre,' he said, 'I will make good. I will protect Monique and will get her away if it is what you want,' he said.

'Auguste, how can you make good? You are helping murderers and afterwards saying you will make good. You cannot bring back the dead. The slaughter has already started.'

Odette placed a hand on Pierre's shoulder.

'Pierre,' she said, 'don't be too hard on us. How could Auguste stop being a policeman? He believed the Germans told the truth. We know now. We will get away and help in any way we can.'

Auguste said, 'I have something to do first.'

Pierre said, 'You have?'

'You remember that horrible road accident in which the plumber Leclerc was killed?'

'Yes. The wife was injured too.'

'The daughter, Bernadette was murdered. I think Brunner, the SD Major did it. I want to prove it and have him guillotined before we escape.'

'Leave it with me. We will put a bomb under him and teach him to fly.'

'And the reprisals? Can you live with them?'

'Of course. You maybe never read Lenin. If you want to make an omelette you have to break eggs.'

'These eggs you talk about are the people you grew up with. Your neighbours, your friends.'

'They were never friends. I never had many of those. I'm a Jew and always was. I could see it in their faces every time I went to the market. It was a look in their eyes if nothing else.'

'Pierre,' Odette said, 'you are so unfair. What about us? Murielle was my closest friend. I was there for you when she died. You know it.'

He turned towards her, his eyes slit-like and dark in the candle-light.

'Odette. You were Murielle's best and closest friend. There was no one else who was there for me. You and Auguste. I will never forget it but I have to defend our country. I have to fight for my people.'

'Which people?' Auguste said, 'French or Yiddish?'

'You know the answer. It is the same answer you would give in my place.'

'Yes, Pierre. I do know. I just...'

'Papa?'

Monique's small treble cut the atmosphere, like a hawk descending on its prey.

Pierre, startled by the sound, turned and his arms opened wide. She ran to him.

'Ma Petite, my little one, Bubeleh. Oh how your daddy missed you.'

She said nothing. Auguste could see how she drank in his presence, his embrace; it drove all his doubts away. He knew where his first duty lay. He had to save his family and Monique was now his family too. And Pierre? He was as close to Auguste's heart as anyone else was in the world. Like a brother. Like his alter ego, who had become the man he should have had the strength and courage to change into. Why had he never believed Pierre, never tried to change it all?

He saw Odette reach out to stroke Monique's little hand, as the child held on to her father. Monique clutched him, squeezed his hair, his coat. It was a hopeless grip; a hand clenched in desperation holding onto all she loved in the world. Auguste knew Monique recognised how fleeting it had to be; for her years, she had a strangely adult view of things. Pierre's very presence here put them in danger and they all knew it.

2

Time passed and no one spoke. Auguste retrieved the cigarettes and lighting one, pondered their predicament. Even if Pierre had the list of Jews, shifting all of them abroad would require resources even the Maquis could not boast. Internment for many would be inevitable. He hated the thought he would be responsible, yet he could not run away like Pierre. Brunner had to pay with his life.

'Papa?' a small voice interrupted his thoughts. Then, 'Uncle Pierre!'

It was Zara. She ran across the stone flags and Pierre reached out his free arm to embrace her too.

'Does no one sleep in this house?' Auguste said, 'Zara, what will we do with you?'

Extricating herself, Zara came to him and sat upon his knee. As the pre-dawn light began to show itself, they sat enjoying an island of time as two families, combined into one. Auguste felt the scene was one of normality in a very abnormal world. It was a moment stolen from the clutches of an evil future and he knew it could not last.

'Pierre, it is getting light.'

'I know. I must go.'

'Papa,' Monique said, 'can't you stay? We can hide together when the bad men come.'

Pierre stroked her cheek.

'Bubeleh, if I do not go, I cannot fight for us. It must be so. Auguste and Odette will look after you until it is time.'

'What if they kill you?'

'They won't kill me. I am like Joshua. I will blow my trumpet and their walls will fall down. You remember?'

'Yes, Papa. Will it be soon?'

He brushed away a tear at the corner of her eye.

'No, not soon. Perhaps years.'

Auguste swallowed away the lump in his throat as he watched Monique cuddling her father.

Zara said, 'Uncle Pierre, who are you fighting?'

Pierre said, 'Why, the Germans, of course, Zara.'

'But they said in school the Germans would not hurt us if we do what they say.'

'No, my little one. They won't hurt you. They hate Monique and me because we are Jewish. They want us dead, so I fight.'

'Why do they hate you?'

Auguste said, 'Now, now, ma fleur. Enough questions. Pierre, I will see you out. I need to give you the list.'

He went upstairs and searched his uniform jacket. He was glad to escape. He found it hard to witness the goodbyes. If he had to part from Zara under similar circumstances, he wondered how he would cope.

Pierre stood at the back door when he came down the stairs. Auguste handed him the list.

'You will warn them?'

'Of course.'

'Will they listen?'

'Who knows? They may not believe me. We can help them get out but if they won't go there is nothing we can do.'

'No, I suppose not.'

'You have done a good thing here. When all this is over, I will remember.'

'That is not why I have done it.'

'I know.'

'I will go out first and check around. I don't want to know where you are going. It's safer so.'

Auguste checked the grounds and came back.

'It's safe I think. Go through the woods. No one is up I think.'

'Auguste,' Pierre said, 'you'll take care of my little one?'

'Pierre, we are brothers. I would never allow her to come to harm.'

'No Auguste, we are not brothers. I am a Jew. You are a Catholic and yet we are as close as friends can become. I'm sorry I misjudged you.'

'You did not misjudge me. You were right about everything. I have learned the truth and I will fight in my way, but I will also escape with our children.'

'Go with God, yours or mine, I don't care anymore.'

They embraced. Slinging his gun over his shoulder, Pierre turned and jogged away towards the tree line. Auguste stood watching as his friend disappeared into the wood. They both knew the place as well as if it was the old schoolyard, where they had played as children. Turning to the back door, he could not help but wonder if he would see Pierre again. He supposed in some way it did not matter, he had shouldered the responsibility of protecting Monique in any case and he knew he would fulfil it.

CHAPTER THIRTEEN

1

The church of St Jacques de Compstelle was not popular with many of the inhabitants of the city. Most preferred the larger and more recently built church of Notre Dame. Auguste liked St Jacques because it was old and the sense of being where worship had taken place for hundreds of years had always fascinated him.

The yellow stone building, restored a hundred years before, stood near the river and Auguste felt nothing but relief as he climbed the rough stone steps, holding Odette's hand with his left and Zara's with the other. No military vehicles were parked nearby and no ominous black cars stood in the street to herald concern.

Père Bernard greeted them at the door. His white robes seemed a mockery of the dark times to Auguste, but he smiled to his priest and they entered the church. Each of them knelt and dipping their fingers in the holy water by the aisle, they made the sign of the cross. They advanced, looking straight ahead along the red carpet. It put Auguste in mind of the carpet in the Medical College and he found it hard to shrug off the image in his mind of Himmler and his talk about the final solution. He wondered what Pius XII would have said if he had been there. He was sure he would have fought, using all the church's weight to protect the innocent. Was it not the Church's teaching over the centuries to protect them, whether they were Jews, Pharisees or Samaritans?

Auguste smiled and greeted the members of the congregation with whom he was familiar. They sat at the back of the church and he hoped Zara was invisible from the door. He still had an irrational fear Brunner, in some absurd way, might appear in the church or be watching outside.

When the service began, he listened to the liturgy and he knew he should not take communion. He became convinced he was guilty of mortal sin. He dredged up feelings of guilt and remorse too. He was sure the church would not condemn him for a crime never openly condemned by the Pope, but the guilt was for a sin in his heart, in the fibre of his being.

Odette stood to take communion. He felt the tension build. He could not remain seated yet he knew he was wrong to partake. The struggle made him sweat. He had not been strongly religious but the church had been part of his life and he felt taking communion now was a betrayal of his own beliefs. He wondered how many betrayals he could commit in his life; the Jews, Bernadette and now his faith. Had he lost faith? Had he succumbed to the evil Brunner and his fellows spread and promulgated?

'Come,' Odette whispered as she took his hand. Like a lamb to the slaughter, like his Lord led to Calgary, he allowed Odette to lead him from his seat, as he heard the Lord's Prayer. Through the Agnus Dei thrusting itself into his hearing, he felt like crying aloud 'this was a sin.'

He stared as father Bernard broke the host and placed it in the main chalice. He felt remorse again as he heard the words.

'This is the lamb of God who takes away the sin of the world.'

'If only,' he thought. 'If only it could take away my sin. Those poor people, separated, imprisoned, work camps, dead.'

He looked up at Père Bernard as he approached. Despite all, he opened his mouth and the wafer felt dry and bitter to him. It was all in his head, he knew it, but the bitterness seemed symbolic of the guilt eating away at him at that moment, a moment of truth. The wine, sour and strong seemed to cloy in his mouth and his emotions brought unsteadiness to his gaze.

And then it was over. He rose as if from some mortal trial and he wondered why he had been so scared. Odette took his hand as they walked back to the pew. Zara looked up and smiled.

'Is it next year, Papa?'

He shook his head. 'What?'

'Confirmation,' Odette said.

'No,' he whispered, 'in two years.'

'Oh,' Zara said and she smiled up at her father.

Auguste smiled back, reassured by his child. If all else came apart in his life, at least there was one anchor to keep him sane. Zara was all, even if Odette left him for the evil he had allowed to happen, he would still have Zara's love. Yet, he also knew Odette was his woman, his adult life, his linchpin; having both of them made his existence worthwhile. He would do what he could in this mess of a war and he would protect Monique too. For Murielle, for Pierre.

The end of the service came and Auguste realised he had paid no attention to it. He had not worshipped, he had ruminated. He crossed himself, facing the altar on the way out.Père Bernard shook his hand as he left.

'I was glad to see you here my son.'

'Yes, Père,' Auguste said, 'I was glad to be here.'

'Perhaps you wish to confess? I am here all afternoon. I know you are busy, but it has been many weeks. You must not leave the Lord and his Holy Church, my son.'

'No. I can come today if you think it is necessary.'

'Only you, my son, know if it is necessary. Take some time first to prepare and then come to me.'

They both smiled artificial smiles and Auguste felt like a man who refuses a forceful salesman but feels guilty all the same for not buying his expensive goods.

He stopped in his tracks on the steps. A black Mercedes stood parked in the street outside, next to his own battered car. Brunner. If the SD Major was here, he had his story prepared but it was thin. Because it was transparent, he knew there would be consequences.

It was almost with relief he saw Linz emerge from the vehicle, his black uniform smart and pressed as ever and Auguste wondered whether French hands or German had been employed in the pressing. He could imagine Linz working with Brunner raping and torturing Bernadette and he had an unreasonable urge to pull out his weapon and kill him. The thought was as fleeting as the smile one might offer to a passing stranger and Auguste smiled to the SS officer.

'Scharfürer, how nice to see you,' he said.

Linz gave his usual, smart, unwelcome 'seig heil' and this time Auguste gave him room for manoeuvre.

'Major Brunner presents his compliments,' he said, 'he requires your services tomorrow.'

'My services?'

'Yes. It is necessary to find and arrest a man in the area east of here and he wishes you to accompany me.'

'You?'

'Yes, he has other things of greater importance to attend to.'

Auguste was tempted to ask if it meant leaving listening devices in someone else's office but he resisted the temptation. He stood square in front of Zara. The chance of his hiding her completely was remote but he thought there was some possibility the arrogant German would not bother with a child, a French child in particular.

'That is all,' Linz said.

'Where? When?'

'I will pick you up from the Prefecture. At seven.'

'No, you will wait for me outside at eight-thirty. I have things to do first.'

He watched Linz's face as it changed from brash arrogance to puce irritation.

'I was told...'

'Damn it man. You are not in charge of civil matters. You are a soldier and do not direct me in these things. I will look for you at eight-thirty and you will not be late. If I am late you will wait anyway, clear?'

'Heil Hitler,' the SS officer said. The salute was less smart and it gave Auguste a childish satisfaction.

Linz opened his car door and got in. With a splash from the white-walled tyres of the black Mercedes as it decimated a puddle, his driver and he left the scene and Auguste prayed he had not noticed Zara.

2

As the Ran family drove home, there was silence in the old car at first. Auguste, deep in thought wondered whether the invitation to ride with Linz next morning was a pretext for something else. Had they become suspicious? Had Bruner sent Linz to identify his daughter?

It seemed unlikely. If Brunner suspected anything, he would have searched the house and he had not. No. Brunner would hardly describe Auguste's child to his junior officer.

Presently, Zara said, 'Papa, who was the man in the black car?'

'He is a German, a soldier.'

'Is he the one Pierre wants to kill?'

'No. Pierre wants to kill all of them and there are many now in our country. We have to protect Monique from them, because they would want to kill her if they knew she was with us. I told you. If they find her in our home we will all go to a prison camp.'

'I want her to go home.'

'Darling we should always be kind, it is what Jesus taught us,' Odette said.

'Yes, never refuse to help a friend who needs you. Haven't I told you many times?'

'But she is Jewish and we are not. Besides, she takes my toys.'

'She has none of her own. Pierre only brought one dolly when he brought her to us. Is it so bad to share?'

'Why should I share all my toys with a Jewish girl?'

'You have played together all your lives. She is your best friend, Zara,' Odette said.

'Zara. Please try to understand. These are much more grown-up matters than dollies and toys. If the Germans come they will kill Monique and maybe us too for sheltering her.'

'I don't understand.'

'Ma fleur, I hope you never find out. We are a family and we are together, it is all that matters.'

He was sure Zara understood nothing. He wondered how she could. A nine-year-old child he thought, could not have any concept of the evil adults could perpetrate upon each other. He realised Zara must see it as unfair, but he knew equally well there had to be a balance in life. He had to protect them both and if God allowed it, get them out of the country. At the same time, he had to keep his family together.

When the car drew up outside the house, crunching on the grey gravel by the front door, Auguste began to fear the worst. The front door was ajar and although there was no sign of forced entry, he worried the SD had found him out.

'Stay here, both of you,' he said, his heart racing.

He drew his pistol with a sweaty hand and approached the door. He moved with caution and made little sound. With his back to the door, he sidled in and heard a fat cough from the kitchen.

'Who is there?' he said.

'Oh, Inspector. I am sorry. The door was open and I knew you would be in church, so I thought you would not mind if I waited here in the warm kitchen. It is so cold outside.'

'Dufy, if you came here to steal, I will arrest you and let Judge Dubois deal with you in the morning. Empty your pockets at once.'

Auguste pointed his weapon at the old man. François emptied his pockets. Auguste detected an aroma reminiscent of dank ponds mixed with sweat as the man moved. Dufy was perhaps sixty years old or so Auguste estimated. He had clear, blue eyes and a scarred, grubby, bearded face. He wore a beret sitting perched at an angle on his large head. He wore a thick tattered, woollen coat.

Auguste looked at the pockets' contents. In one, there was a button, a Laguiole knife and a few francs. In the other was a soiled handkerchief and a folded piece of Manila paper, perhaps torn from the back of an envelope.

Auguste poked the note with the barrel of his gun.

'What's this? You can write?'

'Naturally I can write, Inspector. It is the reason why I am here.'

'What, writing?'

'No, to deliver a message.'

'Push it across the table.'

Auguste took his eyes from Dufy only long enough to pick up the scrap of paper. Scrawled upon it was:

> Auguste,
>
> I am compromised. SD officers are searching for me as I write this. I have given it to Marquite and she will see you get it. I will say nothing. Is there anything to say in any case?
>
> Colonel Andre Arnaud.

Auguste felt a cold hand grip his neck.

'Where did you get this?' he said.

'Well Inspector, I was delivering some beautiful trout to Madame Arnaud and she asked me to bring this to you without any delay.'

'You have read it?'

'Inspector, I am a poacher, you know that. I have been to prison; you know that too. I have not sunk so low in the scheme of things to read other's correspondence.'

'François, you do not speak like a poacher. Who were you before the war?'

'I was as you see, a man who enjoys living off the land.'

'The truth.'

'I was a school teacher in St Cypriene. But you know how, if you like a drink, they condemn you out of hand. It was most unjust.'

'What do you know of this matter? What happened to Colonel Arnaud?'

'Why, the Germans took him. I am sure he will be released.'

'Sure?'

'Well what would they want with such a man?'

'That is for me to know and you to keep quiet about. You understand?'

'I am in touch with certain people whom I come across in the woods from time to time. If you require me to pass the odd message, it is no problem.'

'Who have you been speaking to?'

'Speaking? I don't understand.'

'Why would I want a message passed?'

'Perhaps it is good to stay in touch with old friends. My mother often said, you should always care about small cuts and old friends.'

'Damn it man. Speak plainly.'

François whispered, 'Plain can be dangerous. Just remember, if you need a message sent, old François could perhaps be of service.'

'I don't know what you mean.'

'Of course you don't Inspector. My lips are sealed. May I go?'

'Yes, go. Next time don't break in, wait on the stairs.'

'Perhaps it would be unwise. May I use the back door?'

'Go.'

The door closed behind the old poacher.

Auguste jumped at the sound of a voice behind him.

'Papa, who was that old man?'

'Never mind darling. He was a messenger.'

'He smells of fish.'

'Never you mind. You must let Monique know we are home.'

'Why me?'

'But you know what to do. Run along now and when you are both here, we can eat. We have beef from Duboef's farm today and if we ever get the smell of the old man out of the house, we will enjoy our lunch.'

She scampered up the stairs to the attic. Odette stood in the doorway. Her worried face hid nothing from Auguste.

'They have arrested Arnaud.'

Odette said, 'Auguste?'

'I don't know whether it is a danger to us or not.'

'Does he know about Monique?'

'Do you think I have become a fool? No, of course he doesn't. He does know I planned to warn the Jewish families whose addresses I gave to Pierre.'

'Will he talk?'

'They all do. Whether they will ask the right questions or not is another matter. There is no reason why they would ask about me and maybe the old soldier will not mention me either.'

'If they suspect a conspiracy in the police they might. Oh Auguste, what shall we do?'

'Odette, my love, we sit tight. There is still a chance I can trap Brunner. If I can remove him, the SD will have no reason to go after me. They will replace him and his successor will not look in my direction. I just hope Arnaud doesn't talk.'

'But he will, if they ask him.'

'Yes.'

He crossed the kitchen and held her in his arms. He kissed her forehead. They embraced and he held her as tight as he would the edge of a cliff from which he had slipped. He felt like a plummeting man. Piece by piece his life was falling apart; danger seemed to lurk around every corner. For Auguste it was as though the German occupation had taken his neat, tidy policeman's life, twisted it and lacerated it. Even his religious beliefs, such as they were, seemed challenged. Was he losing his faith? Was he becoming like Job—a man whom God had selected to suffer?

CHAPTER
FOURTEEN

1

Auguste asked Édith to check on Arnaud before leaving his office. He made sure it was an audible request. He wanted Brunner to know he had no knowledge of the old soldier's whereabouts.

He left the building with all the fears expressed to Odette on his mind. Getting into the Mercedes with Linz required effort, but it was an effort he was ready to make; he had no wish to arouse suspicion. It was a cold day, even for February, with grey rain clouds overhead, but Auguste found the car's heater adequate; it converted his cold sweat to a higher temperature. It was sleeting outside as they hit the main Sarlat road. They headed east towards Beynac and he knew they would turn left towards St Andre L'Abeille. It was a small hamlet and Auguste wondered which of the three houses they would be searching.

'Who are you looking for?'

'You do not need to know,' Linz said.

'If you wish me to be involved, you will need to tell me won't you?

How can I arrest a man if I don't know his name?'

'Jules Aubrac, if you must know.'

'He doesn't live there.'

'We know he is hiding there.'

'Ridiculous. He was a bricklayer in Pont-de–Cause, it's the other side of the Dordogne valley.'

'No, we have information he is hiding in St Andre.'

'Even so, he is not a traitor. I can vouch for it.'

'I suppose you would have vouched for Colonel Arnaud?'

'What do you mean?'

'Nothing. We have a job to do. There is no need for conversation.'

Silence descended then. Auguste wondered what was happening. Had Arnaud informed on this man Aubrac? Had Brunner sent them off on a wild goose chase to hide some other activity?

The car turned off to the left as soon as they neared Beynac. Auguste could see the ruins of the Chateau high above, perched on a high hill as if Richard the Lionheart was still peering down at him from above. The wicked English, the "Rosbifs", were rumoured to haunt the ruins, though Auguste paid no attention to such childish ideas.

They drove up a steep hill passing neat tilled fields cut out of the forest on their right side. To the left the terrain was rough and wooded, a steep embankment rising above them. The road twisted, turned and by the time they reached the church of Cazenac Auguste felt a faint nausea, despite his empty stomach. He was relieved when the road opened out a little and they headed for St Andre.

The car descended a rise and passed an embankment on the right. Forested slopes rose to their left. It was there it happened.

Auguste could recall seeing the logs across the road. He remembered the explosion and then all was black. He had a feeling of flying and then a floating sensation. A bright light shone in his eyes for a second or two and he had vague memories of faces peering down at him.

He awoke lying on the road verge. His head thumped and when

he tried to open his eyes, the lids seemed stuck down by some sticky discharge. It brought a strange memory to mind. He recalled how when he was a small child he had an infection in one eye. The doctor said it was a 'sticky' eye. He found himself imagining he was back there in those times. His mother shaking her head, fussing over cold compresses and eyewash.

He shook his head and his next waking sensation was of being pulled, dragged and deposited somewhere hard. His understanding of events began to spread like a bruise in his mind and he forced his eyes open. Out of focus and smeared with whatever stuck to his eyes, he could make out blurred and grey figures. He seemed to be in a barn or outhouse of some kind, then all went black again.

When he awoke once more, it was to the sensation of someone wiping his eyes. It was no gentle hand. He drew his head away and this time knew he could see. A bearded figure wearing a grey beret stood over him and he realised he was lying on his back. He tried to sit up but a brown-booted foot pushed him down and he found he had the strength of a kitten.

A voice made of gravel said, 'Pierre, he's awake.'

'Let him up, Jules.'

His friend's voice took time to penetrate and he began to piece together what had happened. His head throbbed and he understood he must have hit his head and the eye-stickiness was blood. His captors had tied his hands in front of him. They felt numb from lack of circulation and a dull pain grabbed his fingers like a vice.

Then the man removed the boot from his chest. He tried to sit up but all he could manage was to raise himself to one elbow. He looked around. His head swam.

The driver of the Mercedes lay beside him. He did not move. Auguste realised he was dead. It took little imagination to understand: half of his face and adjoining head were missing.

His voice a dry croak, he said, 'Pierre? Where am I?'

'Don't worry.'

'But...'

'Lie still. There is nothing to do but accept what God delivers.

You have hit your head in the blast. You are confused.'

Auguste looked to his left. He swallowed. A shiver ran down his spine. He could see Linz. They had torn his uniform from his body. They had hung him upside down, stuffed rags in his mouth and tied them with a cloth gag. The German wriggled. He squirmed.

The bearded man crossed to the suspended German and stood next to him with a Laguiole knife in his right hand. Auguste knew, despite his confused mind, what was going to happen. He looked away. He was glad there would be no screams. He was not a squeamish man but he had no desire to hear the cries of a man dying in agony. Icy fear gripped him. He knew the Maquis would never let Linz live. He knew they wanted some kind of reprisal for their friends and relatives, tortured in the Mairie by Linz and Brunner. Would they butcher him too? Would they hang him up like a carcass? Was this how it would end? Pierre—would he allow it?

2

Despite turning away, he heard whimpers from Linz. The bearded man, Jules, described what he was doing.

'First we remove the testicles.'

'Pierre, don't do this,' Auguste heard himself say.

He heard more whimpers, obstructed by the gag but still audible. Pierre crouched to him.

'Listen to him, Auguste. Jules is doing what they do to our men, our comrades. It is a good sound. It is the sound of revenge. This one tortured and killed Jules' brother. We knew he would talk so we moved camp, but he was noble, strong. He kept silent for twenty-four hours, as we have all agreed to do to give the group time to move on. The SD dumped his body at the edge of the woods. They had removed his scrotal contents and choked him with them. Look. It is justice. Just look.'

Pierre tried to push Auguste's chin to make him see. Auguste shoved his friend's hand away with his tied hands.

'Are you becoming like them? By doing this you become them. Don't you see?'

Auguste got to his feet. He swayed as he gripped Pierre by the lapels. In his peripheral vision, he saw blood pouring down Linz's stomach and chest as he wriggled and squirmed.

'Don't you see? You cannot defeat a demon by becoming one? Kill him Pierre. Kill him. For the love of God.'

For a brief moment, their eyes met. A heated glance. A fiery flash of understanding and Pierre turned, rifle in hand. He raised it to his shoulder. With a speed to make any huntsman envious, he planted a bullet in the German's head. The exiting slug took half of the skull bone with it and brain and blood sprayed behind in a gory mess on the straw. The report, in the confines of the barn, made Auguste's already ringing ears sting with tinnitus.

Jules turned, knife in hand.

'You bastard. You know what you have robbed me of?'

'We don't have the time. The woods will be alive with Germans in half an hour and you want to spend time doing this? Call Josephine and let's go.'

'What about him?'

'I'll take care of him.'

'You want the knife?'

'No. I'll do it my way. Now go.'

A look of fury wreathed the man's face but he left. Auguste could hear him calling to Josephine.

'You're going to kill the man who protects your daughter,' Auguste said.

'How can you be so stupid? Lie down and keep quiet.'

Auguste did as Pierre asked and he looked up at his friend, uncomprehending.

Pierre raised his weapon. He fired it in the air and winked at Auguste. Auguste watched as Pierre ran to the barn door and slammed it shut, leaving him alone with the two bodies. He heard a truck start up and wondered what would happen now. He could do nothing. If he left and found his way back to the main road, Brunner might accuse him of complicity in the killings. If he stayed where he was, they would assume he was next, but the attackers had no time to dispose of him. He waited.

CHAPTER FIFTEEN

1

Rain made a gentle pattering sound on the windowpane as Auguste sat in the hard-backed chair. Brunner's office, illuminated by two table lamps, appeared comfortable and as well appointed as a hotel lounge. On the right hand wall was the stolen painting and the bookshelves opposite seemed filled with old books. An antique inkstand adorned the desk in front of him, no doubt stolen from somewhere, Auguste mused. He detected a faint smell of mothballs but could not localise its source.

He was uncomfortable. His head ached and his back felt bruised. His left elbow had ballooned with a bruise but he knew there were no bones broken; he could still bend his arm. Brunner's office was warm at least but nothing could make Auguste enthusiastic about what he knew was to come.

German soldiers had taken him from the barn. They refused to speak to him but did not handle him in a rough or disdainful manner. The journey back had been a bumpy and painful one. Only when they arrived at the Mairie did they cut his bonds. He wondered on the journey if there was a German word for suspension, for none seemed prevalent in the mechanics of the armoured truck bringing him back to Bergerac.

Presently, the door opened and Auguste looked over his shoulder at Brunner. For once, there was no bonhomie, no smile and no humour.

'Helmut,' Auguste said, 'I need to get this cut dressed.'

'Yes, Inspector, but we must talk first.'

'Inspector? This is unusually formal.'

'It is a serious matter.'

'It certainly is. I need to get home, let my wife know I am safe and get my cut washed and dressed.'

'Linz.'

'Yes, poor fellow. I saw his body when they got me out of the place.'

Auguste noticed he was speaking much too fast and managed to regain control and slowed down mid-sentence.

'You did not witness it?'

'No, I awoke as the soldiers dragged me out. I'm relieved they didn't fire the barn before leaving. I presume it was the Maquis?'

'Yes. I'm interested in why you say "they"? How did you know there was more than one?'

'The driver and Linz and me. How could one man have taken us to that place on his own? Partisans work in groups, you know that.'

'Linz suffered terribly.'

'Perhaps God was kind and made him faint before the end?'

'It is unusual with what they did to him. Usually they scream and bleed but if you press hard on the wounds, they stop bleeding. One can keep such pain going a long time without too much blood loss.'

'You seem to know about such things?'

'One reads, you know. I have read many firsthand accounts by torturers. You could say I have made a study of it.'

'It is not something we use in the police force.'

'No, but the stakes are different, are they not? Police-work is about obtaining information freely given and piecing it together. My work is different. It is an inquiry but also a punishment; the Spanish Inquisitors understood it. I am sure you understand too in your way. You are, after all, a mature and intelligent man.'

Auguste was silent.

'You see, my little policeman, I have the wider responsibilities of the security of the state, not only a duty to protect a small local population.'

'What do you want to know?'

'What happened, of course.'

'Well, we were on the St Andre road and I recall logs being in the road and an explosion.'

'What happened next?'

'Nothing. I was unconscious until the soldiers came. I recall some dark figures and a feeling of being lifted.'

'Can you describe any of your captors?'

'Helmut. I must go. I've told you all I know. It has not been a good day.'

Auguste knew he had to play his part well. He estimated Brunner was an expert at reading the faces of liars, even when disguised by dried blood, perhaps even better then. It was what Brunner was inured to, it seemed.

'I will not detain you longer. There seems to be remarkably little you can tell me.'

Auguste stood.

'Thank you. I'm truly sorry I could not be of more help.'

'Help? Of course you can help. I will have five local men hanged. Reprisal is the only way to make these insurgents understand the more they cause damage, the more their people will suffer. It will make the Maquis unpopular.'

'Five men?'

'Yes, I will leave it up to you to choose whom you wish to arrest, but as soon as you have had a little rest, I will expect to see a hanging.'

'I am a policeman, not an executioner.'

Auguste stared at the German. A feeling of utter revulsion filled him; it took a superhuman effort to hide the fury he felt. He swallowed. The taste of blood was rank in his mouth. He coughed.

'You protest too loudly, Auguste. My men will hang them. I just want you to select them and bring them to me. We will hang them outside the Mairie for all to see. I will have the gallows built tomorrow. Poor Linz will not go unavenged. The Führer does not tolerate terrorists and nor do I.'

The room was silent and then Brunner said, 'One other thing.'

'Yes?' Auguste said, but he was choking over the emotion welling up within.

'Why do you think they left you alive?'

'What?'

'Well, the driver died in the blast. They took his body to hide it. Linz, they took for revenge and mercifully, they killed him. But you? They left you tied and unconscious. They could have killed you but did not.'

'I...I suppose it was because I am French.'

'You think these vermin see you as French? You work with my men and directly for the Vichy government. Hand in glove. Together. They left you alive for a reason.'

'Perhaps the soldiers disturbed them and they had to get away. Look, my head is killing me. I need to get home. If there is nothing else?'

He noticed a thoughtful frown on the German's face.

Brunner said, 'Yes, Auguste, you may go now. I will order my men to take you home.'

A sudden thought flickered in Auguste's mind.

'Helmut, one thing bothers me.'

'What's that?'

'The girl who was murdered, Bernadette.'

'Yes, a flower of femininity. Such a waste, was it not?'

'She fought her captors.'

'Yes?'

'Yes, there was blood under a fingernail. She must have scratched her torturer on the face.'

'Very natural, I'm sure.'

'You had a scratch on your left cheek next day.'

'I told you, I fell.'

'What blood group are you?'

'What is this? Is the hunter to become the hunted? You think I am involved in such a sordid thing? Are you defending yourself? Have you done something wrong, that you need to attack me? Are you hiding something?'

'No, it was just the way you talked about torture. You seem enamoured of it.'

Auguste wondered if he had overstepped the mark, but he wanted to distract Brunner. He seemed to know so much, yet like Auguste, he had no proof, nothing tangible to offer. No evidence.

'I like my work; that is all. You had better go before I decide to keep you longer. You would not enjoy our hospitality here.'

Auguste rose, he looked at Brunner. It was now as if both of them were fencing. Brunner waved him away. Auguste rubbed his back as he left. He wondered how bad his back injury could be. It was stiffening by the moment.

When the car came, he wondered if anyone would see them delivering him home. He thought it would not be good for his image to return looking beaten and limping in an SD vehicle. He longed for his bed; it had been a bad day.

2

Auguste lay in bed. He was relieved to see the dawn casting its light through the gaps in the blackout curtains. He struggled to move but the pain in his back, which kept him awake most of the night, held him rigid, immobile. The two little pyjama-clad girls, who sat on the bed and bounced up and down now and again, did not help his discomfort.

'No. Please don't,' Auguste said.

Odette lay next to him. She reached out her hand, placing it upon his shoulder and said, 'Auguste, they are only children. Now girls, try to be still. Papa has a sore back and if you jump about it hurts him.'

'Sorry, Papa.'

'Sorry Uncle Auguste.'

He tried to smile but the discomfort stabbed him and he decided to stay where he was. At one point in the night, he had imagined he would lose the use of his legs. Escaping in a wheelchair held no prospect of success.

'I will get you some aspirin, Auguste,' Odette said.

He smiled a tired smile.

'Is Papa ill?'

'No I'm not ill Zara, I hurt my back in a car accident.'

Monique said, 'Was it the black car that came yesterday?'

'Yes, how did you know?'

'I looked out through the window and saw it.'

'Monique my little one, I've told you never to do that. If someone saw you, it could be dangerous.'

'She does it all the time, Papa. I keep telling her not to...'

'No you don't.'

'I do.'

Odette said, 'Children. Stop this arguing and go downstairs. We will have breakfast in a few minutes and Zara must go off to school.'

'It's hard to get up,' Auguste said.

'Shall I call the doctor?'

'No, help me up and I will get ready for work.'

Odette took him by the arm and he somehow managed to swing his legs out of bed and don his slippers. She pulled him upright amid groans and curses.

'Are you going to work?'

'Of course. I have much to do. I told you about the reprisals.'

'What will you do? You cannot possibly comply, surely?'

'I have a plan which may soften the blow. It will still happen but not as Brunner wishes.'

'Papa?' Zara said from the door.

'Downstairs, now,' he said.

Alone again, Odette said, 'Plan?'

'Well you'll see. If it works it will be a half-way house, nothing more.'

'I think the knock on the head has addled your wits. Speaking in riddles now. I have no time for this Auguste, I have one to take to school and one to teach at home. I don't need a riddle-monger in the middle of it all.'

'It's just the less you know, the safer you will be.'

'See. Endless riddles.'

She left him sitting on the bed again, scrabbling in the half-light for his underwear. He dressed with difficulty and managed the stairs. As he moved around, the stiffness seemed to reduce and with an ashen face, he appeared at the kitchen doorway.

'Papa, is your back very sore?' Zara said and ran to him.

He bent his knees and her hug gave him encouragement.

'Zara, ma fleur. I have a sore back but it will pass. I'll take two aspirins and hey presto, it will be better, you'll see.'

'Papa had a sore back once,' Monique said.

'Your Papa would never give in to such a thing,' Auguste said.

'He said it was because he carried a burden. What is a burden Uncle Auguste?'

'It is something heavy but there are many things can cause it.'

'Burden. Burden,' the little girl repeated as if learning a new phrase or saying.

Auguste wondered whether his burdens might be lifted today. He felt wounded. He loved Monique, not like Zara, but close. He thought he could never forgive himself if the Germans discovered her. He regretted the back pain. He had much to do and it would hamper him. He wondered if he should see Dr. Girard, his family doctor, but there was no time today.

Driving to the Prefecture, he was in agony. He thanked his stars the car had a pull-out gear-stick instead of a normal one for changing gear. He was unsure if he could have driven at all unless it was so.

3

Auguste and Édith now conferred in the women's toilets. They were uncertain even there whether the SD could hear them but it was the one place they had not checked when they had come to place their listening devices according to Édith.

'I will have to telephone from the café next door. I can't believe they would listen to the phone calls made from there.'

'Huh. They listen everywhere Auguste.'

'We are agreed then?'

'Yes, I will have the requisition paid as prisoner transport from our end. Are you sure they won't remove the masks?'

'Why should they?'

'Brunner is unpredictable. He may want to see the suffering on their faces.'

'Let him. It makes no difference. I will have to drive to Lyon to sign the documents. The SD surveillance is a nuisance.'

'What about your back?'

'I'll survive.'

Auguste emerged holding his back but in better spirits. He descended the stairs and walked to the cafe next door, where he made his telephone call. Starting up the old Citroën, he smiled to himself. He would fool them all and then concentrate on Brunner. He had begun to hate the man and he knew it was contrary to his beliefs. The knowledge made little difference to him. He wanted justice and he would have it. He drove to Lyon without stopping. Despite difficulty getting out of the car, he managed what he had come for and he noticed his back was more comfortable on the way home. He wondered if it was his elevation in mood or perhaps a delayed effect of the aspirin. He mumbled a prayer under his breath as he drove and clutched the St Christopher he wore around his neck. He felt he could win this time.

CHAPTER SIXTEEN

1

It was still cold. A thick, white frost had gathered overnight and Auguste's car skidded as he pulled it to a stop outside the Prefecture. His nose told him the bakery had re-opened and it was a welcome greeting as he struggled out of the old Citroën. The bright sky above brought its own sense of hope and he smiled despite his discomfort. Brunner had not been in contact since the night of the interrogation and Auguste wondered if he might have changed his mind. He still felt like a man on a treadmill. He could see where he wanted to go but each step left him stationary. Plans were all he had then, plans and hopes. The insecurities he faced still prodded but now he had a way of fighting back in his own way and it gave him strength.

In his office, he stood at the desk and looking down, he noticed a report on his desk. It was from Claude. Without sitting, he opened the buff folder and read the contents. Claude concluded that none of the neighbours noticed Bernadette leaving her house. This was despite the lateness of the hour and her mother's story of a car picking her up. It seemed to Auguste it was at odds with his own experience of such cases. Someone always saw or heard something in a small close-knit community. It was only a matter of asking the right questions of the right person. He wondered how far Claude would take his ambitions and whether his uncle, the Judge influenced him. Auguste did not doubt someone other than Dr. Dubois had telephoned the Judge, but who? He puzzled for a moment then left the office. If you want a job doing properly, you may sometimes have to do it yourself.

'Édith, I'm going out,' he called over his shoulder as he passed his secretary's office.

She came to the door.

'Where? What shall I say if anyone calls?'

'No one will call. Well, if Brunner calls tell him I'm sick but his delivery of bound and gagged hanging-fodder will be on time at three in the afternoon tomorrow.'

'You have arrested them?'

'Yes Édith, exactly as Brunner asked,' he said louder than he needed. Then he winked. 'They are all local men, four farmers and a baker. People around here will learn to respect the law.'

Édith pointed an index to her forehead signalling her understanding and Auguste made his way down the stairs, holding onto his sore back.

It took him effort and pain to drive to the little cobbled street where Bernadette parted from him, but he put up with the discomfort, determined to find out whether Claude had done his work with the diligence Auguste required of his second-in-command.

He stood at the side of the road. He looked up and down the street. Bernadette's mother's house was at the corner of a bend in the street and Auguste estimated any activity would best be seen from the neighbours' houses across the road rather than the ones on either side.

Three houses sported a view of the street in the area of interest. He began at the first. He knocked.

The door yawned; it creaked as it made its slow journey from ajar to open. It sounded to Auguste like a blackboard screech and he felt his spine tingle.

A small ancient appeared in the doorway. The elderly woman stood hunched forward, her spine ravaged by time and old age. Auguste thought her unnatural posture would make her see people's feet before their faces. She looked up at him with clear blue questioning eyes.

'Yes?' she said.

Auguste introduced himself and she invited him in. He followed her to an upstairs room. A tottering pile of newspapers littered one corner and a lamp stood in the other corner, the shade hanging crooked and sad as if it had lost its meaning and its will to live in the daylight filtering in through the threadbare curtains. The curtains themselves seemed unhappy and Auguste felt they needed or even longed for a man with aptitude for such work to re-hang them, since they were as lopsided and impoverished as their owner.

He sat on a grubby couch and the woman sat opposite. Her face seemed a wrinkled picture of all he wanted to avoid in his own old age. She offered him coffee but he knew it would be chicory and he refused, wishing the offer had been real coffee not a mirage drawn by the Nazi occupation. Real coffee and croissants, coffee and bacon, coffee and eggs. It was a source of pain to him in a subtle way and he knew it was a shared discomfort between him and this old woman whom he had never met before. There was however, a kinship. They were both French and both of Aquitaine. Auguste could feel it, whether her eyes expressed it or not. Perhaps it was in her demeanour, he could not guess.

'Madame, I wonder if you recall a night three days ago when Bernadette Leclerc disappeared?'

'Bernadette. Yes, I remember. I talked to another policeman about it.'

'Yes it was my lieutenant; he questioned you?'

'Yes, Major.'

'I am no Major, only the assistant Chief of Police.'

'Well all the same, I remember.'

'Bernadette disappeared in the late evening and she was, as you know, murdered.'

'Murdered? Yes, your thin young man asked me and I told him all I know.'

'Murdered by very evil men.'

'The black car,' she said, her gaze directed at his knees.

'Black car?'

'It came and took her.'

'You told that to my officer?'

'Naturally.'

'Did you notice what kind of car?'

'It was black.'

She still stared at Auguste's knees and he realised her back prevented her from looking elsewhere.

'But there are many black cars. There are even black French cars,' he said, shifting in his seat.

'It was black as the heart of Hitler himself.'

'But you cannot identify it?

'Of course I can.'

'Well?'

'It was a German Nazi car. You think I could mistake the devils' work?'

She crossed herself and Auguste had to shake off the impulse to imitate it himself. When he noticed his hand reaching upward, he scratched his nose to hide the gesture, but knew he looked foolish.

The old woman, eyes alight, said, 'It had flags. They were mounted one on each side at the front. Nazi emblems. Filth.'

Auguste drew out his notepad. He scribbled as fast as he was able. The old woman stood.

'Can I offer you a brioche?'

'That would be very welcome, thank you.'

He felt guilt then. This old woman could have few means to bake. He felt embarrassed to take her bread. She disappeared into the kitchen waddling like an unsteady duck, then reappeared with a plate and two bread rolls. They had seen better days, like their owner. She offered the bread and Auguste took one.

He munched in silence for a moment then said, 'So you saw the vehicle clearly?'

'Naturally. I am old, not stupid. I told your young man.'

'But just to help me too—you are certain it was a German car?'

'Yes, I told you.'

'You won't have recalled the licence number, I suppose.'

'It began with BE.'

'Ah, a German plate.'

'The numbers were 237.'

'You remember that?'

'Yes, I have a head for numbers. Besides, it was the same number as my mother's telephone.'

'Your mother? How old is she?'

'You are police?'

'Yes.'

'And you think my mother still lives? I am seventy-eight years old. You really think my mother lives?'

'No. How foolish of me. I thought perhaps you might have been much younger. Perhaps fifty.'

The cackles coming from the furrowed face caused Auguste to redden.

'You are such a nice boy. Whatever made you join the traitors? You should be out with the Maquis, blowing up trains and shooting at Germans. Proper Frenchmen.'

Auguste looked down and noticed the old woman had leaned forward and her hand rested on his knee. It was as if a huge snail crawled up towards his groin and he stood up.

'Madame,' he said, 'you may be required to give all this as a statement at the Prefecture.'

'I have already done this.'

'When?'

'Yesterday. What a polite young man he is. What's his name? Charles?'

'No, Claude.'

'Yes, that was it. Funny though; he asked me not to tell anyone what was in the statement. A secret, he said.'

Auguste realised there was much to do. He took his leave after finishing the bread. He heard her cackling as the door shut behind him. Had the woman some sexual intention? He dismissed the thought with a shudder and went on to question the rest of the neighbours; following in Claude's footsteps. The answer was the same. The black German car had been identified by two of the occupants of the opposite houses. He could now, if he wished, prove Claude made a false report.

He headed back. He knew what he had to do but pondered whether it was wise.

2

Auguste had another thing left to do but uncertainty had him in its clutches. He needed to communicate with Pierre. Dufy was the key he thought, but he had no unobtrusive way to make contact. It had to be today.

He wrapped his overcoat around himself, pulled the collar up to warm his neck and climbed the Prefecture steps. Claude was emerging as he entered the building.

'Ah, Claude. I read your report.'

'Yes, I'm sorry there was so little to learn,' Claude said, as the two stood conversing in the doorway. The empty street behind them was white and cold and a wintry breeze curled around their legs. The look in Claude's eyes could have been mistaken for triumph but Auguste knew it was only a minor victory even in Claude's view.

'A great shame no one saw the car. I will have to concede to Judge Dubois we have drawn a blank here. He will not be pleased.'

'Well, if we have no clues and no suspects, there is little we can do.'

Auguste gripped Claude's arm.

'My boy,' he said, 'you will go far in this police force.'

'What?'

'I'm sure your natural ability in police work will further you career, that's all.'

'Yes. Thank you Auguste.'

'Off out?'

'Yes, I've an informant to meet.'

'Well, I won't get in your way.'

They parted and Auguste smiled to himself as he climbed the stairs. He would show Claude how a little subtlety could make all the difference to police work. Oh, yes.

He strode into Édith's office, raising a finger to his lips, to ask her to be silent.

She said nothing as Auguste crossed to her side and taking a pencil, wrote on the blotter. Édith nodded and Auguste left.

An hour later, he drew up outside the Judge's chambers. He kept telling himself he should not appear smug but a flicker of a smile crossed his lips as he opened the tall oak door to the outer office. Juliette looked up.

'Back so soon?'

'Tell him I have to make a report.'

'I'll buzz you through.'

The reply came and Juliette indicated the door. She remained seated. Auguste understood the implication. She would do nothing to help him.

Judge Dubois was standing at his window, looking out at the street below. Without turning, he said, 'You have a report to make?'

'Yes, sir.'

'Well?'

'It is here.'

Auguste placed the buff folder on the Judge's desk and stood back. Dubois turned and took his seat at the desk, indicating to Auguste to sit opposite.

Judge Dubois thumbed through the folder in silence.

Presently, he said, 'Are these witness statements sworn?'

'Naturally.'

'You are certain this car is the one Brunner uses?'

'Yes, I checked.'

'But no blood grouping from the fingernail?'

'No.'

The Judge shut the file.

'It is all circumstantial. For all you know, some other German used the car and the scratch on Brunner's face proves nothing.'

'And the burn marks?'

'Burn marks? That also cannot be used to trace anyone.'

'It might convince a jury. A good prosecutor would convince them.'

'I want you to drop this case. It is important you listen to me this time. A prostitute found murdered by a customer. The customer untraceable. End of investigation.'

'But this is not right.'

'I will decide what is right. There are political matters you cannot understand. Now, if there is anything else?'

'But Brunner did this.'

'Brunner. You are obsessed with Brunner. There is no evidence to connect him to the girl. No, we will not pursue this further. Please leave or you may find yourself in trouble.'

'Are you threatening me?'

'Let us just say, I am warning you for your own good.'

'Or Brunner's good.'

The Judge stood. He pointed to the door.

'Get out while I can still control my temper.'

Auguste rose. The two men glared at each other.

'Things really have changed here since the Germans came. We used to seek justice. Now we do as we are told.'

'Get out.'

Auguste left the office. Juliette looked up at him.

'Auguste...'

'What.'

'Oh nothing. You had better go.'

'You heard? Whatever is going on between us is as nothing compared to what is happening in our town. You know that?'

She looked uneasy for a moment and fiddled with her bracelet.

Looking up at him she said, 'I think the Judge is right. If the murderer is a high-ranking SD officer, he will be above the law. There is nothing the Judge can do about it. You have never been one to listen to the voice of reason, but this is one time when you must.'

'You seem well informed.'

'I am neither deaf nor blind Auguste. I have worked here for years and I see everything. Remember?'

'Are you now one of these people? Can I not even trust my own sister?'

'Goodbye.'

Auguste left and got into his car with slow painful movements. His back pain felt worse, as if it was a reminder to him of his impotence. Judge Dubois was collaborating with the Germans; it seemed obvious. If Brunner had telephoned the Judge, warning him to suppress the case, it would explain everything. For all he knew, both Claude and the Judge were co-operating with Brunner. It all seemed to whirl around in his mind. The pivot for all his troubles seemed to be Brunner and no one else. The man was a sadistic killer and he had to face justice. The thought of Brunner never standing trial kindled such anger within him he began to wonder if there was not some other way to avenge Bernadette.

Judge Dubois had accused him of being obsessed with Brunner. Auguste wondered if he was right. He had only circumstantial evidence but he knew the SD officer was guilty. It might be possible to entrap him but Brunner was clever as well as powerful. He wanted to hear Brunner confess. If he had that, he could testify himself in court, even if it meant involving another Judge or even a Judge from another commune.

He had one last thing to do before driving home. He knew it was dangerous but he had no choice now, or his whole plan for the hanging would go astray.

CHAPTER
SEVENTEEN

1

The headlights' beam cut the dusk like a knife cutting paper. It began to rain but a fog had descended and Auguste heaved a sigh of relief at he drove. He crossed the Dordogne Bridge and glimpsed the brown rushing waters of his river—Pierre's river, where they played and grew up together. How could all this have come about? How could he find himself here, trying to justify his very existence, hiding Monique, meeting criminals in the night?

The road wound away from the river and Auguste turned off onto a small, familiar dirt track. He pictured himself and Pierre wandering here as they did so many times in their adolescence, rifles in hand, looking for rabbits.

He recalled one occasion, faced with a small spring rabbit. It was feeding and somehow, it took no notice of him. He remembered standing still. With the gentlest of movements, he took aim. The small-bore rifle butt fitted snugly onto his shoulder and he drew the little creature into his sights. The trigger pulled, Auguste stared through the smoke. Nothing. He missed at twenty paces and Pierre howled with laughter. He recalled how he blushed, then joined in the merriment. What was there now to laugh about, he pondered.

The scene faded in his mind and he returned to concentrating on avoiding the potholes in the rough grit-strewn road. A mile on and he came to a small cottage. He drew up and parked. He struggled out of the driver's seat, his back paining him still and approached the door. The building was a timber-built house, with one storey and a felt roof. It stood on the edge of the forest, isolated and bleak with no others within half a mile. A low veranda faced the dirt road. The garish red-painted door stood out like a pimple.

Auguste knocked. He heard a dog bark somewhere at the back of the house. No answer. He waited in the gloaming. No lights lit the interior, but he looked in through the window in any case. François Dufy was not a man who would frequent the cafes in town and Auguste knew it.

He had almost decided to leave and hoped he might contact him in the morning. The silence broke. He started. He heard a sound behind him. It was a familiar sound. A gun cocking.

Turning, Auguste said, 'François?'

Silence. Auguste saw no one.

'François? Is it you?'

A shadowy figure stepped into the fading light and Auguste felt relief as he recognised the outline of the old poacher.

'What do you want? You are alone?'

'Yes. I need some help.'

'Help? What can a man like me do to help the police?'

'I need you to pass a message.'

'You are sure no one followed you?'

'In the fog? I would have seen the lights.'

'Perhaps. If I was following I would not have betrayed myself by putting on headlights.'

'We don't need to play this game. I need something from you; that is all.'

'And you come here? You are incriminating me.'

'No one followed, I am sure.'

The old man grunted.

'Follow me.'

Dufy turned and Auguste followed around the side of the house. He swore as he stepped on a pile of dog excrement and he heard Dufy smother a laugh. He wiped his boot on the grass and followed the poacher to a small shed behind the house. A Border Collie chained to a post outside a makeshift kennel, snarled at him and he took a small detour to avoid its quivering snout. Dufy called to the dog and it sat, head cocked to one side, eyeing Auguste as if he was some kind of unusual fish. Dufy opened the door. An oil lamp swinging from a string hooked to the ceiling illuminated the windowless structure. A musty, damp smell pervaded the place. Another door, no bigger than a hatch, occupied the lower part of the far wall.

In one corner, a mattress lay, covered by a military-style sleeping bag with a stained, blue-striped pillow lying askew at its head. The floor was earth and sand and Auguste realised the old man lived here and not in the warmer confines of his house.

'You sleep here?'

'Yes, it is safer; my dog warns me if anyone comes to the house. The SD are not after me as far as I know, but things can change anytime.'

Dufy looked at Auguste and smiled. He said, 'No-one is immune from arrest, even you. And they all talk in the end.'

'You need have no fear of that. I know nothing. It is safer for everyone concerned.'

'Yes, times have changed. Now we communicate less, because we know the more we share, the greater the danger. Once the opposite was true, is it not so?'

'Yes.'

'What message?'

Auguste could smell old sweat and the man's halitosis made him take a step back.

'I have a list of five names. These men must be taken out and hidden.'

'Traitors?'

'No local farmers, men with families. If they remain, the SD will hang them as a reprisal for Linz, the SS officer the Maquis killed.'

'They will only pick five more.'

'I have a plan. I can't tell you what it is. The less you know...'

'Alright. I'll take your message, but if there is an answer, how do I deliver it?'

'Just stand in the market square and sell your goods. I will send a man to arrest you.'

'What?'

'If we arrest you it will look like your usual spell in the cells.'

The old man grunted.

'Oh, by the way, if you are in my office, you cannot speak freely. They are listening.'

'Even you?'

'Brunner.'

'Maybe old Arnaud talked.'

'No it was before they arrested him. I think Brunner was worried in case I could prove he murdered a girl in our town.'

'Who?'

'Never mind.'

'If the SD come tonight, I will know you have set me up.'

'I was with them once, but I have realised who they are. They are messengers from Hell. I serve only France. I needed to see it that was all.'

'Then long live that. I will have to go now if I am to deliver your message. If I am successful I will be in the market square.'

'Good luck.'

The old man grunted and held the door wide for Auguste. As he stepped past, he caught the heavy animal smell on the old poacher again. He held his breath.

Avoiding the dog, he found his way to the car, stumbling in the dark. He wondered why his back felt better and wondered if the relief of getting everything done had relaxed him. He took a few moments to consider his position.

He thought about Bernadette, her voice, her face as she sang in the restaurant. He could hear her as she stepped from his car.

'Te absolvo.'

Absolve him of what? Had she said it predicting the future in some kind of riddle? Her words haunted him. They festered. He felt his only absolution would come through vengeance and justice. If he could achieve it, he thought, there might be some chance of reclamation for him.

He had been so stupid, so naive. How could he have been fooling himself all these months believing the Germans were humane employers of Jews in work camps in Germany? He had seen what he chose to see. He remembered the look in the Jew's face on the hospital steps and it made him want to shout aloud in anger and frustration. And now, he was in deep. He felt the risks were worthwhile. The thought salved his conscience to some extent. He felt better about himself though he knew he put Odette and the children in danger. He could not avoid it. Odette understood. Had she not taken on the risk of sheltering Monique herself?

Starting up his car, he turned towards the dirt road and switched on his headlights. It was a frosty night, the fog froze hard and solid on his windscreen, despite the salty water with which he washed it down. He did not mind the effort, it was nothing compared to what was to come and he knew it.

2

A tall fair-haired SS officer knocked on Brunner's office door. Auguste smiled but the man's face remained serious. The SS officer went in and presently, held the door open for Auguste to enter.

Brunner stood when Auguste entered and gestured for him to sit. They remained silent for a moment and then Auguste said, 'The gallows are built I see.'

'Yes,' Brunner said, unsmiling, 'my men are quick workers, unlike you French. Germans do not stop to drink wine and eat frogs in the middle of their work.'

'Frogs?'

'Well whatever they eat. You eat horseflesh do you not?'

'I came to discuss the internments before the prisoners arrive.'

'Yes, of course. What is on your mind?'

'I heard you had arrested Arnaud.'

'Yes, poor Arnaud. He must have known a lot about the Maquis. Pity.'

'He is talking?'

'Not very loudly. He died.'

'What?'

Auguste sat forward in his chair. He examined Brunner's face. It betrayed no hint of any traceable human emotion. It was as if the German had become impassive, blank and neutral.

Auguste said, 'you shot him?'

'No, no, no, Auguste. We would never shoot a man of Arnaud's rank without a trial. We are not barbarians. We obey the law. He had a heart attack under questioning. Hardly said a word.'

'He was no traitor.'

'No?'

'No.'

'We questioned a man. He was Maquis and he told us. Not immediately but all the same...'

'You tortured him?'

'Well, we tried to coax him. Eventually our methods of persuasion work on anyone. Susceptibility had nothing to do with it.'

'But sometimes they would say anything would they not? Incriminate anyone, just to make you stop.'

'Yes, of course. However, we look carefully at the logic of what they say and seldom act unless we have more than one statement corroborating the other. In this case, I had suspected Arnaud for a long time. Our singing Maquis-bird only confirmed what I already thought.'

'I knew Arnaud to be a loyal soldier in the First War. My father often talked about him as a hero. He would not betray his duty.'

'Did you know he had a radio?'

'Of course, he would have wanted news the same as anyone of us.'

'No, a radio transmitter.'

'I don't believe you.'

'Truly, it was hidden in a closet at his home.'

'You think he would be so stupid as to keep it in his home?'

'It was an old model. One like they used in the last war but our prisoner told us he used it to stay in touch with the Maquis and the British.'

'Preposterous. I knew Arnaud. He was no traitor.'

'We will never know for certain. He never lived to tell me. So, it does not matter. There are many more traitors.'

Auguste looked at Brunner. He struggled to hide the hatred he felt. This man had taken a loyal old French soldier and intended or carried out torture, on the word of a man who had given any information to make his torturers stop. Auguste pressed on in any case. Arnaud was dead. Nothing would bring him back and he needed to concentrate on the living.

What was it Arnaud had said? 'La bonne chance', life was a gamble and he was sure the old soldier would never have incriminated him even under torture. If only Brunner knew the truth. Auguste was sure he did not, but he also knew it was only a matter of time before he tortured the right man and Auguste would disappear like Arnaud.

Auguste said, 'The problem I now face is, I have no one in the Gendarmerie with whom I can deal. I have to have both their cooperation and their trucks for the internment. Arnaud also had the list of Jews. If you are right, he could have passed it on to anyone.'

'This is true. But you said yourself he would not betray his government.'

'And if you are the one who is right?'

'Well, it will become messy that is all. You will have to occupy yourself and your men with hunting down the missing Jews.'

'Not my job, Helmut.'

'Auguste, you seem to misunderstand. Your job is anything I say it is. Matters of state security are my domain and you must co-operate, you have orders, do you not?'

'Is it not enough you have made me into an executioner's lackey, to fetch men for you to hang?'

'Ah, so that is what's bothering you? Can you not see by hanging these men, you are protecting your people? They will never support the murderers if they know any of them can be hanged for a reprisal.'

'I understand the logic. It will tie the Maquis' hands.'

'Exactly.'

Brunner looked at his watch.

'Your men are bringing the prisoners at three o'clock?'

'Yes in ten minutes.'

'So we have time. A little music perhaps?'

Brunner stood and Auguste noticed for the first time there was a phonograph on a low table in the corner of the office. He watched as the German extracted a black vinyl disc from its sleeve, careful not to touch the glistening black surface. He placed it upon the red leather turntable and wound up the motor.

A soft crunching sound began as Brunner placed the needle into the outer groove. Music filled the office. It was Bruckner. Auguste knew the piece. He had heard it once when a German orchestra had played it in Lyon, on one of those rare occasions before the war when Odette and he had been able to take a short holiday.

The music started soft and gentle and rose to an early gradual crescendo. The loudness subsided only to approach again and as it did so, Brunner began to wave his hands as if he had become the conductor. He was smiling and Auguste realised this whole pantomime was symbolic. He thought Brunner really believed he was conducting everything in Bergerac, right down to the hangings they were both about to witness. He had an urge to shoot the man. It would be so simple to draw his gun and put a bullet into the SD Major's face while the music blared. He imagined he could do it during one of these loud, ungainly and unsubtle German crescendos and perhaps no one would hear, but he knew it was foolishness. Someone would hear. They would arrest him. They would execute him. No, he must goad the man into confessing Bernadette's murder. Only then, could he go through normal channels and arrest Brunner. He knew his murderous thoughts were sinful but they seemed to well up within him unbidden and foreign.

CHAPTER EIGHTEEN

1

Auguste recognised hate as a difficult emotion to control. He knew it was sinful too. Did not Christ preach forgiveness? It disturbed him he had no capacity in his heart to forgive Brunner. He detested the man and he knew it. The depth of his hatred seemed boundless in those moments before the hangings.

They descended the ornate staircase accompanied by six SS soldiers and the tall blond officer who showed him into Brunner's office. No one had introduced Auguste, but manners aside, he had no interest in the man. He was German. He was Arian and worst of all he was a Nazi. Auguste surprised himself with the thought. He wondered if he was becoming as bigoted and anti-racial as these men with whom he found himself today, but in reverse. He hated them, all they stood for and most of all he hated Germany.

One of the soldiers opened the doors for the group and they emerged into the small cobbled square outside the Mairie. Five gallows stood there, sinister and forbidding in the sloping drizzle. Auguste wished he had brought his raincoat with him but he braved the cold, wet weather all the same. They stood on the steps and surveyed the scene. Half a dozen men and women stood under umbrellas at the far side of the square. There were no smiles and no one talked. This was no wedding after all.

Auguste glanced at his watch. It was three minutes after three. The prison-van should have been here by now. He noticed he was sweating. His mouth felt arid and he could feel his heart thumping against his ribs. He had to slow his breathing down for he realised it had begun to be noticeable.

Brunner stood next to him. The German was impassive.

Presently, he said, 'Auguste, I am amazed your men do not take this more seriously. To be late at a hanging is worse than tardiness at a christening. In any case I do not want to waste too much time over this.'

'No. I would rather be at the Prefecture. Ah, here they are.'

Auguste pointed as a green van turned the corner into the square. The rear compartment had windows with bars. It stopped beneath the steps and the driver emerged. He looked up at Auguste and said, 'Inspector Ran?'

'Yes, that's me.'

'Would you sign here please,' the man said, indicating a clipboard. 'All duly present and correct. They have been gagged and the sacking masks have been applied as you instructed. They won't give any trouble.'

'Thank you. As soon as the sentences have been carried out, you can take the bodies away and you can go.'

One by one, Brunner's men pulled five men out of the van. A sacking mask, tied around the neck, obscured each man's face. Auguste noticed they stumbled and he realised some kind person had made them drunk or drugged. He felt as if his heart would burst with fear. He hoped with mounting desperation, nothing would go wrong. The unpredictability of the situation had him on the verge of running.

Each of the prisoners had a sign hanging around his neck with a name scrawled upon it. None of them tried to speak. Auguste supposed it was a combination of helplessness and alcohol but then remembered he had ordered them gagged. A soldier to each man, the prisoners staggered up the steps of the gallows. No priest came. Brunner had forbidden it.

Auguste watched as the soldiers slipped the nooses over the men's heads and pulled them tight. A large knot sat at the side of each man's neck. One of the prisoners leaned to one side as if the rope was the only thing holding him up. Auguste reflected he must have been on the verge of collapsing. He said a Hail Mary under his breath.

He looked at Brunner. The man still showed no emotion. The pallid, expressionless face remained a mystery to Auguste and he wondered what the German could be thinking.

'Pity,' Brunner said.

'Yes. It is a terrible thing to hang an innocent man.'

'No. It is a pity I cannot see their faces. The look in the eyes as they tighten the noose is something one never forgets. It is a look of fear or sometimes resignation. Perhaps we should take off the masks? Their people in the square might learn the lesson better. What do you think?'

'I... I... it would be a mistake. The victims are quiet now. If you take off the masks, it may not be as peaceable as you had wished.'

'All the same...'

'Trust me. I have seen many hangings and the less the victim knows, the better. I once saw a man fight so hard, the knot loosened and we had to go through the whole process again.'

'When were you ever involved in a hanging?'

'Didn't you know? I worked at the Regional Prison before I became a policeman. I was on the... how do you say it in German? The 'Die Todesstrafe' cells?'

'Yes, though we don't call it that. Well, we had better start. One at a time or all together? A difficult choice.'

'All together would be quickest.'

'Auguste. You French. You have no sense of occasion. Very well, they are your prisoners after all. Do you want to give the orders?'

'No,' Auguste said. 'It is your privilege.'

Feeling relieved, he looked at Brunner's face and saw him smile. Brunner stepped forward. He raised his hand. He licked his lips and smiled. Once he had the attention of all five soldiers, he drew his hand down in a chopping motion. The German's pink, soft tongue still circled his lips. Auguste continued to stare at Brunner who appeared not to notice. He was intent on the prisoners.

The trap doors clicked and Auguste could guess without seeing, what kind of scene must have unfolded in the little square, in the rain. He swallowed. He felt nausea rising from the pit of his stomach and fought hard to control it. No leniency would be offered if he threw up on Brunner; he knew it.

He looked across the square, his gaze avoiding the five swinging corpses. The watchers stared. One of them, perhaps a reporter, paper and a pencil in hand, was alternately scribbling and looking at the dead man. Auguste realised he was noting the names and it gave him a glimmer of hope his plan had not been in vain.

The face of a woman he recognised imprinted itself on his mind. She was a salesperson in a shoe shop who had sold him a pair of shoes the previous summer. He had not at the time, ever imagined her as someone who might attend a public hanging. Her face displayed a look of anger, mixed with horror. The expression characterised the emotions stirring in his own mind. He identified with her. He could feel the exact feeling in her head, even without looking at the dead men who hung there, the mark of Brunner's reprisal. How could she know he felt as she did? No one could know. It was a burden of loneliness and he felt it more and more as the days wore on, particularly now, since he had realised where his true allegiance lay.

What made this war crime even harder for Auguste, was the way Brunner had forbidden a priest to be present. Of course, Auguste did not know if any of the dead men were Catholics but to deny a man extreme unction when close to death was tantamount to wishing him to Hell. He had not been to confession in two weeks and he made up his mind to do so soon. He endured such a weight of sin upon his shoulders now, he wondered if the priest could ever offer him absolution.

Yet, love and forgiveness went hand in hand in his beliefs. He believed implicitly that God forgave. The concept of forgiveness was the one thing making him dubious of the existence of Hell. Perhaps Hell was here. Here in France, in Aquitaine where innocent men were supposed to be arrested and killed for German spite and vengeance.

He closed his eyes. If only he could wish himself away from here. He knew however, he could not run, at least not yet. He steeled himself to stay long enough to avoid suspicion, for it would have seemed strange if he had disappeared immediately after the hangings were completed.

Brunner slapped him on the back. The man was a beast.

'So. All is well then. Linz is avenged, the Maquis are discouraged and the townspeople will learn to hate them. A good day's work. Come, let us open a bottle of wine and celebrate.'

Auguste went inside with him. He climbed the steps with a mechanical tread. Following Brunner to his office he stood, numbed by what they had forced him to witness. All his wishes to leave, to run and to escape, hung by a thread, and the name of that thread was Bernadette.

2

There was a chill in Bruner's office. It was as if the warmth of humanity had escaped through the door when they entered. Auguste shivered. It was involuntary but he understood what he felt and equated it with the presence of the Devil himself. He wondered if he had come into a nightmare world, presided over by Satan, and Brunner was the embodiment of that very evil.

Brunner said, 'Come, sit my friend. We must have wine. Beautiful French wine. It is the one thing you French do well, compared to us.

Of course, it is the climate; what do you call it? Terroir; isn't it so? If Germans lived here of course the quality would no doubt be even better, but your wines are of course, entirely acceptable.'

Brunner buzzed through to the outer office. It was such a familiar sound, Auguste almost expected Édith to appear with a file. Instead, the tall fair-haired SS officer appeared.

'Ah, Schultz, there you are. Go down to the basement and fetch a bottle of the '23 Malartic Lagraviére, would you? And bring two glasses. My friend and I are celebrating the demise of the Maquis. Isn't it so Auguste?'

'If you say so Helmut,' Auguste said.

Animated, Brunner seemed to be even more disgusting than before. He was cheerful and almost expansive. Auguste still had homicidal thoughts but the impossibility of those thoughts brought a kind of apathy and hopelessness. How could he ever engineer a situation where he could trap this evil man?

And then it came to him. Wine. It loosened tongues; in vino veritas; it made men tell the truth. Yes, it could perhaps be a godsend if they drank enough.

He said, 'Helmut, only one bottle? Are you becoming selfish? I never normally get such wine. We are celebrating.'

'Of course, there is nothing else on the agenda today. Schultz. Oi. Schultz.'

Schultz returned and Brunner asked for two bottles.

Auguste said, 'Oh by the way. The night Linz was so cruelly murdered; I think we got off on the wrong foot entirely. I hope you didn't think I have a problem with anything you do. I am, as you pointed out, at your disposal Helmut. We work well together.'

Brunner looked at Auguste. A flicker of doubt appeared in his eyes. In moments however, as far as Auguste could tell—and he was sharp, the look faded and Brunner smiled.

'Of course not, my dear friend. We do work well together. I must admit though, I had doubted whether you had the Arian strength of will. I wondered if you would disobey me over the reprisals. You have proven yourself to me this afternoon.'

'It should not have been necessary. You know I am a loyal servant of the Government. There is no other role for the Vichy Police but to facilitate the smooth running of the country.'

'Of course. I just had the impression you disapproved, if you take my meaning.'

'No. Disapproved of what?'

'Well, the difficulties we have in gaining information from your stubborn countrymen. They don't like to part with their secrets, do they?'

'No I suppose not. Whatever is needed for the state security, as you say, must be the most important factor to us all.'

'You are a Catholic aren't you?'

'What?'

'A Catholic.'

'Yes. I was brought up as one, but I hardly practise any religion now. I have lost my faith long ago. I only go to church because it is expected.'

As he spoke, he could almost hear the words, 'you will deny me three times before the cock crows.'

'Well, sometimes a little religion does no harm. Ah here you are, Schultz.'

The arrival of the wine interrupted them. Auguste noticed Schultz had only opened one of them to breathe.

'Perhaps open both. It will be interesting to see if the difference in timing will affect them in different ways.'

'You think half an hour would make a difference?'

'Naturally. The wine is a living thing. It needs to breathe whether the drinkers are thirsty or not.'

'Schultz, open the other bottle.'

Brunner poured some and they drank. Presently, Auguste sniffed his glass, he set it down on the desk and swirled it around, then again savoured the aroma.

He said, 'This is beautiful and subtle. There is a little cedar and tobacco box on the nose.'

Brunner sniffed his wine with an air of desperation, 'Really?' he said.

'Yes, peppery in the mouth and a clean fruity finish. You have wonderful taste.'

'Er... thank you. I know what I like, though I don't bother with the snobbery of terms.'

'No, of course not,' Auguste said and he poured them both more wine.

'My mother likes wine.'

'Really?'

'Yes Mutti consumes great quantities of German wine. She prefers the Auslese, they are sweeter because the grapes are picked late.'

Brunner smiled as he spoke. Auguste wondered whether he had been wrong about him and the man had a heart after all.

'Really?' he said.

'Yes, she is a wonderful woman. When my father died, she was strong too. I miss her.'

'My mother died...'

'She always wanted me to be a train driver. I was out of work a long time in the early thirties. Happily I have found my calling.'

'It is nice to see a man who enjoys his work. It is rare these days.'

'Rare? You must enjoy your work too, do you not?'

'Of course. What can be better than serving one's country?'

'Yes, you are right. Here's to serving one's country,' Brunner said, raising his glass. Auguste clinked his glass against Brunner's and he realised an outsider would have thought they were friends. It filled him with revulsion after the scene he witnessed outside half-an-hour before.

Auguste made small-talk for the next hour. They discussed the forthcoming internments and the logistics of transport and personnel. Brunner poured the last of the second bottle. His hand was a little unsteady, Auguste noted.

'Such a shame to finish now, so early,' Auguste said.

He raised his eyebrows at Brunner across his almost empty glass and the implication was obvious even to an inebriate. Brunner banged on the desk and shouted for the long-suffering Schultz, who came with no apparent reluctance or irritation.

'More wine waiter,' Brunner said and he laughed.

Schultz said, 'Yes sir.'

Auguste looked at Schultz. A trace of intolerance crept into the eyes this time and he wondered if it was something to work on. The thought of having the power to cause dissent among the Germans seemed attractive.

Brunner seemed drunk. His head wagged from side to side when he spoke and a trace of spittle appeared in the corner of his mouth from time to time.

'Your mother, Auguste, what was she like?'

'My mother? She was plump, feminine and she loved me. Like my father, she struggled in their early life bringing up two children on a farmer's income, but I have no doubt she loved us, me and my sister.'

'I did not have that kind of life as a child. My parents struggled too in the years after the last war. My father had no job and he was always away seeking work. I think it killed him in the end.'

'That is very sad, Helmut. But your mother was there for you?'

'Well yes. She is not a—how do you say it—a demonstrative woman. No hugs, no kisses but times were hard for her in those days.'

'Of course they were,' Auguste said. His responses became mechanical. He felt only anger.

'Do you think a man's parents shape his adult life?'

'I suppose it is so in many ways. Why?'

'I often thought as I grew up how I wanted the normal expressions of affection from my mother. Longed for it in fact. She was not emotional, more formal than most I suppose. It caused a kind of pain at first you know? No, maybe you don't. You had a very different life, after all.'

'Yes. My parents were always there for me. Never a raised hand, seldom any beatings like my friends at school.'

'Ha! German discipline. It is why I am so different to you. Had it not been for my father's discipline at home I would never have appreciated the things I do now in life.'

'Discipline?'

'Yes. When a child misbehaves, he needs beating. My father was very good at that, I can assure you. It made me the man I am now, rigorous, disciplined and loyal to the Fatherland and the Party. He was a noble sort.'

'I don't beat my daughter and never have. I think children respond better to being shown the way, rather than punished for transgressions.'

'No. The German way is the right one. It enforces the laws of society and makes a child understand how to conform to its rules.'

Sick of the German's soliloquising, Auguste said, 'So Helmut, tell me the truth.'

'Truth?'

'Yes, can pleasure be gained from another's pain and suffering? You strike me as a man who enjoys his work'

'Yes, but I do it because it is my duty. For the Party and my Fürer. I feel I stand guard against the ungodly forces of racial mixing, protecting the purity of the Aryan race.'

'You really enjoy it though?'

'You really want to know?'

'Yes, it is beginning to interest me. I puzzle over it sometimes and I must confess to being curious.'

'Well. Where should I start? There are two types of inflicted pain. One is to gain information; it is what my men do downstairs. Linz was good at that though unlike him, it gives me no pleasure at all. The other, I hesitate to admit, comes from the admixture of pleasure and pain.'

'Pleasure?'

'Yes, it can be sexually arousing. Do you never slap your wife's rump when you make love?'

'Of course I do,' Auguste lied, 'the harder the better.'

He tried to offer a nonchalant laugh but all he could conjure up was a choked giggle. Auguste realised Brunner had to drink most of the next bottle and knew he had to slow down his own consumption. He would make it happen.

'It is something special to hear a whimper from a young woman as you give pleasure and mix it with pain, is it not?'

'Yes, but I am a married man and there is so little time for lovemaking when you have young children in the house.'

'It is not a problem I am burdened with now I am in France. Here I feel I can indulge myself a little.'

'Fascinating.'

'That is not all; the power of life and death is equally fascinating. Linz understood. He was a man who showed keenness and under-standing.'

'Yes poor Linz. They did terrible things to him.'

'I thought you were unconscious?'

'I saw the body as they lifted me out of that terrible place,' Auguste said with haste.

Brunner's eyes lit up. He became animated again. The subject now stimulated him and Auguste for his part, felt only deeper revulsion if such were possible. It was like poking a snake. One moment you experiment to see what it will do, the next, you jump away in case it bites.

Halfway into the third bottle, Auguste enjoyed the sensation of being over-refreshed but he had all his faculties, if not his reflexes.

'I often wondered what it would have been like to make love to that girl Bernadette. You know, the singer in the restaurant, the one who died.'

'Her? Why do you bring her up?'

Brunner's eyes narrowed.

'Well, she was beautiful. I bet she wouldn't have minded a bit of pain.'

'Her? No. Too young. Stupid girl, no sense of fun. She made me angry. I don't tolerate rejection by girls like that who have no morals. The way she moved when she sang, even when she walked was provocative.'

'All the same, a beautiful body.'

Auguste's mind wandered back to the mortuary and the last glimpse he had of Bernadette's body. It had been a mortal shell, emptied of love. Emptied of life as well as the organs making life. Despite his revulsion, he continued.

'Whoever killed her must have enjoyed her. I wish it had been me.'

'You wouldn't say that if you knew the truth.'

'But it could only have been a sweet fuck.'

'She fought. She cried and there was no pleasure at first.'

'You know?'

'What?'

'You know how it was?'

'No, no. I am only using my imagination.'

'Of course. All the same, my imagination tells me it must have been an exquisite pleasure with a young beautiful body like hers.'

Brunner was silent. He stared into the distance for a few moments then seemed calm and cold.

'I tell you it was no pleasure. The girl fought tooth and nail all the time. As soon as I released her wrists to tie them above her head, she bit me. You saw how she scratched me. She had no capacity for pleasure yet she taunted men with her body. I would have let her live had she just once expressed interest in me. Her death was the only way I could obtain anything other than screams and crying. To be honest, I didn't mean to kill her. I just wanted her to stop screaming.'

'But Helmut, why did you not confide in me before? What did you think I would say?'

'You seemed so keen to arrest the killer. It hardly seemed a sensible move to explain then.'

Brunner stood up. His chair toppled over with a dull thud; he waved his arms.

'If that is all France can offer in the way of women, then you,' he leaned across the desk, scowling to Auguste, 'can keep your French whores.'

Auguste said nothing. The wine dulled him enough for him to react with a slow, careful line of thought. He finished his glass.

'Helmut, it's been a really pleasant afternoon but I simply must be going back to the Prefecture. We must have this discussion another time over some more of your excellent wine.'

'What?'

Brunner swayed back and forth. A greenish colour began to evolve on his face and it gave Auguste a deep satisfaction and pleasure to imagine the wine jettisoning from the German's gullet. It was as if such a beautiful, living thing might have the power to reject Brunner and not the converse. It would be symbolic; the wonderful wine of France rejecting the German.

'But you can't go now.'

'We could perhaps manage another bottle?'

'No. I don't think so. Maybe you are right, the day is waning.'

Brunner tried to raise his right arm in a salute, but his left failed to support him and for a moment, he fell across the desk. He recovered with speed but it was clear to Auguste now was the time to go. He had learned enough. In court, he would be solid and truthful. Brunner would go to the guillotine.

He stood, saluted and said, 'Auf wiedersehen Major.'

Brunner looked up.

'Yes,' he said.

As Auguste made for the door, he glanced over his shoulder. Brunner sat with his head in his hands, his shoulders rose and fell and Auguste felt satisfaction at last. The beast was weeping.

He smiled as he descended the stairs. Germans. They can engineer, they can build armies, but they cannot tolerate good French wine.

3

The rain ceased when Auguste parked outside the Prefecture. He looked back at his car then realised one wheel was on the pavement and one of the windows was still open. He descended the stairs and corrected his inebriate parking, shut the window and thanked his lucky stars there was no one to challenge his drunken driving. It would have looked bad, though of course there were no other consequences for a policeman of his rank.

Once ensconced at his desk he stared straight ahead and despite his lack of sobriety, he began to think things through. Brunner had admitted the murder. It was a triumph but he needed to be cautious. If Judge Dubois were an accessory, then Auguste would have to be secretive too. He needed to commit the entire conversation to paper. He had no wish to involve Édith; it was a safety issue. He could not afford for her to be a target of the SD.

He wondered what Claude might do if he found out about the hangings. Most likely, he would never find out the hanged men were not the ones Brunner expected. If Claude was in league with Brunner then he would have to be excluded, but he was an unknown quantity now.

Édith knocked and entered.

'Auguste, there is a small silly matter...'

'Oh?' he said.

'Have you been drinking?'

'Well I had a few glasses of excellent Bordeaux and I don't care.'

'Auguste, do you need to go home?'

'Yes, yes, but later. I have some things to write.'

'Dictate them then and I will type them up.'

'No, it is a private matter. How can I help you?'

'Help me?'

'You said there was a matter...'

'Yes. It's that poacher, François Dufy again.'

'Dufy?'

'He has been arrested again.'

'What for now?'

'He was doing almost the same thing as last time.'

'Which was?'

She held an index finger to her mouth.

'Which was?'

'I... I...'

'You can speak freely.'

'He was in the market place again selling game. He was shouting things.'

'Well?'

'Fat trout, not as fat as Göring.'

'What?'

Auguste smiled and he saw the glimmer of a smile on his secretary's lips.

'One of your constables picked him up. Claude questioned him and cautioned him.'

'Send him up. I will have to reprimand him myself. He takes no notice of Claude.'

Auguste sat alone. He tapped an index finger on the desk. He knew the SD were listening. He knew he had to make it good but he had doubts about his ability to be subtle after a bottle and a half of beautiful Bordeaux. He had to concentrate. He poured a glass of water from the jug on his desk and glugged it down, hoping it might sober him up.

The old poacher's knock came before he was ready, but he put down the glass and looked up.

François said, 'Now what? I hoped you would let me rest in the cells.'

'Dufy, you are a fool. This is the second time you have been spouting insulting remarks about the German High Command. What have you to say for yourself?'

He raised his index finger to his lips, indicating silence.

Dufy said, 'But you arrested me because I said my rabbits were as fat as Göring. Now you do the same when I say it is not true.'

'You think you are funny? See if you think this is funny.'

Auguste smacked his closed fist on his palm. He hoped it made the right sound but it seemed limp.

'Get up Dufy, you reprobate. I don't ever want to see you here again. Wait. On second thoughts, I will escort you out. I don't trust you not to steal something on the way down.'

He got up and took Dufy by the arm. He walked him down the

stairs. Close to the door, he whispered, 'well?'

'I delivered the message. The five men are safe and their families know what to say.'

'Good. Tell Pierre I have proof of Brunner's guilt and I will need to see him in a couple of days.'

'He won't come. It is too dangerous. He came to you once and that was enough risk. You can't ask him to do it again.'

'Just tell him the old tree stump, ten o'clock at night tomorrow. I will have news.'

'He won't come.'

Auguste smiled. 'He will come.'

'Here, have you been drinking?'

'Shut up François, go now.'

Auguste was still smiling as he climbed the stairs back to his office. He wiped his hand on his jacket as if the old man might have contaminated him. It was the first time things had gone right for a long time. He felt confident he had enough on Brunner to prosecute and nothing would stop him now.

CHAPTER NINETEEN

1

Auguste slipped in the dark on his doorstep when he came home. The evening frost had begun its shiny, white encroachment onto the porch. He saved himself from the fall by grabbing at the clematis adorning the wall next to him. The plant, an ancient remnant of years gone by, ripped from its wires. It hung dejected in his hand. He giggled. His head spun and he realised his back pained but the discomfort was not as severe as he expected. Wine, it was clear, dulls pain. He repeated it to himself as he took off his shoes.

Entering the kitchen, he bumped into the doorframe and cursed. Odette, eating with the two girls looked at him and smiled.

'You've had an argument with a bottle I see, you naughty man. You know you shouldn't use such words in front of the children, you of all people.'

'Sorry. Yes, I did have a few bottles of an excellent '23, an ethereal pleasure, but a formidable one.'

'I'm glad. It is the first time I've seen you smiling when you come home for a long time.'

'Not much in my day to smile about but some hope has come. I will tell you later.'

'Papa,' Zara said as she hugged him.

Monique too, left her plate and he drew her in as well.

'My little girls. How have you been today?'

'Well...' Zara began and she launched into a blow-by-blow account of her school day, pausing only to breathe.

Auguste sat down and looked at his wife as Zara continued her tale of events.

'Papa, you aren't listening,' she said.

Auguste propped his chin on his hand but his elbow slipped from the table edge so he sat back and tried to pay attention. It was as if he had managed to remain attentive to events until now but the relaxation of homecoming had released the alcohol in his veins, trapped there through tension and fear.

He felt good. True, he had much to do, but he thought he could see an end to his problems. Brunner would pay, somehow Brunner would pay.

'Uncle Auguste,' Monique said.

Her voice seemed to jolt him. He opened his eyes wider and tried, despite his inebriation, to concentrate upon the little beings who now occupied all the attention he could muster.

'Yes, my little one?'

'I saw a black car outside today. I hid myself in the attic like you told me.'

'Good, good,' he said.

'I'm sorry I looked out. I heard it and I'm sure no one saw me. I didn't know whether to hide in the attic or not.'

'You are a good girl.'

'Papa, you told her not to look out. I told her too. Tell her off.'

'Now, now,' Odette said, 'you must stop telling tales on Monique and causing trouble. How many times do I have to tell you?'

'You never listen to me,' she said.

'Dear Zara,' Auguste said, 'I always listen to you. What a lovely day you have had.'

'No it wasn't. See. You didn't listen.'

'I love you anyway. Never forget it.'

'No you don't. You love her.'

Zara pointed at Monique.

'I love you both but in different ways because you are different people. One can love many children. Now eat your supper and don't fight.'

The girls finished their food in silence.

Odette said, 'You girls go upstairs now and don't forget to brush your teeth. I will come and tuck you both up in half an hour.'

'Not yet Maman, please. I want daddy to put us to bed.'

'I will come up too. Now run along my children. The day is nearly done and a new one will dawn just for you, before you know it.'

Monique looked at him with curiosity.

'What do you mean, Uncle Auguste?'

'Well, just... just that it... Oh never mind. Off you go.'

His momentary confusion cleared and he realised he was talking rubbish. He knew he was still drunk and since he had taken less of the wine than Brunner had, he hoped the German would not recall the whole conversation.

'Odette,' he said, once he could hear the girls' footsteps upstairs, 'I saved five men's lives today.'

'The reprisals? There were no hangings?'

'Well there was a public hanging but the men who were hanged were not our local farmers.'

'Who then?'

'You remember Duboef the prison Governor in Lyon? He has been a good friend ever since I left the prison service. He helped; he understands. I had five condemned criminals from Lyon transferred here for execution but told Brunner they were local men.'

'But Auguste, Brunner will find out as soon one of his informers spots even one of them.'

'No, that's the beauty of it. I passed a message to Pierre to get the five men away and they will be safe. No one but me and a handful of partisans will ever know.'

'But...'

'Really, it will work. It has only to work long enough for me to arrange Brunner's arrest.'

'Arrest?'

'Yes. He confessed to the murder of Bernadette Leclerc. He drank a lot of wine and told me.'

'Do you think the Judge will listen to you? He refused before. What has changed?'

'I can give evidence in court. It is worth a try.'

'Brunner will have you arrested, Auguste. You will disappear and we will never see you again. Dubois was right; you are obsessed to the point of now risking your own life.'

'He is a sadist and a murderer. He must face justice.'

Odette stood up. She leaned towards him, her mouth set. Their faces close, she said, 'I have married a fool. You risk everything. Do you hear? Me, Zara, Monique. We will all be interned and killed. You cannot do this.'

'I must.'

'What was she to you? That girl, Bernadette, you hardly knew her.'

'She was a young woman, as Zara one day will be. Brunner tortured her for sexual pleasure and then killed her. If it was our daughter, how would you feel about it?'

'She wasn't our daughter. Our daughter is the one whose life you are risking by pursuing this.'

'A man must have some principles.'

'Men. You and your principles. You are all the same. You and your wars, your killing. I's all right to die for a principle even though you take everything from your family in doing so. And always the women are left behind to suffer, to manage. What is the saying? In peace, men bury their fathers; in war, men bury their sons. Who thinks about the women in the middle? You men? I think not. You don't grow up from the age of seven when you play at soldiers in the woods.'

'Odette, what kind of world would we have if such crimes were allowed to go unpunished? We have a duty to God to protect the innocent and punish evil.'

'There is no teaching in our church which says you need to give your life needlessly for a principle.'

'But God watches us all, all the time. To allow a sin like Brunner committed to go unpunished is a sin in itself.'

'Maybe you should ask Père Bernard. He will tell you. You are becoming obsessed and ill with all this.'

'No. I am drunk, tomorrow I will be sober, but Brunner's evil will still be here. It is like a stain on my conscience. Bernadette must have justice.'

'Auguste,' Odette said, her voice softening, 'please consider the danger. I could not bear it if anything happened to you.'

She reached out a trembling hand and touched him on the shoulder, across the table. He turned his head and kissed the proffered hand and he saw tears in her eyes.

He understood it all. He knew she was right from a woman's perspective but he was like a terrier gripping a rabbit in its teeth. He could not let go for any threat, for any personal danger. Yet here Odette needed the security of an endurable everyday life. He was threatening her security. She needed him to desist, yet despite his love for her realised he could not. It was as if a maelstrom gripped him and it dragged him in, defenceless and powerless against the force of the whirling currents of his wish for justice.

2

The old stairs creaked as they ascended hand-in-hand to put the two little girls to bed. Auguste sat on Zara's bed and Odette upon Monique's. A single nightlight burned on a table in the opposite corner of the room and Auguste squinted at the flickering illumination. He stroked his daughter's forehead and hair; a gentle

repetitive motion. The caress always sent her into the familiar pre-
sleep state all parents recognise in their offspring with such expert
ease.

He glanced over his shoulder and saw Odette held Monique's
hand and the child's eyelids were drooping already. When he glanced
back at Zara, her eyes were wide open.

'Off to sleep now ma fleur. Tomorrow is another day, just for you.
Let it come. Today is finished.'

'Papa?' she said.

'Yes, my little one.'

'Who is Bernadette?'

'What?'

'I heard you and Maman talking downstairs about a girl called
Bernadette.'

'She was a girl who died and Papa wants to make sure no one else
will die as she did.'

'How did she die?'

'Well, ma fleur, sometimes people die even when they are young.'

He evaded the question. How Bernadette died was the last thing
he could tell her.

'Will I die?'

'Not until the Lord sends for you.'

'Will I go to heaven if He sends for me tonight?'

'Naturally, my child. All children do. It is the grown-ups who have
sinned whom God punishes. But nothing will happen to you tonight.'

'Have I sinned?'

'Now, enough of this, you must sleep or tomorrow you will be too
tired to do your schoolwork.'

'Yes Papa.'

'Papa loves you. Now off to sleep.'

Moments later, both girls were fast asleep and Auguste and Odette
returned to the kitchen. Auguste began to feel famished. The kitchen
still smelled of rabbit stew and he found his mouth watered as he
pictured it.

'Any stew left?'

'Yes, I'll warm it up.'

'It is better warm, is it not?'

He placed a hand on his wife's buttocks and kneaded, soft, gentle movements.

'Keep your mind on the food, you animal.'

She smiled but pulled away from him.

'It is the only thing could keep me from your rabbit stew.'

'Well rabbit stew is all you get tonight, my husband. I don't make love to drunks.'

'But I'm sober now.'

'Not sober enough, my friend. How can you think of sex at a time like this anyway? You've seen men hanged and heard a confession from an evil man. How can sex even enter your mind?'

'Perhaps it is a release or even a distraction. I don't know.'

He sat down.

'Where did you put those cigarettes?'

'Here.'

Auguste lit one. His head felt light and the room spun for a moment or two. He blew a smoke ring and stared at it as Odette busied herself with the food.

'You know, Odette, we must be ready to leave quickly if it becomes necessary.'

'Leave?'

'Yes, we will have to go to the Swiss border, but we must travel light if we do run. There are military checkpoints on most roads and we can only travel by car as far as maybe Sarlat.'

'We can't walk all the way to Switzerland.'

'We may have to.'

'What about food?'

'We take as much as we can carry then live off the land. People will help us I'm sure.'

'Not if they know who you are. Everyone hates the police.'

'They won't know me near the border. We can maybe cross the border south of Geneve. I think it may take up to a month of walking, but much depends on how far we can go in the car.'

'We can't carry a month's food. Do you think Pierre can help?'

'Maybe. It will not be for a while, but I have to go before the internments. I have sent word to all the Jewish families. If most of them escape, Brunner will suspect me. If I can arrest him then we may be safe. I don't know.'

'Auguste. As long as we are together I will not fear anything.'

'I know.'

'Enough of this now. Here, eat your food and we will go to bed early.'

'Promise?'

'No. I need to hold you, that's all.'

Auguste smiled his understanding and ate in silence. It seemed as if they had made a decision. They would have to leave. Now they had a plan he felt in less doubt and it seemed as if he had been shown the way. He decided to tackle Judge Dubois in the morning. He could hardly wait. Justice was beckoning him and it felt good.

CHAPTER TWENTY

1

A cold sun shed cloud-filtered rays through Judge Dubois' office window. Auguste sat in silence in the ornate Louis Quinze chair opposite the carved oak desk. Thrumming his fingers on the arm, he noticed he was sweating though it was cool in the office. He ran his fingers around the inside of his collar and reflected it felt too tight. Looking at his watch he realised it was nine-thirty, there was no sign of Dubois and he came to the conclusion it was no wonder legal matters took so long, if even the Judges led such relaxed lives they could turn up for work at this hour.

Auguste jumped when he heard the door behind him open. Juliette entered with a coffee cup.

'I thought you might want this.'

'Thanks,' he said.

He took the cup and held it with both hands, looking up at his sister. It was real coffee and he savoured the aroma.

'Funny life isn't it?' Auguste said.

'What?'

'Well thirty years ago, it would have been blackcurrant juice.'

'Yes. Those years have gone by like lightning.'

'Like a passing moment.'

'Yes,'

'You remember how Pierre used to fancy you?' he said and smiled.

'Don't be silly.'

'That was what I told him at the time.'

Juliette looked down; she smiled. Auguste felt surprised. It was the first conversation in which they had engaged without anger creeping in, for years.

'Such a pity,' she said.

'What? That I put him off?' Auguste said.

'No, don't be stupid. It's such a shame he is Jewish.'

'Don't you like Jews?'

'That is offensive. No, the Germans don't like Jews and it is they who rule our country. Through Pétain but all the same...'

'We should maybe expel them then.'

'The Jews?'

'No. The Germans,' Auguste said.

Their eyes met. Both of them smiled and Auguste began to wonder if there had been a softening in her stone-like heart. He had always wanted to be friends again but he had been unable to pay the price. Such is pride, he reflected and they were both proud.

'The Judge seems to think they will always be here and we had better cooperate or die.'

'He's wrong. Do you remember the hamster?' he said.

'Hamster? You lied to me.'

'Well it wasn't exactly a lie. It had reddish fur.'

'But it had a long tail. You said it was a hamster. I spent the better part of a month allowing it to crawl all over me before Maman explained what a rat looked like.'

'It was funny. It was like what is happening in Bergerac.'

'Oh?' Juliette said.

'Yes. The SD create an illusion of law and order. They pretend they wish to follow our laws, but what seems to be right is wrong and what used to be good is no longer good.'

'I know. I wish they could all be blown up.'

'What? Are you a partisan all of a sudden? You, who works in the Judge's office?'

'No. I'm just trying to warn you. Don't push the Judge too far he is...'

A high-pitched masculine voice interrupted them.

'Juliette. What is happening?'

It was Judge Dubois. Auguste rose and said, 'We were just talking about our childhood.'

'Oh. Yes, of course. What are you doing here? Juliette, why did you let him in?'

Auguste said, 'Are you afraid I will steal an ash-tray, or look through your files?'

'No. I just don't like unexpected visits. I have much to do.'

'So much you turn up here at a quarter to ten? I have been waiting forty-five minutes.'

'You did not have an appointment.'

'Do I need one when it comes to the law?'

'No.'

Dubois glared at Juliette and she turned and left. The door clicked behind her and Auguste began.

'This is a transcript of a conversation I had with Brunner. It is self-explanatory. I want to arrest him.'

Dubois removed his overcoat. In no apparent hurry, he hung it on a hanger and hung the hanger on a hook on the wall. He looked thoughtful. He placed his hat with care, balanced on the hook. Still in no haste, he turned and looked at Auguste in silence. His face was strained, lines furrowed his forehead, and there were bags beneath his eyes. He did not read the transcript.

'Did you hear me?'

Dubois frowned. He said, 'It is not my hearing which seems to be the problem, but yours. I told you to drop this case.'

'But this is fresh evidence.'

'I don't care if he said he had murdered that Churchill fellow with a frying pan. Leave Brunner alone.'

'He is a sadistic killer. He murdered a young lovely French girl for his own sexual pleasure. Why are you protecting him?'

'Protecting?'

'Yes. You ignore everything I say about the case. What more do you need? A confession, witnesses stating they saw her enter his car. The scratch on his cheek. If I can't convince a jury with that, there is something far wrong with our justice system.'

'It may be so. I still do not think you can bring this case. First, because there are no witnesses to the crime. Secondly, because this so-called confession is not admissible in evidence.'

'It is a sworn statement.'

'It is your word against his.'

'He did it.'

'You can't prove it. There is no evidence.'

'He admitted it.'

'There is no evidence I tell you.'

Auguste tapped the scrawled transcript with irate fingers.

'This is evidence.'

'If I bring this case against Brunner bad things will happen. He will pick selected members of the community and hang them. He told me so,' Dubois said.

'And so you let him remain free to do this all over again?'

'He swore he would never do it again.'

'What is he threatening you with?'

'Nothing.'

'He is.'

'No.'

'I can see you are scared. What has he threatened?'

The Judge sat down. He put his head in his hands. To Auguste's utter amazement, Dubois began to weep. His shoulders heaved and he groaned. He looked up, eyes red and wet.

'He has my son.'

'What?'

'He has my son locked away in the basement of the Mairie. The only reason he is still alive is my cooperation with Brunner. I cannot bring this case to court.'

'Another Judge?'

'The crime was in my jurisdiction. No other Judge can take it.'

'I can't just give up.'

'The girl will have to be forgotten. If you pursue this matter I will have to have you sacked.'

'What?'

'Can't you see? My hands are tied.'

'You are like Pilate. Your hands are tied? You are a man with no honour Judge. I never minded the nepotism when you appointed Claude. I tolerated your interference in police matters too. I stood by and watched as you allowed Brunner to ruin our legal system. What angers me most is your cowardice.'

'Inspector,' Dubois said, 'it is easy for you to talk. It is not your child Brunner has imprisoned. How would you behave if it was?'

'I would fight. I would not abandon everything I have spent my life building. Trading your principles because of fear.'

'There is nothing you or I can do.'

Auguste was silent.

'You had better go. Don't mention this matter to me again.'

The Judge sat back in his chair. His face displayed his emotions and although Auguste suspected he hated Dubois for his weakness, he recognised there was a grain of truth in his words. He wondered what he would have done if Zara was the one in the cells. Would he have tried to get her back? Would he have fought?

'Is there nothing we can do to get your son released?' Auguste said.

'Don't be stupid. Why would Brunner throw away his trump card? He controls me and will soon control others too. His influence is like a cancer spreading through our town,' Dubois said and he thumped his fist on his desk. 'There is nothing I can do.'

'If Brunner was removed, would they not release your son?'

'There is no way to remove him. He has contacts in high places and he will act as soon as he suspects I want to arrest him.'

'There is one thing I can do.'

'You're a fool. It is hopeless.'

Auguste stood up and walked with heavy footsteps to the door. He heard Dubois weeping again. Resigned, he walked through the outer office and down the ornate stairs. The realisation that Brunner held all the cards, struck deep. The Judge's son was another pawn to be sacrificed in this game of chance. He wondered how such a turn of events could affect him. Everything had changed. The Judge was useless to him and all those rules he once valued and lived by, seemed tattered and torn. He still wanted Brunner to pay but there seemed only one way now. An impossible way and one condemning him forever.

2

The sky formed a uniform grey canopy above, threatening rain as Auguste drove to his office. He was smoking again. The bitter-sweet taste of the aromatic Gitanes cigarette filled his mouth and its pungent smoke filled his lungs. He inhaled deeply and his head spun as he drove. He tried to distract himself from the thoughts welling up inside. He thought about his first cigarette. He had been thirteen and Pierre and he had stolen a packet from the kiosk in the central market.

Pierre said, 'You have to be careful to do it right.'

He had always seemed so knowledgeable to Auguste. He had been one of those teenagers who possessed an innate ability to convince. One who seemed to be 'in the know' and Auguste had always looked up to him.

'Like this?'

'No, you have to take it into your mouth and then you breathe in.'

Auguste tried and the coughing fit lasted minutes and when it passed, he vomited.

'You will never make a smoker. Look.'

Pierre inhaled and although his facial colour changed to a faint green he did not acknowledge it, nor did he vomit. Their relationship had always been like that. Pierre—determined and strong, Auguste—wishing he could be like his friend but never daring.

He frowned thinking about how it had all changed when the Germans came. He had been instrumental in reducing his friend to the status of sub-human. A being with no rights, disenfranchised and despised. He wondered if he had harboured some kind of jealousy and it had come to the fore when he registered his friend as a 'Jew'. Had this jealousy made the process easier? Whatever the motivation persuading him to play along with the Nazi scheme, he knew now his better self, the man within, was at last fighting back.

Brunner. His hatred for the SD Major came back too. The injustice of Brunner living and breathing filled him with anger. It was now a cold anger, an anger making him sly, devious. Auguste lived all his life for the law. It always equated in his mind with justice but he felt bitter and disillusioned now. No justice through the law would materialise in this case. Brunner had the power and he had already won.

Auguste wanted the man dead. He wished he had obeyed his impulse to shoot him in the face before the hangings. A few grammes of lead in the man's brain and he could have solved the problem, but it was not so easy. He pondered how the German had gloated when he described the rape and murder. Auguste wondered whether, had it not been for the wine, he could have shot the man as easily after the executions as he could have before.

And where was his God in all this whirlpool of events and emotions? He thought for a moment he had lost his faith, but the thought did not linger. It would have made it too easy. If he did not believe, he could, without doubting his absence of faith, kill Brunner and never lose sleep over it. Life must be so easy for an atheist. No heaven, no hell. No concept of sin or its consequences. But such was not Auguste's nature and he knew it. He had doubts, yes, but he did believe in Christ, the Passion, the Resurrection and the Church.

He knew what Odette would say about it all. She was a pragmatist, one who could always see the practicalities of life. She had steered him through his adult life in this way and kept him sane in a mad world. She would advise him to forget. She would tell him it was not now important to avenge Bernadette. The dead look after themselves.

Her question on the previous night rankled now. What was Bernadette to him, or more rightly what had she been? He had not loved her. No physical contact occurred, no promise of sweaty groping in the car. His feelings, he thought, had been innocent, yet her presence had stayed with him long after she had skipped to her mother's doorway.

Auguste wondered whether he had become a child-chaser; she had been eighteen years old. He was old enough to be her father. The more he thought about it the more he realised it was that connection he had felt. She charmed him and he had fallen for her, but as a father might love a child. He calmed at the thought. It had not been sexual; he reassured himself.

He looked up and realised he had parked his car outside the Prefecture. His driving had been automatic and mechanical, transported far away by the depths of his thinking. He continued to sit in the car. Returning to work now seemed pointless. It had no meaning for him anymore. Without truth and justice, where was the purpose in being a police officer?

He lit another Gitanes inhaling with appreciation. He needed to kill Brunner. He had to get Odette and the two girls away afterwards and it had to be quick. He would do it, but he had to make preparations. They would have to leave as soon as the killing was done.

When? Soon, he thought. He would lure Brunner away somewhere where no one would find his body and then shoot him. In the back? No, too easy. He wanted Brunner to know what was coming and why.

More smoke. But it would condemn his soul forever. It was a mortal sin. It would be unforgivable in the eyes of the Church, in the eyes of God. He also knew his countrymen were fighting a war all around him. Was this not an act of war, to perpetrate on an enemy of his country? Had not millions died through the centuries in the name of God? Did God seek vengeance on soldiers, fighting for the faith? He recalled how in the Bible, Joshua had annihilated whole cities of people, even women and children, in the name of God. Auguste wondered whether he wanted Brunner dead in the name of God or was justice so far removed from God, he was making himself into an instrument of vengeance and ultimately Satanic.

'No,' he thought. 'I know God will forgive me. It is all because I care. I care about the life Brunner took. I care about the evil this man is still free to commit. I believe it will be God's justice and it is He who commands me, guides me. Brunner must die.'

Auguste felt he needed help. He needed to talk to someone who would not condemn him, who would not judge him. In his mind, he cried aloud for help and there was nowhere to turn. He knew all the likely answers. He knew what everyone in his life might say. He felt a fool. He had little hope if he ran and even less hope if he killed Brunner.

He needed Pierre. Only his childhood friend would know what the next step should be.

CHAPTER
TWENTY ONE

1

Auguste entered Édith's office at speed. She looked up at him and he made the usual gesture for silence. He indicated for her to accompany him and they went together down the Prefecture stairs.

Outside, Auguste offered her the crook of his arm and she took it, looking at his face as they walked.

'What is happening Auguste? I have worried all day. Where have you been?'

'I tried to convince Judge Dubois to prosecute Brunner. He refused.'

'Did you expect him to agree?'

'Yes. The Major confessed to Bernadette's murder. I would have given evidence in court.'

'It would mean nothing. A man like Brunner would protect himself. He has escaped your clutches, my friend.'

'He has escaped the law. He has not escaped God's justice.'

'Oh?'

'Yes. I will have to help things along. They know how you and I have worked together for years. After I have done what I must, you may need to get out yourself.'

'And where would a sixty-year-old widow run to? The south? Lie in the sun, until they come for me one day? Or should I go to England? A place of fog and rain, for the rest of my life? No Auguste, I will not run. They have little or no reason to come for me in any case. Have they not monitored the conversations in your office? They will always think I am an innocent victim of your machinations.'

'You are certain?'

'Naturally.'

'Then may God go with you Édith. You have always been loyal and I want you to know...'

'Don't say it. It can only cheapen it by speaking it aloud. I have always admired you. You have a capacity for justice not mirrored by anyone else in the Prefecture. If we never speak frankly again, I want you to know I will pray for you.'

He smiled to her and realised she was one of the few people he trusted in all this mess of killing and plotting. It struck him hard. It was as if he had marched through his life without noticing her and here she was, supportive and loyal. He wanted to kiss her but he knew a man who kissed his secretary on the steps of their place of work would raise more than a passing glance.

'I will never forget you,' he said.

'No. I will always pray for you Auguste. I know you are a good man, but we have together, been forced into such a terrible situation. You will not return?'

'I'm not sure. My justice may take time to execute.'

'Execute is a good word to my ears.'

'I still have doubts. I don't know if I can get my family away.'

'You must,' she gripped his lapel, 'you keep them safe, you hear?'

'It is all that matters to me now.'

'Then may God be with you.'

They parted at the Prefecture steps, she ascending and he watching. Emotions rose within him. He still needed help but felt there was no one to turn to. Odette would never agree to his plan. He wondered if the simplest solution would be to ask Pierre to set a bomb under Brunner, but he felt Brunner was his problem alone. It was his duty to ensure Bernadette's murder was avenged. The Maquis might fail and they would lose more men. No. This was something he needed to face by himself, but the aftermath was the part with which he needed help.

He needed to see Pierre. The only contact he had for that, was François Dufy. He hoped Dufy delivered his message and Pierre would meet him in the forest. He decided to go home. It seemed pointless to be working. He would be away from here soon enough. Even if it looked suspicious to Brunner, he did not care.

2

It was on the drive home he began to have second thoughts. He drove past the church and he felt as if it beckoned him. He pulled up.

He wondered if what he wanted to do was wrong. He was racked with pangs of guilt over the murder he planned. To kill an enemy in cold blood and look him in the eyes as one does it, takes a special kind of man. Pierre was one of those, but Auguste had never killed anyone and he was now eaten by doubts whether he could do it when the time came.

He had known killers. He even flattered himself he knew Brunner but he had never even shot someone in the line of duty. It must be a sin. He was not the most devout and accepting Catholic, but even he knew what the church would say. Mortal sin, eternal damnation and hellfire. Christ had never killed nor had he ever condoned it, yet millions had died in the name of Christ.

He began to agonise over the rights and wrongs, the moral view of what he was about to do. He knew he had made up his mind, but wondered whether he had the strength to carry it out. From his car, he noticed the church doors were open as he drove past. Five minutes later, he turned his car and returned. He parked outside and crossed the street to the church doors. He stood there. Doubt gripped him and he was about to turn away when Père Bernard called from inside the church.

'Auguste. You have come at last. You have prepared for your confession?'

'Confession? Oh, yes, that is why I came.'

'Come then, I will get my things. My surplice is in the vestry.'

Auguste followed and when the priest opened the door, he stood waiting. The wait took him back to his teenage years when he and three other boys had been on meditation. Père Bernard had taken them to a Cistercian monastery in Perigeux. The monastery had been winter-cold and damp and he regretted not bringing enough warm clothes. He recalled how, feeling cold and tired, he sat down with the monks and ate their bread and cheese, wondering what such people would get up to in the evening. The meal finished, the Abbot unlocked a chest standing against the dining hall's wall. It contained bottle after bottle of red wine, some of it very fine. He learned a great deal about the Church, about theology and about drinking wine. The mental picture made him smile, for he had also learned the infinite capacity the monks possessed to imbibe their local wines.

Père Bernard returned. Auguste made the sign of the cross and the priest followed suit. They entered their separate confessionals and sitting down, Auguste waited, he felt a tension in his stomach and he was sweating. It was like visiting an elderly relative, much loved, but of fearful temper. He could not understand the tension within him. It was only confession. One of thousands in his life, yet there seemed to be something more serious, more significant to him this time. The hatch slid open between them.

Auguste said, 'Bless me Father for I have sinned. It is three weeks since my last confession and I beg forgiveness.'

'Tell me your sins, my son,' the priest said; his voice flat and non-committal.

'My venial sins are small and require little discussion: I have a much graver matter to confess'

'If you require counselling you must make an appointment, you know how to make your confession.'

'Yes father.'

Auguste admitted his venial sins and cited their circumstances. He explained about his dishonesties, his carnal thoughts and his outbursts at home.

'But I am in danger of losing my eternal soul, Father, and I need your guidance.'

'But you have not committed this sin?'

'No.

'Then it is a matter for counselling. Your penance is fifty Hail Marys and a gift to the church of fifty francs. God, the Father of mercies, through the death and resurrection of his Son, has reconciled the world to himself and sent the Holy Spirit among us for the forgiveness of sins; through the ministry of the Church, may God give you pardon and peace. Te absolvo in nominis Patris et Filius et Spiritus Sancti.'

'Father , I need to speak to you.'

Père Bernard said nothing. He blessed Auguste with the sign of the cross and pressed an index to his lips. Puzzled, Auguste followed him to the door of the church. The priest took his arm in a large firm hand and walked him outside.

'Here, walk into the graveyard with me.'

Still puzzled, Auguste went with him.

Père Bernard said, 'there is a listening device in one of the confessionals and I cannot find it.'

'A listening device?'

'Yes, it has been there a long time but the SD imagine I do not understand.'

'Father,' Auguste said, 'I need your help.'

'Well?'

'Is it wrong to take a man's life if he deserves it?'

'No man deserves death, you know it.'

Père Bernard patted him on the knee. It brought back memories of a similar conversation when Auguste had been a child. He had enquired about communion and its meaning. Père Bernard had made as much time for the seven-year-old as he might have for an adult.

'I have already allowed people to be killed by the Nazis by a mixture of indifference and ignorance.'

'Jews?'

'Yes.'

'The indifference is more serious than the ignorance but it would only be mortal sin if it was committed with forethought.'

'Their blood will be on my hands all the same.'

'I believe so. It is still not a mortal sin.'

'How can it be so?'

'His Holiness has said in his Christmas speech, the Church condemns, and I quote, the marking down for death of people by reason of nationality or race. He did not invite us to take arms against them.'

'The Church then, does not encourage us to stand up to the Germans for this reason?'

'What is on your mind Auguste? Here, sit.'

They sat on a stone bench in the graveyard, a weak sun trying to give some warmth from a cold sky. Auguste could hear a pigeon cooing nearby in an old apple tree over the cemetery wall. It reminded him of happier times.

'Auguste, my son?'

'Sorry. I... I...'

'Auguste, tell me what has happened.'

Auguste began with Bernadette's murder. He explained about the torture, the conversations with Brunner and Brunner's confession.

'So he killed an innocent child?'

'He admitted it.'

'And now?'

'He will not face justice unless...'

'It is a mortal sin and you know it.'

'But he is a killer. We are also at war with Germany. In war killing is not murder.'

'You imperil your immortal soul. It is not the fact of killing, it is the premeditation which makes a soldier in battle free of sin and a murderer guilty in the eyes of God.'

'And if the killing is just? In God's eyes? How can it not be?'

'Killing for vengeance is not man's role here on earth. Vengeance is God's. Men like Brunner will never enter the afterlife and all you would do by taking the law—God's and the State's, into your own hands is to join him in Hell.'

'You knew Bernadette?'

'Yes, of course. I christened her. I held her in my arms just so,' the priest said, as he formed a cradle with his arms. 'I confirmed her too. You may recall her singing in the choir. The voice of an angel.'

The priest sighed. Auguste looked in his face. He could see unmitigated sadness as if the old man mourned the girl as much as Auguste felt he did.

Presently, Auguste said, 'Père Bernard. If I do nothing, that monster will kill more girls for his depraved pleasure. I know it and I must stop it.'

'For whom do you want to do this? To protect others? For God? Or is it for yourself? I cannot force you to any course of action, only warn you of the consequences.'

'Do you not think God is more forgiving of us than the Church would have us believe?'

'The Almighty Father forgives everyone.'

'Then how can Hell exist?'

'You are truly like Thomas Didymus my son. You want my reassurance God will forgive you for killing another with forethought and for revenge. I cannot give it. Is there no way to change your mind?'

'All I know is Bernadette has a right to justice. In this war, justice has died. Evil sits in the Mairie and laughs at us. I have to eradicate it and I believe it is God's justice as well as man's.'

'It saddens me to hear your determination. I will pray for your immortal soul and beg the Lord's forgiveness. I understand why you want to do this, as any man would, but I cannot condone it.'

'And the Maquis? Are they outside the Church's grace too?'

'Many of them are Jewish and Communists. They are not of my flock. If they do their work with Christ's name on their lips they are mistaken.'

Auguste stood up. Père Bernard looked up at him and shook his head.

'Go with God. I pray He will turn you away from this course of action.'

'Goodbye Father,' Auguste said.

He reached the bars of the cemetery gates and the rusty hinges made a sound like the groans of a dying man to his ears. He did not look back. He felt lonelier now than when he had parked his car outside. The sun hid behind a shroud of dark grey clouds and he reflected it might be symbolic. He had not lost his faith in God but he wondered whether the Church had let him down and eclipsed his only hope of salvation.

In the car, he thought about his conversation with Père Bernard. It had been foolish to imagine the priest would collude with his plan. He trusted the old man to keep silent but he questioned his wisdom in confiding in anyone, holy orders or not. He thought he would not tell Odette what the priest said. She would abhor the risk in any case and she had similar principles to her priest, Auguste knew that.

CHAPTER TWENTY TWO

1

Odette cleared the table. She was efficient. In less time than Auguste would have taken to get the plates and cutlery out she had washed up and put everything away. Auguste, sitting at the kitchen table felt the surface with a flat hand. He noticed a scratched area where as a teenager he once scrawled the name of a girl. Enamoured by her he had etched her name at every opportunity and could think of nothing but her for weeks. His father had used his belt to discipline him and tonight, he realised he was no different himself. Had he caught his thirteen-year-old son carving a name on his kitchen table he had no doubt about his feelings.

He got up and retrieved his walking boots from the porch. He sat back down in the kitchen and began lacing them.

'Where are you going? It's almost ten o'clock,' Odette said.

'I told you. I need to meet Pierre. I need to know the best route to take when we leave.'

'Are we really going? Leaving our whole lives behind? I don't know how I feel about going away. I have lived here all my life. So have you. There is Zara's schooling too. She will lose everything.'

'We have to go. We have Monique to think about and now I have pursued Brunner, our lives will be in danger. We can't stay.'

'Are you sure about this? Is there no other way?'

'No. As long as we are alive and together it will be alright.'

She crossed the kitchen. She stood over him until he had laced his boots. He stood and took her into his arms. He kissed her on the cheek and she hugged him as if they were parting for a long time.

'You think Pierre will be there?'

'If the old poacher got the message to him then he will come. Did you know Dufy was a teacher once?'

'A teacher?'

'Yes, but he likes to drink and he lost his job.'

'So?'

'I mention it only because it shows what kind of small-minded place we live in. It may be good for us all to get out. Get away from the Germans anyway.'

Odette stared at the floor. She said nothing. Auguste had no need of imagination to understand what she must have felt. He knew. A grain of sorrow persisted in his mind but he valued his principles too much to abandon them. It was not at any cost, he reassured himself as he shut the backdoor. It was perhaps at the cost of leaving his home behind, but staying was becoming impossible.

2

He felt for his gun in his pocket. He gripped it as he walked. It gave a firm metallic reassurance. He was a good shot but he knew he would hesitate to shoot anyone, even a German soldier. He walked the path through the first section of forest and turned left at a tall pine tree. He knew the tree well. It was older than he was and he recalled how he had carved that girl's name there too. Foolishness of youth.

For a second he thought he heard a twig snap behind him. He stopped. He strained his ears to listen. Light descended from a half-moon high above but the trees grew close together and little light illuminated where he stood. An eerie silence enclosed him. He waited, wondering if perhaps Pierre was following him. No more sound. He wondered if he had imagined the sound. He continued his walk. He missed his dog, but he knew even if she had been here, she could not come with them to Switzerland. A dog would have been a liability.

Fifteen minutes later, he reached a moss-covered tree stump. It stood at the side of a small clearing, a dark coffin shape in the moonlight. The long shadows of the pine trees drew a spider's web pattern on the grass and he looked up at the moon. He wondered why the moonlit sky betrayed a red tinge behind the screen of black, waving boughs whispering together above him in the breeze.

Auguste stamped his feet. He looked at this watch and the luminous dial showed it was five minutes to ten. He waited. Sitting on the tree stump, he searched in his pocket for his cigarettes. He refused to admit to himself he was back in the habit of smoking, but had bought another pack on the way home in any case.

He tapped the end of a cigarette on the box to remove the loose tobacco and placed it in his mouth. He lit the Gitanes and inhaled. The smoke was thicker in this cold and he saw it rise like a plume of dense white as he sat on the tree stump. The damp of the moss seemed to penetrate and he felt his backside to see if it was wet.

A sound. It struck his ears like a drum in the silence surrounding him. Another sound; this time unmistakeable. A loud whisper. He looked over his shoulder in the direction from which the sound had come. More silence. He stood, facing the sound.

'Pierre?' Auguste said in a whisper loud enough to be heard.

'Keep still,' the voice came.

'Pierre, it's me. Where are you?'

'Here.'

Auguste spun around and heaved a loud sigh.

'Pierre, why did you sneak up like that?'

'I needed to circle you to make sure no one followed you.'

'No I wasn't followed. I did hear a single twig snap behind but it was fifteen minutes away and there was nothing more.'

'What have you made me risk my life to hear Auguste?

'Are you not relieved to see me unscathed after the bombing?'

'Of course I am. I knew you were unharmed. Come old friend, what am I doing here?'

'I have to get the girls and Odette out.'

'Where to?'

'I plan to get to the Swiss border. I have those letters of transit. I can get Odette and Zara across and I plan to take Monique overland south of Geneve. They can't police the entire border and there will be places to cross over.'

'It is possible, but how will you get there?'

'We will walk.'

'It is over five hundred kilometres. With two children, how do you propose to do that? Even twenty kilometres a day, it will take a month. You will never get past the road blocks and the German patrols near the border without help.'

'Can you get us out then?'

'Impossible now. Since we killed that German bastard a lot of people will not support us. The escape lines are stalled for the time being. Why don't you wait? In a month or two...'

'I can't wait. I have to settle a score with Brunner.'

'The SD Major?'

'Yes. He tortured and raped Bernadette Leclerc, I told you.'

'Yes you say so endlessly. I thought you were going to arrest him.'

'Judge Dubois is protecting him.'

'Dubois? That is news. I will pass it on. So he is a collaborator. But Brunner goes free?'

'No. I will kill him.'

'You? Don't be stupid.'

'Yes. I cannot leave unless I do it. Bernadette must have justice.'

'Don't bother. My people can do it and we won't even charge you a fee.'

'No. it is something I have to do. I started the investigation. He boasted about it to me and I must do it.'

'Don't be foolish, man. You would risk everyone you love to get vengeance?'

'No. It is a matter of honour and justice. He has to know why he is to die. You think I would endanger my very soul if I did not feel strongly?'

'How will you do it?'

'I haven't decided. I will do it.'

'Sounds half-baked to me. I will try to persuade my men to look out for you. When do you leave?'

'Tomorrow night or maybe the night after, it depends on whether I can get Brunner on his own.'

'What do you want me to do?'

'We will need some route maps and some idea of where the patrols are. It is not information I can get without arousing suspicion.'

'You leave tomorrow night?

'Yes, we will drive to St Andre and bypass the Sarlat road and then head towards Lyon. There are no roadblocks on that road. After Lyon, we head for the mountains until we turn north. I don't know the way after that.'

'I will send someone to guide you. We will watch to see when you go. As you drive up the Cazenac road, look out for a man with a torch. If you are lucky and you have the support of my friends, you might be able to drive all the way. We'll see what they say.'

'Pierre, Monique will be safe. I swear it.'

'You cannot swear to something out of your control. But I hear you.'

Auguste stepped forward and embraced his friend. Uncertain for a moment, Pierre kept his hands at his sides but seemed to change his mind. They embraced like brothers and when they broke, Auguste said, 'Wish me luck.'

'You don't need luck you need divine intervention.'

'Ha.'

'Good hunting my friend. I will see you again.'

'Yes.'

Pierre looked over his shoulder and strode into the darkness around the clearing. Auguste lost sight of him in seconds. Standing alone, he lit his last cigarette and walked towards the tiny path where he had emerged into the clearing. He wondered whether his communication with Pierre had been worth the risk. He might have written it down and sent it via Dufy, had it not been for the danger of any writing these days. If a written message fell into the wrong hands, all would have ended. Ended with pain and death.

3

He reached the tall pine tree. He heard the sound of a soft footfall behind. He stopped. He glanced over his shoulder. Nothing. Waiting, he placed his hand inside his coat pocket, gripping his pistol. His thumb slid the safety catch to 'off'. When it happened, it made him jump.

'Stop. Put your hands up or you're a dead man.'

He let go of his pistol. He put up his hands. Listening, the night was dead and nothing moved.

A faint lunar radiance surrounded him and all around was bible-black. He wondered whether, if he leapt to one side out of the patch of moonlight, he would be invisible to his assailant, but he hesitated. He did not know how many he faced. They could encircle him for all he knew. Silence surrounded him. The absence of sound convinced Auguste he had to get away. He wondered later whether Pierre's "divine intervention" played a part in the events that stimulated his actions.

An owl screeched close by. The sound, like a baby crying made him jump. It was a split second decision, but he made it. He risked much then. He threw himself headlong. He rolled. His body did not stop until it came to rest against a log. Lifting his head, bushes scratched him and he realised he lay hidden, by luck or by design, he had no inclination to decide. Auguste knew he had no time to reflect either.

A shot rang out in the wood. Like an icon lit by candle's light, he saw a figure illuminated for the fraction of a second by the flame from the barrel of a gun. In silence, he drew his weapon from his pocket. Arms up in front, leaning on his elbows he pointed his weapon. Silence. Black, dark silence.

Auguste felt the ground around him. A deadwood branch lay close. He gripped it with his left hand, keeping his weapon pointed in the direction of the gunman. In silence, he launched the stick. He heard it fall into a bush to his right.

Another shot rang out, but he saw it before he heard it. He fired at the ghostly figure. It was a split second reaction, a reflex and he heard a cry. It was a cry of pain.

Had he killed or disabled his attacker? Uncertain what to do next he knelt in the underbrush. All was quiet. Listening, no sound broke the palpable, solid silence around him.

Minutes passed, he realised he was shivering, not with cold but a more basic emotion. He was scared. Then he heard it. It was a whimper. A cry of pain but low in volume, short of strength. Auguste stood then and made his way towards the sound. The moon emerged from behind a cloud and scarcely visible, he saw a shadow on the ground, beside the old pine. It looked as if someone had dumped a sack of waste. He knew what it was.

He approached the body with caution. His eyes, used to the gloom, sought his assailant's hands. The man lay face down. He began to stir. Auguste groped in the dark around the injured man. His heart leapt when he found the gun. It was a Luger. German SD issue.

Reaching for the man, he turned him over.

The pale face, almost indistinguishable, seemed familiar. It puzzled Auguste.

'Who are you?' he said.

The man groaned.

'Who are you? Auguste said, but louder this time and he shook the man's shoulder.

'Where am I?' the man said.

'Claude? What in Heaven and Hell, are you doing here? You fired at me.'

'I... I remember now. My head...'

'Here let me look.'

Auguste lit a match. Claude's head was drenched in blood. The bullet, by luck not design, had creased his skull, leaving a long gash at the side above his ear.

'Can you sit up?'

He propped Claude against the tree. He wondered what the boy knew.

'What are you doing here?'

He had to lean close to hear.

'I... I followed you. Watching your house for days. I saw you with the partisan.'

'Why follow me?'

'Orders.'

'I give you your orders. Who ordered you?'

Silence.

Auguste shook his injured colleague.

'Who ordered you?

'Brunner.'

'Brunner? But why?'

'He knows you are linked to the Maquis.'

'He's wrong.'

'I saw you.'

'It was an old friend, nothing more.'

'You can tell it to Brunner soon enough. He's coming for you.'

'What?'

'He's... coming...'

Auguste tapped Claude's face with impatience.

'When? When is he coming?'

Claude said nothing.

'We had better get you out of here,' Auguste said.

Claude made no response. He realised he could neither leave Claude where he was, for fear of his freezing to death, nor could he easily take him to his home. He opted for the latter, determined to keep him prisoner until the family and he were safe and away.

He lifted Claude's left arm onto his shoulder and stood up. Claude stumbled to his feet. His right arm hung limp at his side.

'Can you hear me?'

Claude said, 'I know, I know, I know.'

He stopped then, seemed to swallow and began again, 'I... I... know.'

'Make sense man,' Auguste said, supporting him and half dragging him along the path. Claude became heavier.

'Come on. You have to help me.'

'I... I...'

'Damn it man. Talk sense.'

Auguste stopped after ten minutes. It was as if he was carrying his lieutenant. He eased his burden to the ground by the thick trunk of an oak tree and propped him, head hanging, against it.

'Claude.'

The man seemed unresponsive.

'Claude.'

This time he slapped Claude's face.

'Wake up.'

Claude, despite the stimulation, remained with his head lolling to the right. He made an odd movement with his left arm and leg. They went out straight, the hand twisted outwards at his side. Auguste lit a match and held it to the young man's face. His eyes remained closed. He opened the lids and the pupils were widely dilated, like cat's eyes on a dark night.

In desperation, he shook him. Nothing. He shook him again, calling his name and Claude lay still. The moon came out again, its baleful light illuminating the scene to Auguste.

He felt Claude's pulse. Nothing. He felt again at the man's throat.

No neck pulse. It dawned upon Auguste this was a corpse. He had killed him.

He stepped away. He stared as the fact of it stabbed his mind. He had killed Claude. Auguste knelt again. Desperate, he tried to find some sign of life, but there was none, not even detectable breathing. No pulse in the neck revealed even a faint spark of life. He had been right first time. What to do now?

He had killed his subordinate; it was a fact. He stumbled backwards and tripped, ending sitting on a pile of leaves. He stared at the moonlit form before him. Emotion stirred. He felt a tightness in his throat. Here was a man. A man he had known. Claude had done nothing wrong as far as Auguste could see. Yes, he was a little ambitious but all young men are like that. He would no more have wished him dead than he would have informed on him to Brunner.

Yet, Claude had reported to Brunner. He had betrayed Auguste and he had followed him tonight and tried to arrest him. Monique said she saw a black car. Perhaps it was Claude in an SD vehicle. Perhaps the SD picked him up on the day when Auguste had left him to get statements in Bernadette's street. No wonder he got back so fast. Brunner himself might have picked him up and ordered him to keep the witnesses quiet.

He felt as if he was beginning to understand the depths of what had happened. His folly and the machinations of the SD Major. Pieces in a jigsaw puzzle. If Claude worked for the SD behind Auguste's back then Édith was right. Auguste should never have trusted him. He felt foolish then. It was because he wanted to trust someone, anyone and he had fooled himself into doing it. As a police officer who had seen the worst of humanity, he should have known better.

He felt stupid then.

What had Claude said? Was Brunner coming for him? Was he going to arrest him? When would he come? Was it true or just a dying man's spite? If Claude had tried to unnerve him he would have been delighted at the effect it of it.

Auguste began to panic. Would he find the SD vehicles parked outside the house when he returned? Was Brunner really coming for him?

He knew he had to hide the body. He checked a third time for signs of life but of course, there were none. He puzzled over how Claude could have woken and then died. Perhaps the Judges' brother could have told him but it did not matter now.

He dragged Claude's body to a hollow fallen tree-trunk. Memory thrust a picture in his mind of Pierre crawling out of it, shouting, 'I win, I win.'

It was like living a nightmare. Good things mixed with horror. The memory made him shudder. His nerves were on edge and he knew it. He shoved Claude's body into the hollow trunk. It was an impossible task, because the feet stuck out and he had to gather fallen branches and armfuls of leaves to hide them. Anyone walking the path in daylight might have spotted the corpse otherwise.

Within ten minutes, he had buried the evidence. Gone but not forgotten, he said to himself and he laughed a small laugh then realised he was becoming hysterical. He shut himself up with difficulty. The nightmare of Claude's death seemed to follow him somehow and he tried to focus on what to do next. It became a struggle with his sanity. He felt alternately like laughing and crying all the way to his back door.

Standing at the door, he took a deep breath and opened it. He stopped in his tracks. Uncomprehending, he said, 'What for the love of Christ, are you doing here?'

CHAPTER TWENTY THREE

1

It was Juliette; she sat, nursing a cup of some hot beverage in her hands. She stared at her brother. Auguste could see a look of horror on her face.

'Juliette? Why have you come?'

'I...'

Juliette's mouth worked as she regarded her brother.

Odette said, 'Auguste. Are you hurt? Your shoulder.'

He thought she looked frightened. She stepped towards him, the speed of her steps betraying her urgency, as he looked where the two women stared.

His shoulder was a mess of red and dark crimson. He pictured at once the bleeding wound on Claude's head and he shuddered.

'No. I'm alright. It isn't my blood.'

'Whose is it? Are you sure?'

'Of course I'm sure. I would know if I'm hurt or not, wouldn't I?'

'Yes, I suppose so,' Odette said, 'but whose blood is it?'

'Juliette, what are you doing here?'

'I came to warn you.'

'Warn me?'

'You must get away. Brunner is going to arrest you.'

'I heard.'

'You knew?' Odette said.

'Well, I heard.'

'How would Pierre get such information? He is hiding in the woods. He can't...'

'Never mind who told me,' Auguste said, sitting down at the table, 'let's just say a little sparrow whispered in my ear. The same little bird whose blood sits on my coat.'

'Whose blood?'

'Someone was hurt, I'll tell you later, nothing to worry about.'

Juliette said, 'Auguste, this is no joke. I heard Judge Dubois and Brunner talking in the Judge's office.'

'The Judge called him?'

'Yes. Brunner wants you out of the way. He called you troublesome. He said as he left, he would deal with you tomorrow.'

'When was this?'

'Before I went home.'

'Well, you'll get your hands on mother's house then won't you?'

Odette said, 'Auguste. What are you saying?'

'Oh, nothing. I've had a bad evening. Sorry, Juliette.'

His sister stared at him. An uneasy silence seemed to fill the kitchen.

Odette broke it.

'If Brunner wants to arrest you, won't he have to have some kind of evidence? He has none does he?'

Auguste said, 'A man like Brunner requires no evidence. He can arrest and question anyone he wants. Look at poor Arnaud. Brunner said he died of a heart attack. Well I can imagine what brought it on. Filthy sadist. Well he won't get us.'

'He could be on his way,' Juliette said.

'No, these things happen in the small hours. It is a technique. People are at their least aware between four and five in the morning.

He will come then.'

Odette said, 'What are we to do?'

'Hush now my love,' Auguste said, 'I must think for a moment.'

Minutes passed. The two women stared at Auguste and he, for his part, stared at the table. He reached out a flat hand and felt the scratched and pitted surface. It reminded him of so much. He recalled his mother and wondered what she would have said. She had always been pragmatic like Odette and Auguste often wondered whether men marry women who are like their mothers or whether they seek similarities in their partners to justify their marriage. Somehow, his mind refused to cooperate. It was blank apart from memories of his childhood, his home and his parents.

'Auguste,' Juliette said, 'you have to leave and quickly. That filthy German will come soon. You have to hide.'

'Yes, I know, but I told Pierre it would be tomorrow. If it is tonight, I will miss the Maquis guide Pierre was arranging.'

'Pierre? He was arranging something?' Juliette said.

'The less you know, the less they can get out of you, my sister.'

'Yes, I'm sorry. I should go.'

Auguste stood and scrabbled in the drawer by the range where Odette had hidden his cigarettes. He noticed with satisfaction there was another packet of Gitanes. He took them out and pocketed them. Presently, his hand emerged holding a set of keys.

'Here,' he said to Juliette. 'Take these. They are the spare keys to the house. When we are gone, you can live here. Protect it; you know.'

'No, I cannot, mother willed it to you.'

Auguste slammed his fist on the table, overwrought, he cried, 'Damn it woman, those things don't matter anymore. We might be back, but I have a feeling we won't. At least if you live here, it is still in the family.'

'Auguste...' she said. Her hand reached out for the keys and she gripped them, not in triumph but shedding tears as if they were some kind of holy relic to which she had prayed over long years.

Odette said, 'Juliette, you have done a great thing by coming tonight, but you had better go, before the Germans come. I have much to do if we are to leave tonight.'

'Yes. I understand. Auguste...'

They stood and Auguste looked at his sister. He felt for an inexplicable reason it would be the last time he would see her. He crossed to her and took her in his arms. She could not respond at first but in a moment, she hugged him back.

'Juliette, all this time.'

She said, 'I know. It has all been foolish pride.'

'My sister, if only we could have those years back, but we can't. We leave tonight, for a better life somewhere where the Germans and their Nazi doctrines won't harm anyone. Pray for me. I will pray for you.'

Juliette had no answer but tears. She pushed him away and made for the door.

Odette said, 'Goodbye Juliette.'

She did not turn or speak but walked with rapid determined steps, her high heels clacking on the wooden boards.

Auguste and Odette heard the door close and they looked at each other. It was time to talk, to plan and perhaps to cry.

2

It took an hour before they finished loading the old Citroën. Auguste packed four canvas back-packs and enough food to start a journey but he knew it would not be enough.

They roused the sleeping girls and Odette explained what was happening as well as she could. Both children stood, half awake, rocking on their feet awaiting instructions.

Auguste said, 'Now girls, we are going on a journey. You must each take your favourite toy, one each and we will set off very soon.'

'But I was sleeping. Are the Germans coming?' Monique said.

'Soon.' Odette said.

Auguste said, 'There is something I must do first.'

'But what about us Papa?' Zara said.

'I will take you to the edge of the woods and you will hide. I will be back very quickly.'

Odette said, 'Auguste. Can we not just go?'

'No. We discussed it fully, you know that.'

'But what if...What if you don't come back?'

He smiled a strange smile.

'If I don't come back then you will have a long walk. You have the papers and the money?'

'Yes, but I wish you wouldn't go.'

'I can do nothing else. If I leave him behind me, he will come after us. Besides, you know what I feel.'

'You and your stupid ideas. What was she to you anyway? Did you... did you?'

'Of course not. She was a young and talented French girl. She deserved to have a life. A good life. He took it away. He has to pay.'

'Who has to pay?' Zara said.

'Never you mind. It is too complicated to tell you now. Now, you all have to get into the car. Let's go.'

It was cold and icy outside. It crossed Auguste's mind to leave and never come back, leaving Brunner's men to make their fruitless raid. He and Odette could be many miles away by the time the SD gave chase.

Something stopped him however and he knew what it was too. It was a deep and vital anger. It was a towering rage for his country, fed by the German presence, but there was guilt too. Guilt because he had been so slow to react. He had allowed his life to become complicit, treacherous. He collaborated with the Nazis and it betrayed all he valued. How could it take him so long to realise the width of the chasm between good and evil, displayed before his own eyes. The thought nonplussed him.

He wondered as he drove, whether God was guiding him but he put away the thought. He was killing God at the same time as he would kill Bruner. His denial of the mortal sin of murder was the same as if he denied Christ, denied the whole Church and its holy laws. He felt as if some unrecognised hand guided him. If it was the Devil, then so be it. If it was Satan then he felt Satan was right. And what did it make him? He knew he loved Christ. He loved his Church but he felt forced now to go against it all for the sake of honour and justice. He felt everyone around him had forgotten those concepts and now he alone stood between humanity and the abyss.

Five miles out of Bergerac, on the Sarlat road, he dropped off his family. To his right was a canal running parallel to the river and he ensured Odette and the girls hid well out of sight, on its bank under some bushes.

Odette hugged him. He had to tear himself from her arms and he dared not look back, he was leaving his heart behind. Zara whimpered. He knew what he had to do. Nothing would stop him.

CHAPTER TWENTY FOUR

1

The dark streets of the town, illuminated by his headlights, seemed almost to warn him. They spoke to him. He was leaving; leaving Bergerac, leaving God. Giving up his soul in exchange for his own sense of honour. Why would not God, the Church, Père Bernard understand? He had a responsibility to the people of his town and community. It was what he had taken on when he became Police. The duty had always been a serious and solemn one for him and he never deserted it even if time had now shown how his morals had become tainted.

For Auguste, the Jewish murders were a matter of shame. Could it have been a simple blindness? Or perhaps a voluntary shunning of the truth? All those dead people. Families. Children. They stretched out before his mind's eye like some killing field, limbs grey and bloodless reaching out to him. And what suffering would he be prepared to face on their behalf? Was he trading his immortal soul for them? No, it was for all of those Frenchmen and women lying in their beds, wondering who the SD would kill next or even where their next meal would come from. Brunner's death was a key to it. A key to freedom.

The only Jew he knew well was Pierre. His old friend was like a brother, as far as they could ever become kin, with their separate blood-ties and separate religions. But he cared for Pierre as he cared for no other man alive. Monique too. He loved the little girl and in one sense for Auguste, everything revolved around this one child. He could no more abandon her for the Brunners of this world to butcher, than he could desert Zara—his own flesh and blood.

A cat skittered across the road in front of him and he swerved. The skid almost caused him to hit a streetlight. The car stalled. He turned over the engine and set off again.

He felt a wave of remorse now. Had he taken on too much? Could he really kill Brunner? Perhaps the man protected himself. He had not thought of it before. Auguste had imagined he would go into Brunner's house, shoot him and leave. What if there were guards— heavy security? No. He had been to Brunner's house before. The barred gates were always locked but he knew Brunner would not want his men to be too near him. He was smug. Auguste recalled the hangings and the satanic eagerness of the man. Brunner loved seeing those men hanged. That alone was a reason to hate him. Auguste reasoned however, killing the Major because he hated him, was the wrong motivation. It had to be cold. It had to be the administration of God's justice. Not revenge, but execution and he wanted Brunner to know why he would kill him. He wanted to see remorse in the man's eyes. No. Remorse might turn his hand. Remorse might weaken his resolve. He wanted Brunner to repent. Like a sinner before God's avenging hand, before the inevitability that was death. And Auguste felt he would be God's vessel of justice. Not only for God but also in some way, for France and the evil these Arian, Nazi demons had visited on his country.

Presently, he saw the street where the SD Major lived. Brunner had commandeered a small house on three storeys facing a cobbled street. It was near the main church of Notre Dame. A single streetlight shed a bright circle of light outside the doorway. The house itself was set back from the street by a six-foot cobbled frontage, and a high barred, wrought-iron gate separated the doorstep from the street.

He saw no cars parked. He knew Brunner used a driver and he had never seen him drive. Perhaps Brunner was afraid of bombs. A hundred yards from the house, Auguste parked. A slogan was painted on the brick wall across the street. It read 'Traison, Famine, Prison'. He smiled. It was a common act of resistance to change the Vichy government's propaganda words 'Travaile Famile Patrie' into this popular slogan. The shade there hid his car, like a shroud. It would not be easy to make out or identify later. He checked his pistol before he got out. He had taken the Luger, though he had never fired one before. He wished then he had practised a few shots but he knew there were only five rounds left in the clip. He knew the writing on the butt, 'Deutsche Waffenund Munitionsfabriken' abbreviated to only a lower case 'm' and it struck him there was poetic justice in killing Brunner with a weapon made in the heartlands of Germany— 'Das Vaterland' indeed.

He pulled up the collar of his coat as he walked towards Brunner's house, a meagre protection against the cold breeze. He checked his watch. It was close to midnight.

He tried the green-painted wrought iron gate, but it was locked. A bell-pull hung suspended beside it and he gripped it with shaking fingers. He heard the ringing as a faint, far-off sound somewhere inside the house. He waited, his heart beating a tattoo against his ribs and his mouth arid as desert.

No reply. He rang again, harder and longer. Auguste pictured Brunner awakening, confused in the dark of his bedroom, reaching for his alarm clock.

A light came on in one of the upstairs rooms. The window opened.

'Who is this?'

'It's me Auguste, Helmut.'

'Auguste? What do you want at this time of night?'

'I need to speak to you Helmut. Can I come in?'

'No. Can't it wait until the morning? My office.'

'No. It's urgent.'

'What is it about?'

'It's Claude. I have to speak to you. Do you want the whole street to know a matter of importance to the SD?'

'We will speak in the morning, one way or another,' Brunner said.

The strange tone in his voice revealed exactly what he meant, to Auguste's mind. He would torture him in the morning. Electric shock. Red-hot irons. Beatings.

'It is a life or death matter. I have to speak to you now or it may be too late.'

'You had better go home. I have nothing to say now.'

Brunner began to lower the sash.

'Helmut, wait.'

'What is it now?'

'Claude has evidence about the dead girl. He has spoken to Barbie. There is more.'

'Is that all?'

Auguste lowered his voice a little to give the impression of complicity.

'I need to tell you more. You can't trust Barbie. I cannot tell you out here.'

Brunner considered in silence for a moment.

'Oh, very well then. Wait there.'

Auguste stood where he was. He was banking on Brunner's insecurities. The thought that Barbie in Lyon, might comply with a subordinate's arrest was an attractive one. Auguste was a patient man but the wait had him rattled. Sweat dripped down his back; his heart still thumped and his back began to ache from the muscle tension. He pictured Brunner making a telephone call, he imagined him checking his gun. Auguste gripped the Luger in his pocket. His thumb slipped the safety. He was ready.

2

Auguste did not measure the time it took, but he felt he must have waited minutes. He almost made up his mind to run; to discard his weapon and flee. It was a split second's decision but as if in a vision, he pictured Bernadette's body on the porcelain mortuary slab. He knew he was compelled to stay. He also knew deep inside what was right. At last he was resigned to the task he had taken upon himself.

The front door opened and there was Brunner, in dressing gown and slippers. It seemed absurd to see this man dressed like any other domesticated person. He wondered if all such scenes had a ridiculous side to them. It seemed surreal to Auguste, who had only seen him in uniform or dark suits.

Brunner unlocked the outer gate and stepped back. He kept one hand in the pocket of his gown and indicated to Auguste that he should go first.

'I will follow when I have locked the gate.'

'I will wait, Helmut, it is no trouble,' Auguste said.

He did not intend to let Brunner escape. He wanted to keep his eyes fixed on the man.

The gate locked, Auguste said, 'After you my friend.'

'No, after you.'

'Please, you know the way.'

Brunner shrugged. He led the way up a flight of stairs and then to the right into a living area. Had Auguste been capable of taking it in, he would have been horrified at the contents of the room. It held works of art such as any museum would have been proud. A thick Persian rug adorned the floor space, a Louis Quinze low table stood in front of an antique sofa. An antique silver-inlaid walnut chiffonier stood against the wall and pictures by Degas and Renoir hung on the walls, looking down from their gallery-lit positions..

None of this was apparent to Auguste, whose heart felt as if it would leap from his throat at any minute. Brunner turned.

'Can I offer you a glass of wine?'

'No. No thank you.'

'Now then what's all this about your lieutenant? He's spoken to Barbie about my little indiscretion?'

'He was working for you, wasn't he?'

'He is ambitious. He does a little service for me now and again. I reward him. Is it a crime? I don't think so.'

Auguste, unable to contain himself and make more small talk, drew his weapon. The Luger was heavy but he held it with a firm but sweaty grip. Beads of perspiration formed on his forehead.

Unperturbed, Brunner said, 'What's this? A French policeman with a German gun? Are you going to arrest me?'

'No. I'm going to kill you.'

'If I might say a word about that?'

'Talk is useless. You tortured, killed, raped a young French girl. It is impossible for me to indict you, but you confessed to me. For me, it is enough. You will pay the price; before God you will pay the price of His justice.'

'She was nothing in the scheme of things. She gave a little pleasure and now she is dead. It is a nothing.'

'You're a murderer.'

'Yes. Are you not also a murderer? What about all those arrests?'

Murderer? Auguste pictured Claude's body, his frantic attempts to verify the man was dead.

'I've never killed for pleasure.'

'Please, there is much to consider here, besides your small-town morals. Let us sit down and take some time to talk about this.'

'Time? You want to spin this out, don't you? What did you do? You telephoned, didn't you? They're coming aren't they?'

'Nonsense! Whom would I telephone? Sit; let us discuss this like civilised men.'

'When are they coming? How long?'

'Please Auguste, there is no one coming. Tell me what troubles you.'

'No. I'm finished talking. You die even if you beg.'

'Beg? I will not beg. I am a German officer. I have more pride than that. But I need to live. If you go now, I will give you time to get away. I will not look for you until morning.'

'No.'

Brunner changed then. His voice took on a hard edge, his eyes narrowed and his jaw set.

'I'm not scared of you, you stupid little French policeman. My men are going to arrest you and your family in only a few hours. It will go ill with you if you shoot me. I am your only hope of life. I can be lenient, you know. My successor will not be, I assure you. They will be here soon.'

'I cannot. I am here to see you get justice.'

'Should you not make sure the safety catch is up? It would not be of much use as it is.'

Auguste did not take his eyes off the German.

'You can't fool me. I have handled weapons since I was a child.'

'Then you should know better. The Luger has a safety catch that is on when it is pushed down and off when it is in the up position. Shoot, if you don't believe me. It won't function.'

This time Auguste's anxiety got the better of him and he looked down. It was long enough. With a speed taking Auguste by total surprise, Brunner stepped forward and struck his clenched fist into Auguste's face. He made a grab at the Luger. The gun went flying, to rest against the wall beneath a Degas depicting a ballet dancer who peered down unsurprised at the weapon.

Dizzy, Auguste remained standing. Time seemed to pass faster than he comprehended. His next aware moment came seeing Brunner on one knee scrabbling for the gun. Auguste stepped forward onto his left foot and kicked with all the strength his dazed mind could muster. He struck Brunner on the side of the head.

It was Brunner's turn to drop the pistol. He fell back and Auguste dived for the gun. Brunner was quicker. He had the gun now in his right hand and turning fast onto his back, he tried to level it at his prospective assassin.

Auguste grabbed Brunner's wrist. He squeezed hard, using his left hand. Brunner could not bring the weapon to bear on his foe. They lay there, Auguste on top, Brunner with the gun in his hand. Each of them strained against the other with all the strength he could muster.

The pistol began to descend. Brunner was stronger. He was using his right hand. Auguste grasped it hard. The pistol still descended. It was slow, but inexorable. The barrel almost reached Auguste's face.

For one second, he had a fleeting glimpse in his mind of Odette's face, Zara and Monique standing behind. It was as if his whole life floated, suspended before him in one moment in time. One tiny second of weakness and all would be lost. Not only his life, but the lives of the ones he loved most in the world.

His whole brain screamed 'No!'

In this one vital moment, he felt the release of a cryptic, unfathomable strength. It was as if some superhuman force took his arm. He jerked his hand with all his weight. It was with a strength born of desperation. It was enough. Brunner's wrist bent. The arm gave way. The pistol lay between them as they struggled for control.

To Auguste the report felt as if a horse had kicked him in the solar plexus. It threw him bodily off the German. In panic, he glanced at his chest. A powder burn and blood, thick red blood, stained his coat.

Yet he could move. He could stand. He had the use of his limbs. Glancing at Brunner he realised he himself was unscathed. Brunner lay sprawled, eyes wide, the gun still in his hand. Blood welled up from the hole in his chest and from behind; it pooled and layered around him. Auguste watched as it seeped between the floorboards into the dark places below. He breathed hard. He checked himself again and floods of relief washed over him. He sat down on a chair and dizziness threatened to drop him to the floor.

It was over. He had done it. He forced himself to his feet. He checked Brunner's dressing gown pocket but there was no weapon, only a neat folded handkerchief with the embroidered initials HB. He used it to try to wipe the blood from his overcoat but in seconds realised it was hopeless. It was like wearing a red badge proclaiming he had shot Major Brunner of the Bergerac SD.

Panic took him then. What if some neighbour heard the shot? The Germans were coming. There was no time. He realised he needed to leave as fast as he could. He could not walk down the street in his blood stained coat. Without a coat, he would look even more suspicious. He ran into an adjacent room. He found a wardrobe. He pulled open the door, finding a leather coat with a wool lining. It was not as warm as the one he wore but it would have to do. He donned the coat and bundled his own beneath his arm.

He stopped then. Should he leave Claude's weapon or take it? He decided to leave it and at least no one could link it to him. A wine rack stood at the bottom of the stairs. He could not resist it. He reached for a bottle and in the lamplight shining through the open door, he read the label.

'Chateaux Malartic Lagravière; Grand Cru Classé de Graves; Pessac Leognan 1923.'

He shrugged and took the wine too. He walked with a brisk but unhurried step to his car. Thrusting the soiled, bundled coat in front and setting the bottle between his legs, he started the engine and drove. In the rear view mirror, he saw trucks arriving. Turning the corner at the end of the street, he saw green uniforms on soldiers emerging from the trucks. He knew then they would soon pursue him if they gained access to Brunner's house. Would Schultz prove as evil as Brunner? Would he be as intelligent?

He felt safe. He would be out of Bergerac in minutes, before they even found the Major's body. It would not be long before a general order of arrest circulated.

It struck him how in the end, Brunner's death was not the execution he had planned. The gun went off by accident. Perhaps his soul might be safe. He knew however, deep inside, his thinking was flawed, but he clung to his thought as a man may cling to a denial of marital infidelity or a dying man to a crucifix.

CHAPTER
TWENTY FIVE

1

Auguste drove with care. He kept his speed down because he wanted to be certain to arrive without skids and without mishaps. He felt as if a tremendous burden had been lifted from him. His goals now had a clarity he had not experienced since the letter from Tulard arrived from Lyon. All he wanted was to find Odette and the girls. He wanted them safe from the Germans, from the Brunners of this world. He knew also he had only cut off one of the hydra's heads. More would come, more Brunners, more evil people spreading their message of cruelty and in-tolerance. He had now freed himself of it all. A new life and a new beginning awaited. Switzerland beckoned. They must need police officers there. He could become another man. He could become less confused about good and evil. In a neutral country, surely the margins were not as blurred as they had become here, in his home, his Bergerac.

He drove the road out of town until he came to the canal. He pulled his car up on the grass verge getting out with care. His head buzzed from the blow Brunner had dealt him and his stiff back ached again. Wondering if his fight with the German had caused his back pain, he walked up the bank to where he had left his family.

'Odette,' he called.

Silence greeted him.

He walked to the bushes where he had left them. No sign of them. Walking along the bank, he called Odette's name repeatedly. A deep loneliness filled his heart. Anxiety now replaced the release he experienced over Brunner's death. He had done his part, where were they? Had a police or military patrol picked them up?

Walking further, he decided to turn back and wait. At the bushes, he stood, feeling cold. He shifted his weight from foot to foot, he kept his hands in his pockets, then lifted them out. He paced and he turned back again. The cigarette packet in his trouser pocket summoned him. He took one and tried to light it but the breeze extinguished the match as soon as he struck it. Only five matches remained in the box. Placing the cigarette in his mouth, he opened his coat and obtained enough of a windbreak to light up.

The smoke burned his throat but the nicotine was welcome. His head whirled for a breath or two in the familiar carousel-ride reminding him of his youth.

'Auguste?'

He turned. It was Odette.

'Where have you been? I've been waiting for ages.'

The two girls, unanimous now, ran to him and he knelt before them, arms wide to receive their hugs. It made his heart soar when they threw their arms about him.

'A military patrol came so I took the children across the road to the wood.'

'We must hurry.'

'What happened?'

'I'll tell you in the car,' Auguste said.

They crossed the grassy slope and got into the car. Auguste noticed an early frost had made the grass yield a crunchy feel underfoot and he realised time was passing.

'Well?' Odette said as he started the engine.

'We have nowhere to go. We have to wait until tomorrow evening before Pierre's man will meet us on the Cazenac road.'

'What happened?'

'Brunner?'

'Yes Auguste, I am not enquiring about Pétain, am I?'

'Sorry. Perhaps we should talk when the girls are asleep.'

She looked at him, a quizzical look adorning her round face. He glanced at her and he smiled.

'Enough to say, it is a threat which will no longer bother us.'

'You took a big risk. If anything had happened to you, what would we have done? I would have been lost and alone.'

'Alone? With these little monkeys in tow?'

'Yes, alone.'

'I know.'

'Where are we going?'

'I'm not sure. We have to hide and hide the car too. Do you think we can find a barn big enough for the car? Maybe a farmer would let us hide.'

'Maybe the farmer will turn us in to the soldiers. You are not the most popular of men in your uniform.'

'No. I have clean clothes in the back.'

They drove on in silence until Odette said 'They sleep. Now tell me what happened. You killed him?'

'Yes... No.'

'What?'

More silence.

Auguste said, 'We tussled over the gun. He hit me and as we fought, the gun went off. It blew a hole in his chest.'

'Papa who are you talking about?'

Odette turned and said, 'Hush now ma petite. Try to sleep while we travel.'

They waited longer and drove through St Cypriene. Auguste turned right at the end of the big pond. The open Sarlat road now lay before him and he found his breathing settled down and he no longer sweated.

'Auguste, tell me properly.'

Auguste told her the full story. She nodded and sucked her teeth.

'It was close then?'

'Yes.'

'But you are sure he is dead?'

Odette glanced over her shoulder to ensure the girls slept.

'He is dead. Justice has been served and I did not kill him. It was an accident.'

'It makes no difference Auguste. You went there to kill him and you did. I hope there is a just God in heaven. I fear for your soul, my husband.'

'This is war. There are no peaceful options for men like me. I am glad he is dead. I am glad he will not do to any others what he did to Bernadette.'

'Did she really mean so much to you? You hardly knew her.'

'Odette, if you had seen her tortured body in the mortuary, you would understand. She had a voice like an angel and she was beautiful. Then she was dead on a porcelain slab. You think I can breathe the same air as the man who did this?'

He reached down to the floor. His hand emerged holding the bottle of wine.

'I took this,' he said.

'You stole?'

'No, the owner was dead. Would you have left this for the Germans?'

'Where are we going?'

'Do you remember when Pierre's men killed Linz? They did it in a barn near Le Castanet. I think I can find it. We can hide the car there and sleep. Tomorrow evening we drive down to Beynac and then take the road where we meet Pierre's man.'

'They will be searching for us. Is it safe to hide in one place for so long?'

'We have no alternative; I don't know where we can cross the border. The Maquis know every crossing place.'

'The Maquis hate you and see you as a collaborationist. They may not help. Oh, Auguste I wish none of this had happened. We have lost everything.'

'No. We have gained our honour as French people everywhere one day will do. We are together and it is all that matters.'

She reached for his hand where it rested on the gearstick. The contact reassured them both as Auguste turned off the main road. Five miles on after ascending a steep incline, Auguste got out, outside the barn where Linz had met his end. A farmhouse perched on the top of the hill a quarter of a mile further up the road.

He changed his clothes and trudged up the icy slope towards the farmhouse. He hoped they would help. The farmer had to have Maquis leanings or they would not have chosen his barn.

The farmer and his wife took little persuasion once they saw the children in the back of the old Citroën. The farmer's wife warmed soup for them all and they hid the car in the barn.

As Auguste shut the barn doors behind them, he realised people like the farmer and his wife were the true patriots of France. The men and women who supported their countrymen, who changed German slogans on walls, who resisted in the only ways they could. He realised also he had joined them. Despite his fears, a relief descended on his troubled, anxious mind. He was home.

2

'I have a corkscrew on my knife.'

Odette said, 'We have no cups.'

'Do we need them?'

'You will drink it all. I know you.'

Auguste smiled.

'Here,' he said and gestured with the bottle, 'Madame should taste the wine perhaps.'

They drank from the bottle, the wine felt like a mouthful of blackcurrant mixed with plums and cedar wood. Odette looked up at her husband. Her careworn face lit up with a smile.

'You were right to take the wine. It is too good for those German palates. I love you, my husband.'

'Are you sure they sleep this time?'

'We have only a few hours before dawn. Should we not sleep too?'

'Sleep is good. This is better,' Auguste said.

He reached for her and their lips met. His hands were everywhere, furtive, desperate. She responded mechanically at first; then over-whelmed by her feelings, she yielded to the passion welling up inside her. The pace of their touches and kisses slowed. They made love with gentle unhurried movements for they knew each other's bodies, and they both felt they had a right to this moment together. He, feeling desperate to blot out the world around and she, determined to take this one moment in a world where the future loomed uncertain.

After they finished, they lay on the straw of the stall and he drew her in close, to warm her and caress her. Auguste sighed, hearing the children moving in the straw behind the slats of wood separating the stall from where they lay. He closed his eyes and recognised he should have made different choices long ago, when it mattered. He knew also it would have changed nothing in the long term, unless he had become a political figure or fled the country. Exile in London with the Free French held no attraction.

He wondered why Arnaud had stayed. His allegiance was with the exiled French army, yet he stayed. He remained ready to create his own form of resistance. Brunner brought an end to it. Auguste was glad the Germans had not succeeded in torturing the old soldier who, like Pétain, was a relic of heroic times in the First War. Auguste wondered whether old soldiers retained their allegiances and if so, what was Pétain doing? He preached collaboration, but it was collaboration with Satan himself. Genocide. Such was unforgiveable in anyone's doctrine. He sighed with relief at his escape from the servitude cooperation which the Germans required of him. He finish-ed the bottle while Odette slept, curled up against him.

No sleep came to Auguste. He could not understand why, but he was fully awake all night. Thoughts about the night before haunted him. He wondered whether all the ruminating and self-examination had been in vain. He had done what he thought was right and the pain of it came now. He kept seeing Brunner's dead body sprawled on the Turkish rug, blood running from it, staining, damaging, as if even in death, the German had been as destructive as he had been in life.

He closed his eyes. All he could see was the front of Brunner's house and the sight of the man in slippers and a nightgown descending the stairs. Auguste sat up, he was sweating and his breathing had speeded up again. He wished his heart would slow but he knew it was simple anxiety. The long stress of what had gone before and the anticipated stress of what was to come combined to permeate his thoughts with fear.

A faint pre-dawn light lit the barn. Auguste heard a cockcrow outside and he realised whether he slept or not the children would soon awaken and need him as much as they needed Odette. He wondered how they would take to a new life in another country. Zara would cope, he was sure, she was clever at school and knew both French and German already. Monique was a different more serious child, but who could blame her? She had no one but Auguste and Odette. He reassured himself they loved her and would do what they could to save her and nurture her when they built this new life, this future in the land of milk and honey.

Dawn broke and the gentle light filtered through the small barred window above the double pine doors. Auguste reflected the day was new and his life too had changed, nascent and fresh, free of the burdens of his old existence. The light in the window brightened and a beam of sunlight reflected off the roof of his battered old car. It formed a cruciate design suspended for a moment or two in the air before it changed and faded.

He was neither superstitious nor did he feel as religious as some but he felt empowered as if a sign had appeared to guide him. He thought it might have been the lack of sleep but the more he considered the more it seemed to be a sign. Was it reclamation? Was it forgiveness? He had no time to ponder as the girls began to stir and yawn.

He smiled. He felt lighter in some way as he stood and brushed the hay from his clothes. Brunner's leather coat had kept him warmer than he felt he deserved and he removed it, wrapping Odette in the black leather. She stirred but remained asleep. He felt a tenderness touch him. She always evoked a feeling in him of wanting to nurture her, protect her. It seemed a contradiction. All he had done so far was endanger her with his personal sense of justice and now it was over, what had he achieved?

He watched her as the morning light waxed, her face illuminated by the daylight, dim and faint still. He thought she looked angelic. He shook his head. He wondered if he was going mad, absorbed in some religious reverie. He had things to do. He had to prepare for a long month of travel and he wondered whether the children would tolerate the hardship of it. He felt like a shepherd, preparing to guide his flock to the market eager to protect them from the wolves that roamed in the night.

He heard the girls, rapt in mumbled conversation, then he heard Monique yawn. He stuck his head around the post of the stall.

'Shh,' he said, pressing his fingers to his lips, 'Your mother is sleeping. Let us go outside quietly and see if we can find something to eat.'

They made their way towards the farmhouse, Auguste, in the middle, holding a girl's hand in each of his own. Another barn stood next to the farmhouse, from which the sounds and odour of cattle wafted on a fresh morning breeze. Auguste thought the farmer might provide some fresh milk. It threatened to be a long day. No one would be there to guide them until nightfall.

3

They rounded the corner of the barn. A military vehicle stood parked outside the farmhouse. Auguste pulled the girls back.

'Papa, will we have real fresh milk?' Zara said.

'Shh. Things have changed.'

'Things?' Monique said.

'There are soldiers here. We must hide. Run down to the barn and wake Maman, quietly now. Stay there. Hurry.'

Auguste stood hidden by the corner of the barn. The cock crowed again. He waited. He had no idea then how many soldiers there might be, but he checked his German-made Parabellum. The clip held eight cartridges and although no match for the semi-automatic fire of a Luger, it was the weapon he had trained and practised with.

He waited. He saw the girls running and they entered the barn. His hands were shaking. He needed to know what the car meant. Had they arrested the farmer? If they had, he would talk. Auguste and his family meant nothing to him after all. To him they were strays and whether or not the army was after them, they could not be worth dying for. He was breathing fast as he flattened himself against the wall.

Presently, he heard voices. He could not make out the words and he leaned forward to see better. He spotted two regular soldiers. Each carried a rifle. He saw one of them pass something to the farmer who smiled and thanked them. He pointed down the hill to where Odette and the girls hid.

The soldiers unslung their weapons and checked them. They were advancing down the hill shoulder to shoulder. They looked clean-shaven, eager and young, hardly older than twenty. Intent on the barn down the hill andneither looked around the corner of the nearer barn. Auguste heard the farmhouse door close. He let the young men walk five paces past him. He stepped out.

'Don't move,' he said. 'I'll kill you if you do.'

The gun trembled in his hand. His knees felt as if they might begin knocking together at any moment. He had an almost overwhelming desire to run. Sweat dripped, tickling, down his spine.

When it happened, it came fast. As one, the two Germans turned. They had no time to level their rifles. Auguste shot the one on the right in the chest. The soldier flew back as if hit with a pile driver.

The second, slower than the first, levelled his rifle. Auguste fired again, higher this time. He thought, through the smoke, he had missed. He threw himself forward onto the mud. His pistol remained pointing forward, ready. Nothing happened. The soldier stood for a moment and his rifle fell from his hands. He toppled forward. Auguste got up and looked. The helmet lay three feet away. A hole, the size of his fist oozed blood and brain at the back of the boy's head. He pushed the body over with his foot. The face seemed marred only by a neat hole in his cheek.

Neither of the Germans moved but Auguste moved. He ran towards the farmhouse. He was breathing fast but he knew the farmer had a telephone and anyone could hear the sound of his gun for miles around. He had no time to lose.

He burst through the door. The man stood with his back to him. He clutched a telephone receiver to his ear. Fury raged in Auguste's head at the treachery. Auguste raised the pistol as the man turned. He brought it crashing with full force into his betrayer's face. It landed with a crunch. The farmer fell towards the wall. The receiver hung from its twisted brown cord and swung back and forth.

Auguste listened. No sound in the house. He put the receiver to his ear. He heard an accented voice say, 'Are you there? Are you there?'

'Yes, I am here.'

'Hello. Who is this?'

'My father is outside with your men. The people in the barn left in the night.'

'They left?'

'Yes.'

'How do you know? You were told not to go near.'

'Your men have checked just now.'

'I ordered them not to do that. They were to wait for the others to arrive. Let me speak to them.'

'They just drove off. Shall I see if I can catch them?'

'No. More men will be there in a few minutes. What kind of car were the fugitives driving?'

'A black Renault. They said they were heading to La Gréze. They looked like partisans to me.'

'Very well. We will pay you well if we catch them. Let my men know when they arrive. Good work.'

The telephone went dead. Auguste wondered where the farmer's wife was hiding. He heard the farmer groaning as he pushed the door open. He ran past the bodies of the two soldiers, but on impulse retraced his steps. Stooping, he picked up the two rifles and although he felt he wasted time, he took a belt with ammunition off one of them. He turned and ran.

Rounding the corner of the barn, he felt a blow on his shoulder. He stumbled.

'Oh, Auguste. I'm sorry,' Odette said. She held a length of wood.

Zara giggled.

'Maman hit Papa,' she said.

'No time,' Auguste said. He picked up the rifles and shoved them into the car.

He said, 'We have to go. Hurry.'

'What is happening?' Odette said.

'Germans coming, any minute now. We have to go and quickly.'

It took seconds to pick up their belongings from the hay and get into the car. They drove out of the barn and down the road.

'Where are we going?' Odette said.

'We have to lie up until this evening. I know a place.'

'A place?'

'Yes. Trust me.'

She said nothing.

Monique said, 'I never got my milk.'

Odette looked at Auguste. She squeezed his hand where it rested on the gearstick. The expression on her face spoke volumes to him. The reassurance of her touch seemed to Auguste like a cool balm on sunburned skin. He realised he had killed two men. He had no qualms now. If his soul was in jeopardy, then it might as well be for something worthwhile and besides, saving his family could surely be no sin under heaven or on earth.

CHAPTER TWENTY SIX

1

Auguste headed north. He was aware his gasoline supply was pre-cious but he had to distance himself from the dead Germans and from Beynac. Two ten-litre cans stood in the back of the car but those were his reserves and he would have to conserve them. After twenty miles on winding potholed roads he turned left and began a climb up a wooded single-track lane. The Citroën's temperature gauge complained on the steep climb but he drove without hurrying, in low gear, and on they climbed.

At the hill's summit stood several buildings protected by a high, whitewashed, rendered wall. At the end of the track, a wooden door stood closed, a bell-pull swinging in the winter breeze. Auguste halted the car; he got out and approached the doors. He rang the bell and waited. He knew there would be a response.

Presently, the shutter opened and a face appeared framed in a brown hood.

'Yes?'

'Father, I am a traveller. I have my wife and two children in the car. I seek shelter and help.'

'What kind of help my son?'

'We are pursued by German soldiers. They are searching for us and can identify our car. We need to shelter until nightfall.'

'You cannot shelter here, my son. We do not take sides in earthly struggles. We can give you food and drink but we cannot shelter you.'

'I have been here before when I was a youth, on meditation with Père Bernard of Bergerac. Would you ask the Abbot? He might consider my pleas.'

The shutter closed. Auguste stood there facing the worn brown slats of wood, hoping. He shuffled from foot to foot. After several minutes, he turned and began walking to the car, shaking his head to Odette.

The bolts on the doors creaked as a monk opened them. The portal swung open and Odette started the engine of the ancient battered car. Auguste followed as she drove it in through the low archway. Entering the courtyard of the abbey, he heard the gates close behind them and saw a monk directing Odette towards a shed whose doors stood open and ready for the vehicle.

Odette approached, holding the children's hands. Auguste picked Zara up in his arms, her weight sitting on his hip as he walked. They climbed the steps and a monk showed them into a narrow cloister. Turning left, they proceeded to a doorway, where the cold stone floor echoed to their footsteps. They waited and the monk opened the door to a large room where long tables with benches stretched before them. It was a high ceilinged room where fifty could sit and eat. Beyond the dining hall, was another short corridor to the Abbot's office.

Auguste knew the layout, he had been here before, after all. He could never forget those three days. They were part of a happier life, one in which the future seemed so clear, so definite. Now all of it had gone, replaced by a shaky hope of better things to come, but a deep river of danger flowed in his path, one across which he knew he would have to venture.

The Abbott stood when they entered. He was an old man now

though he stood straight and walked forward with no visible limp or stoop. Auguste found his face familiar and he tried in desperation to recall the name, though it eluded him.

The Abbott, tall and angular, with a face furrowed by time, wore the same brown cassock as the other two monks and his baldness made his tonsure into a 'u'shape instead of a circle.

He reached forward to Auguste who took the proffered hand.

'I am Abbott Fernand. You are?

'I am Auguste Ran.'

'You have been here before? In happier times perhaps?'

'I was here for meditation twenty-five or more years ago. The memory has stayed with me ever since.'

'You wish to stay?'

'I need only shelter for my wife and children and our car until it is dark. Then we will leave. If the Germans get us we will be sent to Drancy and then? Who knows?'

'Have you committed crimes?'

'Crimes against the Germans. But no crimes against France or our people.'

'You have taken lives?'

'Yes.'

'The Church does not condone killing even by the Maquis. If the Germans find you here, they will shoot all the brothers. You have put us at risk.'

'Would they come here?'

'Perhaps not. We are of little interest to them. The Bishop has made bargains with them and they leave us alone.'

'You approve?'

'I did not express my opinion, my son, but you can guess by your treatment what I and the brothers believe.'

'I understand. I would not endanger you if I had any other choice. I have nowhere to run to.'

'This is your wife?'

'Yes, Father Abbott. Odette,' he signalled her forwards.

Auguste made the introductions and the monk who showed them

in led them away to the dining hall, where they were offered milk, bread and honey. Auguste watched as the children ate, observed by the monk.

His name was Brother Dominic. Auguste recognised the monk's local accent. He estimated the monk was a similar age to himself.

'Brother Dominic, you are from Bergerac?

'St Cypriene.'

'You know Père Bernard?'

'Yes, I know of him.'

'He was our priest.'

'Ah.'

'You disapprove of us, perhaps?'

'I disapprove of violence. I saw the weapons in your car. Bringing them here endangers us all and we believe only in peace and solitude.'

Auguste crunched an apple. He said, 'But you must have a view of what is happening?'

'I follow the views expressed by the Bishop of Rome. Pope Pius has expressed his views and I have no view other than his.'

A quiet voice came from the now open doorway to the Abbott's study.

'You seem troubled by the Church's view of the occupation?'

Auguste turned on the bench and faced the Abbott.

'We were only talking. Brother Dominic agrees only with the Pope, but neither of you knows the true extent of what the Germans are going to do to the Jews.'

'Extent?'

'They intend mass murder of all Jews. They are in league with Satan.'

'Perhaps so. But you have perhaps heard the Russians perpetrate the same inhumanity against Jews as the Germans?

'There are no Russians in the Dordogne Valley. Only Germans and the French people they persecute.'

'The Pope has spoken out against it. In his Christmas speech he said...'

'He did not condemn the Nazi murders of Jews, setting the

Church firmly against them. They are evil and the longer our Church keeps turning aside the more people will die.'

Animated now, the Abbott said, 'Have you not heard how Catholics are helping to hide Jews? How the church is finding ways for them to escape Germany and even France? If the Catholic Church were to speak out too loudly, the Nazi ire would be directed at the Church and we would be powerless to help. We could not save lives with our hands tied.'

'The Church should call upon all Catholics to fight the Nazi evil. Christ would never have allowed such a thing.'

'You speak of Christ? Do you not understand how Christ fought the Romans? He did it with peace and love.'

Frustrated now, Auguste shifted again on the bench.

'Peace and love will not help against a doctrine of extermination. I heard Himmler himself describe what they see as their final solution. They will murder all the Jews. It is evil and every man, woman and child in France, must stand up and throw out the invaders.'

'You are becoming agitated. We do not need to argue.'

Auguste put his head in his hands.

'Father Abbott, You are being kind to us. You risk your own life to help and protect us. Still, I cannot resolve the Pope's reluctance to call a crusade, if it is the right word, against a doctrine wanting to exterminate a whole race of people for nothing.

'Auguste my son, why do you think I am sheltering you here?'

'I... I...'

'It is because we all believe you are right, but our whole lives are spent following the edicts of the Church and the Holy Father in Rome. We cannot transgress. But in the way of Our Lord, if we have a chance to help people who need our assistance we cannot say no, out of charity and love.'

Odette said, 'please forgive my husband. He has been through terrible times. We are grateful and we follow the Church's teachings. We, like you, would never refuse to help one who needs it.'

'There is no need for us to argue. It is as God wishes. He has sent you here and we will do what we can for you.' Brother Dominic will show you where you can rest and you are free to wander the gardens and the Abbey as you wish.'

Auguste and Odette stood up as the Abbott left them. When he was gone, they resumed their meal. He wondered if he had overstepped the mark with the Abbott. He wondered too if in some way he had overstepped the mark with God and the Holy Church. He knew it made no difference. Escape was all that mattered now.

2

Their meal finished, Odette stood up.

'Brother Dominic, would you show the children the garden? If you have time, of course.'

'Of course,' the monk said, but his look was questioning.

Odette said, 'Girls, Brother Dominic will take you to see the gardens.'

'It's cold outside,' Monique said.

'The sun is shining. It will do you good to stretch your legs. Now, don't argue, children.'

They went with the monk. Alone, Auguste looked at his wife with an expression of gratitude as if he found the children a strain.

'What happened back there at the farm?' Odette said.

'Nothing special. We escaped didn't we?'

'Auguste, tell me the truth. What happened?

'I don't really want to talk about it.'

'Please, tell me the truth.'

She reached across the table and took his hands in hers.

'You know maybe?' he said.

'I know there were shots and then you came.'

'Is it not enough?'

'Please Auguste. I have to know how far we have sunk in this mire, this swamp of danger and war.'

'Well, there were two soldiers. Young men. Germans. I gave them a chance. I didn't shoot either of them in the back. I hailed them and told them to drop their weapons but they didn't.'

'You killed them?'

'Odette, you heard two shots. There were two soldiers, what do you think—we played card games?'

'What is happening to you? You killed two young men and you don't care?'

'To be honest. I killed Brunner because I knew it was justice. I have believed in justice all my life, but the system failed me, failed Bernadette. I planned his death but in the end, it was an accident. We are at war with Nazi Germany. Père Bernard told me the Church would condemn me for taking the man's life. He would believe I had lost my soul now. What difference does killing two soldiers make? They would have killed me, but I was quick. If I am damned, then I have leeway in the remnants of this life. Leeway to protect my family.'

They looked at each other. He realised she knew behind the expression on his face, behind the words, her Auguste was suffering. He buried his face in his hands. His shoulders rose and fell and the sobs came too.

Odette came around to sit beside him. Her arm a soft, gentle, weight encircling his shoulders, she said, 'Perhaps the Abbott can help. Perhaps if you give confession to him, he will absolve you.'

'He can't absolve me of mortal sin, can he? I have murdered. I knew what I was doing. I can hide behind the mechanism of it but the intent was there and it sits like a storm crow on a wall, ready to take me to hell.'

'Auguste. All the things we do on earth for the love of God and for those who love us, is seen and judged. The Lord is omnipresent, he knows what you are suffering and he will understand. It is true you took on His role and meted out justice to an evil man but I cannot believe you would face the same punishment as Brunner will. Our God is forgiving and kind. Go and ask the Abbott if he can take your confession.'

'No. I know you are right, but it makes us heretics does it not? To believe there is no Hell and sins are forgiven, when the Church teaches there can only be eternal suffering. So, I felt no pain when I shot those young soldiers. I did it without any feeling at all at the time. Only now, I think they were only boys. They had mothers and fathers, brothers and sisters who will mourn and suffer because of me. I have to live with those thoughts. I don't even know if it is a sin anymore.'

'Auguste, when we get to Switzerland, we have to repair. We will have to find the right road in our faith. Promise me?'

Auguste looked up. Her face shone in his eyes. He knew it was his mind wanting to see her this way, but he felt she radiated faith. It was not her faith, it was his. He believed in her more than he believed in the Church or its doctrines or any of the pressures they had faced or would in the future.

He reached for her hand and turning, he kissed her mouth. It was not erotic, but passionate all the same. She pushed him away.

'Not here. We are in a monastery.'

Auguste smiled. He said, 'I'm sure they would understand.'

'Auguste we were having a serious conversation.'

'Too serious. Come, let us find the children. My mind is so weary. I cannot think about these serious things all the time. We can ask the brothers for some wine. They love a drink.'

'A drink?'

'Yes, if there is one thing I learned last time I was here, it was the holy brothers have a capacity for wine only the Ancient Romans could have matched.'

3

They left the dining room hand in hand, as they walked out into the morning sunshine. Brother Dominic greeted them and smiled with un-expected warmth.

'Monsieur Ran, I have begun to realise what children have to offer, even in this serious place. Do you know what your daughters have done?'

'No.'

'They have begun to create a home over there.'

'A home?'

'They called it a "den". They are using last year's prunings from the trees to build a shelter.'

'Indeed,' Auguste said.

Auguste took his wife's hand and they walked down the hill towards where Brother Dominic indicated. Across a small lawn, they came to a privet hedge, a dubious guardian between the vegetable garden and the cultivated area in front of the abbey. He peered around the hedge.

Branches framed them and he could see Monique and Zara. They had built a lean-to shelter against the hedge. A long straight branch flew from the shelter.

'Got him, filthy German.'

'I'll shoot the other one.'

'Yes,' Zara said, 'kill them all.'

Auguste stepped out.

'What are you doing?'

'We're killing Germans,' Monique said.

'It isn't a nice thing for little girls to do,' Auguste said.

'Well you do it,' Zara said.

'What?'

'You do it. You killed Germans at the farm.'

'I... I...'

'Never you mind what happened at the farm. You should not have been listening in the car,' Odette said.

'Well it's true isn't it?' Zara said, looking at her father.

'We are at war, ma fleur. Not all Germans are bad. Even some of their soldiers are good men who do what their officers tell them even when they don't want to.'

'Then they are wicked all the same. It's no excuse.' she said.

Auguste stood and looked at his daughter. He wondered how one could argue with a child who spoke adult truths from a child's mind. A deep gloom began to descend upon him again because he had no answers. He looked away and then turned and walked back to the dining hall. His feet felt like leaden weights and he stared at the ground. It felt as if his whole world was rotten. He had been one of those people his own daughter had accused and he could not resolve the feeling she was speaking with a perspicacity to which no child was entitled.

Auguste felt like a man who has laboured long, digging in the dark, and when the light comes, he discovers he has dug a pit in the wrong place. If it was so, he felt he might as well jump into it. No absolution would be coming his way.

CHAPTER TWENTY SEVEN

1

The monks, true to their word, fed them and hid them until sundown. Auguste repacked the Citroën and as a red sun descended behind the dark green pines, they set off.

The monks offered no lengthy farewells or tearful adieus and Auguste knew, because of the palpable reality of the danger they brought with them, they had outstayed their welcome. The little girls knelt on the back seat and waved and the absence of similar gestures from their late hosts did nothing to prevent them from continuing until the monastery gates disappeared from view.

Dark descended and large errant snowflakes began to fall, challenging the windscreen wipers to disperse them. Even the heater betrayed an audible struggle and Auguste wished he had a different car in which everything functioned. He knew he would be parting with the vehicle anyway and he had no regrets over it; no sentimental attachment for this lump of metal betrayed him. It had served its purpose and measured against all he left behind, losing his car was a bagatelle.

Twenty miles along the road, they came to the main Sarlat road. The Beynac Chateau glared down at them, an ancient silhouette, a ruined piece of history like his own life, yet he knew it was not the same. He was leaving, rebuilding, reclaiming his life. He had not stayed to become ruined and broken, a relic for visitors to gawk at. He had a nascent future now; one with a meaning for him, and one, which was born of the evil he had escaped.

They turned right once they reached the Sarlat road and within two hundred metres turned right again, heading up through the darkened farmland towards Cazenac. The last time he was here came to mind and he shuddered at the thought of Linz's demise. The climb was steep in places and the car's wheels spun as he took the bends, though he was a confident driver and well versed in winter driving. A mile up the road, he saw the torch. The owner swung it from side to side and stood in a side turning on the left. To the right there were empty, open fields, created by the amputation of trees hundreds of years before.

He slowed at the turning. A tall figure approached. Auguste had his hand on his pistol and he drew it as the man came near. The torchbearer knocked on Odette's window with the torch. She wound it down a fraction, enough for her voice to be heard , but no more.

'Odette, don't you recognise me?'

'Pierre,' she said.

Auguste said, 'Pierre, is it really you?'

'Of course it's me. Are you going to leave me here in the snow?'

'Papa,' Monique said, She opened her door and ran to her father.

'Bubeleh, how I've missed you,' Pierre said. He laughed and Auguste found the sound was as welcome to him as a blazing fire on a winter's night.

Pierre hugged his child and Auguste felt emotions stirring. He knew this meant a lifting of his responsibilities and he relaxed into his car seat. If Pierre was here, he had no need to worry about Monique. He had discharged his duty and his obligations. Pierre knew how they could cross the border. Relief swept over him.

Greetings over, Odette sat in the back with the girls. Pierre occupied the front seat with a sten-gun across his knee.

Auguste drove on, ready to turn towards Sarlat and then Pèrigueux.

'What is the weapon?'

'A British sub-machine gun. They drop them to us with parachutes. Good for killing close up, but no accuracy.'

'I have two German rifles in the back.'

'Not much use to you in the back, my friend.'

'Pierre, how come you are here? I thought it would be someone else.'

'Well, it isn't. Not pleased to see me?'

'There is no one in the world I would rather have with us,' Auguste said and he meant it. 'I just got the impression you would send someone.'

'No. They refused, my friend. When I told them who you were, they refused to risk their lives for you. They know about the Vichy police and they felt there was no reason to risk themselves for you.'

'But I...'

'Yes, I know. They wouldn't help anyway.'

'How can we cross the border without their help?'

'They wouldn't help you, I said. They will help me. There is a boat moored already. We just have to be in the right place at the right time.'

'I have those papers with me. I would give them to you and take my chance with Odette and Zara, but we would not find the boat without you.'

'No, that's true. So how shall we do this?'

'I planned to drive to Lyon. From the hills south of Lyon, we can travel on foot. Two or three weeks,' Auguste said.

'If we can get closer in the car it will cut the time down.'

'I know, can we risk it?'

'We will have to see. North of Lyon would be better. What did you do with Brunner? I heard he had an accident?'

'Not exactly. We fought over a gun. I killed him.'

'We Jews have a saying: "Don't be wise in words, be wise in

deeds". You were wise this time, despite all the things you said about why you wanted him dead.'

'You will never understand. I think I have lost my soul for the sake of justice. I am a murderer.'

'We are all murderers. Joshua was the biggest murderer of all. Men, women, children, whole cities. I don't think he went to hell.'

'He was doing God's work.'

'And you weren't? God had a choice. He could have brought down thunder and lightning to save his poor sinner, Brunner. He didn't. You killed a sadistic German murderer. From the bloody cross on Calgary to the hell-camps in Poland, there is a lot of blood spilled. Hell will be overcrowded if He sends people with your qualifications to that place. Don't worry, my Catholic friend, I'll vouch for you to Saint Michael.'

'Saint Peter, Pierre. Saint Peter.'

'Whoever. You Catholics! You make anyone famous into saints. The Romans did the same. They made their Emperors into Gods. You make your heroes into demigods. What's the difference?'

'Pierre, we are driving into danger, do you want to have one of your religious discussions as we drive?'

'No. It's fine. Let's head towards Lyon and then see if we can get any further. We can have no defined routes without my brothers-in-arms on our side. If we make the border, their boat will get us to Switzerland and then it is all good.'

'Good? I don't know what I will do when I get there. I have no references and no backing for any policing jobs.'

'Auguste, we have another saying: "Make sure to be in with your equals if you're going to fall out with your superiors".'

Pierre's booming laughter came as a pleasant relief. Auguste wondered when he had last heard that sound. He realised it was a sound acc-ompanying his transition from childhood to adolescence and then into adulthood. He knew he loved this man. He felt complete in his company and he believed they could make it now. They drove on in silence and the children slept.

2

They drove north towards Periguex. Snowdrifts hampered them because the tiny unmade roads undulated with deep dips in places. They had to get out at times to push the car. The overriding thought in Auguste's mind was, when would they have to walk? He had brought good warm clothing for all of them and Pierre was used to living in the cold outdoors. Some of the time he questioned whether the entire episode, from Claude's death onwards had gone awry. He had killed four men. Two inadvertent deaths and two shots fired in self-defence, but it ate away at him all the same, as he pushed the car, as he munched his bread, as he cuddled his family.

Using small roads, they drove through Tulle. It was a large market town reminiscent of Bergerac. The town square, submerged by snow now, but tree-lined and no doubt cobbled, Auguste imagined, like home. Balconies peered out at them from grey and yellow houses, with peeling render and missing slates. Pierre guided them. He seemed to know where the roadblocks were and at first they made good time, but a military checkpoint at Ussel drove them north on more small winding roads in the direction of Thiers. Auguste wanted to head south of Lyon but Pierre insisted they head north first; he indicated the roads Auguste wanted to use would be impenetrable and swarming with Germans. By dawn, they were still driving and still undetected. The border became a distant mirage to Auguste. Even if they arrived there, he had no idea what they might find. It could be swarming with German troops, SS soldiers, or SD.

'Here, see the farm?' Pierre said.

He pointed to a light in the distance, shining like a far off beacon.

'The last farm I stopped at, the farmer telephoned the Germans.

He betrayed me.'

'He did?'

'Yes, it was the barn where you killed Linz.'

'You went there?'

Pierre laughed. 'It was the only place I could think of.'

'You are such a novice, Auguste. I'm surprised you survived to get that far.

'Oh, stop it. I do well enough.'

'The farmer, Gaillarde, is a collaborator. We picked his barn because we knew it was isolated and we knew he would have informed on us if we gave him the chance. We tied him and his wife up first before the attack. It was Josephine's idea. She thought there was a chance the Germans would suspect them of complicity. And you went back there. It's a mad world and someone up there must be looking after you.'

'Well, he sent for the Germans. I hit him.'

'I would have killed him.'

'Perhaps, I'm sick of killing. Sick of death.'

'Hah. You should run with the Maquis. Then you would see killing, my friend.'

The car drew to a halt outside the farmhouse. It was at the apex of a triangle of buildings and outhouses. The tiled roof had moss growing on it and the whitewashed walls looked like any other farmhouse in Saone-et-Loire. Auguste realised all his plans had changed since they picked up Pierre. They'd skirted Lyon to the north and headed so far in that direction according to his map they were near Digoin.

Pierre got out and walked to the door. Moments later a rugged looking man wearing a beret and leather jacket opened it. Auguste heard muffled conversation and Pierre signalled for the others to enter.

He had just emerged from the car when Pierre said, 'The farmer is a sympathiser. He said to put the car in the shed over there.' He indicated a dishevelled outhouse, with a gate hanging at an angle and looking as if it would fall off at the slightest touch.

He left Auguste to hide the car and entered the farmhouse.

Auguste did as his friend indicated and rejoined his family. The farmer was friendly and hospitable. He would not allow them to sleep in the barn and his wife arranged bedding for them all upstairs. This was a different welcome from the last one. Auguste remained distrustful but he wanted to believe in these people.

By late morning, Auguste and Odette found themselves alone in a darkened bedroom, the shutters closed and a sense of quiet content pervading the room.

'Did you sleep?' Auguste said.

'Yes, did you?'

'I slept better than for a long time. No nightmares about Brunner or the SD. Do you think we are safe here until nightfall?'

'Pierre said they have passwords used by the Maquis. He identified the farmer using a coded phrase. He thinks we are safe.'

They washed, using the basin and jug standing on the table in the corner of the room and together they descended the stairs. The farmhouse kitchen reminded Auguste of home but the memory caused pain, he knew, after all, he could not return until the war ended, if at all. Upstairs the children slept still and neither Odette nor Auguste had the heart to wake them.

Pierre came in then.

'Well, it seems there are plenty of wandering German patrols in this area. We have been luckier than I had hoped. We may get a clear run to the border north of Geneve, rather than south if our luck holds.'

'I wish I had your faith, Pierre,' Auguste said.

'If you had my faith you would be Jewish not Catholic.'

'Very funny. Are you never serious?'

'No. Seriousness makes me cry. I don't blubber in front of the goyim. So I laugh a lot.'

They ate and went outside to examine their gear. They knew they might have to abandon the car at any time if they were spotted.

'You're sure the boat will be there?' Auguste said.

'Yes. We can drop Odette and Zara at the bridge near Le Crèt. We head north from there along the Rhone for about a mile before the next bridge. It should be there, hidden in the trees.'

'You know the way?'

'I've heard it described. The thing about the Maquis is you can trust them. We fight together and we die together. It is a close bond. Many are young men who escaped being sent to Germany to their work camps, others are like me, yellow star men. Some are communists. No one cares and we are all equal.'

'You are going back?'

'No, my friend. I will never go back to that place. The people didn't protect me. They never lifted a finger. Only the Maquis.'

'You won't miss it?'

'Me? No. I will make a new life. There are Jews everywhere. We stick together. Anyway, it was Murielle's memory keeping me there. I miss her even now.'

'Naturally, my friend.'

They went through their provisions and gear in silence, each with his own thoughts. Auguste began to hope they would drive all the way to the border. But was the border safe? He had never been there and he knew nothing of the river where Pierre said the boat lay hidden. He realised he needed Pierre now. It was as if throughout his childhood and adolescence he had needed this man. Now that dependence escalated. He relied on his friend for his life and for that of his family. If anything happened to Pierre, there would be no border, no boat and no escape. The tension of that thought held him like a stanchion. His back ached, yet all he wanted then was to be on the road, to face what was to come and fight for the chance of deliverance for Zara, for Odette.

When dusk fell, they set off once more on the road to Le Crot. They hoped they would be able to make their way south-east afterwards, and head towards the border.

At the small town of Blanzy, they saw another roadblock, more by luck than design and so had to turn once more to the north, passing through Montsauche. By three in the morning, they stopped in Dun-Les-Places, a small village in Burgundy, far off their course. It became clear they would not reach the Rhone during this night.

CHAPTER TWENTY EIGHT

1

The village of Dun-Les-Places was no more than a crossroad with a group of houses stretching in each direction. Close to the centre they had built a church. It rose fifty feet into the air above the road. A small railing-protected churchyard separated it from the road and the spire looked to Auguste like a huge concrete pillar, reaching up to the sky. The wooden doors stood open even at this hour and he stopped outside, looking into the church. He could see candlelight and the chancel looked well lit, warm and welcoming. Three or four people emerged and he wondered if he had missed a Saint's day with a midnight vigil. He wracked his brain for the date but now he came to think of it, he had no idea whether it was still February or March. He was about to ask Pierre but felt foolish, as if the simple question would give him away, making him look stupid. He thought better of it and said nothing.

Pierre said, 'The village priest is one of us.'

'He's Maquis?' Odette said from the back.

'Yes, non-combatant but one of us.'

'You think he will shelter us?'

'Yes, of course, though we might have to sleep in the church.'

Auguste said, 'It will be a first time for you then?'

'Hah,' Pierre said and got out. Minutes later, he emerged from the church and when they had hidden the car, they entered the church through the front door.

The priest, Père Jean, welcomed them.

'We have an all night vigil in honour of St Romanus of Condat. He was buried near here. You may know?'

'No father I had not heard.'

'Perhaps his life as a hermit in the Jura made him obscure, but the two lepers he healed came from here and so we do this on the last day of February every year. Come, you will of course, be welcome in my church.'

He had grey, thinning hair and a round smiling face. His eyes were wide, brown and sharp. Auguste thought he looked like an old, greying owl.

Père Jean showed them to a corner of the church and pulled pews together to make a sleeping place for the children. When they had settled them, Auguste and Odette prayed.

'Do you wish to make confession?' the priest said.

Auguste looked at him with curiosity.

'I did, only a few days ago,' he said.

'But if your undertaking is dangerous it may be wise.'

Odette nudged him in the ribs. He stood then and Père Jean showed him to the confessional. Auguste went through the first stages of the ritual mechanically. He had no strong wish to comply and he kept asking himself why he was doing this.

He sat in the confessional in silence at first. The priest, no doubt used to hesitant penitents, spoke first.

'My son, what sins do you wish to confess?'

'Forgive me father I cannot wade through many small venial sins when greater ones weigh heavily on me. I cannot think what to say.'

'Then begin with the worst and we will gravitate to the minor.'

His confession was slow at first. With each sentence, the story became clearer in his head. The words became easier to speak and within minutes, he felt he had told all there was to tell about Claude's death and Brunner's murder. He told the priest everything, the places, the circumstances, even the expression on Brunner's face when he drew the German pistol. He left nothing out.

'You see, Père Jean. I am so mired in mortal sin, I cannot be forgiven.'

'What makes you say this? Have you lost your faith?'

'No father, I have lost my soul. The Church teaches that to take another's life knowing beforehand one is going to do it, will lead to eternal damnation.'

'But you were an instrument of justice. God's justice. Were you not?'

'I thought so. I did not do it for a personal grudge. I did it because he was evil, despite anything the church may say to the contrary.'

'Of course he was evil. All of these Nazis are evil. They commit their atrocities and their genocide in full view of the Lord God. Such things cannot go unpunished or unresisted.'

'But the Church does not speak out against them.'

'My son, there has been more evil perpetrated in the name of the Church than I care to think of. It is not the dogma that matters; it is what is in your heart and in your mind. Did you know when the knights went on crusades, there was always a priest to bless them when they boarded ship? He would say that it is not a sin to kill an infidel, it is the path to heaven. If it was wrong, then many went to hell unknowingly. They were good Christians too.'

'I don't understand.'

'My point is this, soldiers of Christ have fought evil for a thousand years, or at least what they perceived as evil. You have only done the same, perhaps not for God, but before God. It is no worse in God's eyes than a soldier in a war.'

'But I killed those two young soldiers too.'

'You defended yourself and your family Auguste. I do not know you, but I understand your motives and I bless you for them. Whatever my Church's dogma may say, you have not sinned and I will give you absolution.'

'But you do not represent the Church in this?'

'Of course I do, I am an ordained priest.'

'Are you not condoning my sins?'

'Not condoning. You care, you see. If you did not, it would be hard to absolve you. Let me give you absolution.'

Père Jean spoke the Latin ritual and for Auguste it was as if it washed over him. The words flowed and although he hungered for it to end, Auguste felt, layer by layer, his sin stripping away. Deeds, words, choices, circumstances, slipped from him. Doubt, anxiety, uncertainty were replaced by a conviction he had been right. When he emerged from the confessional it was as if he was reborn, a weight lifted and his mood elevated. All his ruminant thoughts seemed wasted now. He wondered whether the purging of his soul would make his remaining life safe.

Looking at the priest, his eyes moistened. It was involuntary and he heard Pierre's voice in his head saying 'of all the men I know, you are the most readily brought to tears.' He wondered whether it came from childhood or recent times. Pierre did not understand. It was a matter of soul and conscience. How could a man be unemotional about that? It was a matter of the soul foremost, his very being, according to his beliefs.

Would his soul now rest secure in the arms of this reprieve? Forgiveness was something he believed in but he could still find no trace of it in his heart for Brunner. He remembered the look on Brunner's face when they hanged the five Frenchmen. He pictured how the man licked his lips, the smile at the end and his wish to celebrate. Brunner had been a demon and Auguste knew the truth of it now; he had fought God's good fight and now, absolved, he was free. He felt liberated as never before.

He took the priest's hand and looked him in the eyes.

'Père Jean, I am truly grateful.'

'Bless you my son, but I am only fulfilling the role thrust upon me by God. I will carry your burden for you. Put all those troubles behind you.'

Auguste turned away and as he walked towards his wife, he thought her face shone with the love he felt for her. He felt he was now free to love her, as she deserved, without the fetters of his darkened conscience, without a tarnished soul.

Odette smiled at Auguste as she stood to approach the priest. Auguste touched her shoulder, reassuring and gentle. She smiled and approached Pére Jean. Auguste watched as she crossed herself and entered the confessional. She gave her confession and Auguste noted she prayed for half an hour afterwards. He stood looking at her from the doorway and he wondered what she could have confessed. He could not imagine her to be a sinner. He concluded love alters the way you see other's actions and words.

A hand on his shoulder interrupted him.

'Is your soul cleansed now, my friend?'

'Pierre, you are such an irritating bastard.'

'I'm no bastard. I'm a Jew,' Pierre said, grinning from ear to ear.

They rested for the remainder of the night and Auguste slept deeply, as if the absolution from this renegade priest had taken away his burden of guilt over the killings. When he woke, he began to doubt again whether this priest could, in reality, forgive his crimes. He was certain the larger crime, the internments and arrests under his orders, could not be forgiven and he realised he had never mentioned these to anyone except Odette.

Mid-morning came and went and the girls seemed rested. He walked out but there seemed nowhere to go. A hundred yards along the road, he stared back at the church. A picture came into his mind of bodies, lying haphazard in death, limbs twisted and tangled. Above a figure swung, hanged from the spire. The picture disappeared in a second and did not come again. He wondered at the vision and thought his over-wrought mind played tricks on him. He said nothing but he knew he was still under pressure.

Then he heard the trucks. From where he stood, there was a good view of the northern road and upon it, he saw three military trucks approaching. The pitch of the engines rose and fell as the trucks negotiated the pitted and uneven road and they seemed to Auguste to be moving at a ponderous pace. He ran. He had to warn his family. Where could they hide in the village? If it came to a fight, he resolved they would not take him alive. But what of the children? His heart raced, he sweated and he arrived at the church steps too breathless to speak.

2

'Auguste. What's wrong?'

Odette came to his side, Pierre behind her.

Breathing hard, Auguste said, 'Soldiers. Trucks. Three of them, coming this way.'

Pierre turned. He ran to the back of the church to the vestry. In a moment, Père Jean appeared signalling them to come. Odette and Auguste roused the children. Bewildered as they were, the whole group stood with the priest in front of the altar. Père Jean leaned forward and pushed. The silence gave way to a grating sound and the altar pivoted back revealing stairs to an underground cellar.

'Quick, hurry,' the priest said and without thinking further they descended to the damp earth-lined space below ground.

In seconds, the darkness enveloped them. It felt like jumping into a dark pool and realising there would be no light, only movement. Auguste lit one of his remaining matches. It provided enough illumination to find a small oil lamp standing against the far wall. He lit the lamp and by its poor illumination, they could see they were in a hollowed out space capable of holding twenty or so people.

Auguste held the lamp aloft but there was nothing else to see.

'Dowse the light,' Pierre whispered, his voice conveying the urgency they all felt. August doused the lamp. They stood still and listened. August became aware of a small hand grasping his and he squatted down and picked up the child. He was uncertain at first whether it was Zara or Monique.

'Shh,' he whispered.

Monique whispered back, 'Yes Uncle.'

The sibilant sounds of their voices resounded in the cellar-space and all of them realised the walls amplified every sound. They stood in silence. Monique shivered in Auguste's arms and he held her tight.

There was a sound above them. Auguste could hear booted feet clacking on the flagstones. He felt for his gun, with his left hand still clutching Pierre's daughter. His eyes became accustomed to the dark and he identified a chink in the otherwise perfect blackness above him, where they had descended. The ray of light blinked at him and he knew there were men walking back and forth.

In the silence, they stood waiting. Auguste sweated. He racked his brain trying to recall whether they had left any trace of their night's sleep in the church. He trusted the priest to have checked, but in his policing experience, he had learned to check things himself. He felt his heart beating against his ribs and his breathing quicken.

Auguste found himself praying. He began with, 'Hail Mary Mother of God...' the line repeating itself in his head over and again. Silence reigned all around him. No one spoke and no one moved.

It seemed an age before anything happened. In reality Auguste knew it could only have been half an hour or so, but the time seemed to pass with such dreary sluggishness the little girl he was holding began wriggling and squirming. He let her go and she must have felt her way to her father for he heard the word 'bubeleh' whispered soft and deep. He was on the verge of panic. He wondered if at any moment, the altar would slide away and German rifles would cast a threatening silhouette against the daylight. Worse still, a grenade would be enough to finish them all for good.

He heard the grating sound of the moving altar. The gun in his hand weighed heavy. With legs apart and both hands on the pistol, he stared hard, forcing himself to see despite the bright white threatening to blind him.

No guns, no soldiers. Only Père Jean smiling down at them.

'Come up now my children, come up. They have gone away. They came in, they looked around as they always do. What they hope to find in a church I cannot conceive. They ransacked a few houses and then they went away again. It is a minor annoyance we have to put up with from time to time. Please, come.'

Auguste hesitated. In his mind, he pictured soldiers, guns and threats forcing the priest to call them up. His brain worked as he tried to plan how he would defend them against so many. A police officer not a soldier, he was untrained in such things. Glancing over his shoulder, Pierre seemed relieved and reassured.

The priest's proffered hand and smiling face seemed to pacify, to beckon. They emerged into the church and saw the priest was right, no soldiers were in evidence and Auguste heaved a sigh of relief. He wondered if all the constant stress had made him paranoid, but understood it was caution not some fictitious imagining.

In the late afternoon, Père Jean brought food and they made ready to depart. A clear sky above them and a red sunset ahead, they set off south and east. Luck had brought them this far and Auguste's imagined trek, hiking though unknown woods and forest seemed a long dream away from the realities of travelling with Pierre.

CHAPTER TWENTY NINE

1

They by-passed Autun and kept on farm tracks and small roads, hoping to go unnoticed as they travelled. Auguste concentrated on keeping the little Citroën on the road. A light sprinkling of snow lay around them. Frost began to spread icy tendrils across the tracks and paths. Dark pine forest alternated with desolate unploughed farmland. High up now, the temperature plummeted and the icy journey continued. The travelling was less easy than Auguste had imagined; the ice and frost made some of the roads slow and dangerous.

He knew German soldiers could stop them at any time. They had only to reach a checkpoint and try to flee and it would be enough. Shots would be fired, military vehicles would follow them and it would all end. The border seemed an intangible goal to him then, a holy grail to which he looked for safety and salvation. He said nothing to the others but his anxieties rose and fell almost like the undulating roads upon which he drove.

No more checkpoints barred their way and an hour before dawn, travelling down a forest track; they came to a dead-end, close to the small village of Le Crêt, a kilometre from the Bellegarde bridge. He had driven two hundred kilometres since dusk. It was here they realised the car could go no further. Whether there were reports of their escape or not, the chance of the soldiers recognising the car was a real one and neither Auguste nor Pierre felt the risk was worthwhile.

They stayed parallel to the road, trudging through sparse woodland and fields until houses began to be more frequent.

'How far Pierre?' Auguste said. He was carrying both rifles and a backpack, one hand holding Zara's and Odette beside him.

'I would guess half a kilometre. We have to part at the main road if Odette and Zara are to get across safely.'

'Are there soldiers?'

'Of course there are soldiers. There is a large checkpoint on this side of the river. No one gets across in daylight. We have little time now before dawn.'

Trudging now along the road, they came to a crossroad signposted 'La Route de Chapelle'. There were no cars, and no lights lit the road. They took the westerly road until the road curved to their right. Trees marched either side of the road here and they walked until they could hide in sparse woodland with dense scrub and bushes.

They had almost reached their goal. Could it still go wrong? Auguste dared not voice his fears. He knew both Odette and Zara needed support but he had a growing feeling deep inside there were more dangers to face. He worried the boat might not be there. He knew the guard on the bridge could turn Odette and Zara away, leaving them with the fierce and dangerous choice of the river crossing by boat. It was clear to him if the soldiers spotted them getting into the boat, the entire garrison would be taking aim at them. He pinned his hopes on the letters of transit. Even though Brunner was dead, his signature and the SD stamp on the letters, should add enough weight to the documents. They had to be enough.

Odette had not spoken since they left the car. Auguste looked at her face as they set down their gear in a thicket under a large elm tree.

He knew all the way from the car what she must feel. He had a feeling akin to despair and his chest felt tight as if his heart weighed heavy in his chest.

'You and Zara must go. You have the letters of transit?'

'Yes,' she said.

Pierre embraced her and she knelt to hug Monique.

Auguste took her hand.

'It will be fine, you will see.'

'Can't we all go by boat?' she said. 'I don't want to be separated from you Auguste.'

'This is the safest way. With those documents it is certain you will be able to cross without any questions.'

'Perhaps Pierre and Monique could go.'

'I don't know where the boat is and I have never been here before.'

'But what if they catch you?'

'Then you must make a new life. It will be all right. Come, how hard do want to make this for us both?'

He looked down at Zara, her tired eyes looked up at him and he smiled.

'Papa, where are we going?'

'You and Maman are walking across a big bridge, ma fleur and I will come later with Pierre and Monique.'

'When will you come?'

'Soon,' Auguste said and kneeling among the dark brown leaves, he hugged her to him. 'Never forget your Papa loves you. Never forget it.'

'I love you too Papa.'

He took Odette in his arms and kissed her mouth. He wiped the tears from her face and said, 'I love you my wife. I will see you in a few days. Take care of our little flower.'

Odette said nothing. She looked at Auguste then turned and taking Zara's hand, she led her away toward the road. She did not look back, but Zara did. She waved to Pierre and Monique and then again to her father. In the pre-dawn light, she did not see his tears.

Auguste, Pierre and Monique pushed through the wood to where they could see the military checkpoint. They lay on their stomachs, hidden by a low hedge of rosehip.

Auguste saw Odette did not flinch as she showed the papers to the soldier who manned the checkpoint. He could see the soldier smiling and passing some comment, but his wife and child had their backs toward him and he could not see their faces.

His relief at that moment threatened to overwhelm him. A deep sorrow overtook him too. He had a feeling he would never see them again.

2

'And now?' Auguste said.

'Now my friend, we walk through this wood and cross some fields and then down to the river. With any luck we will get across and meet Odette and Zara in a day or so.'

'It sounds easy.'

'No, better than that. Our freedom is inevitable. Come Monique.'

The little girl took Auguste's hand as if she could feel his pain and with Pierre in the lead, they struggled through the ever-thickening wood. She squeezed his fingers and Auguste who understood her meaning, reciprocated.

Auguste could think of nothing but Odette and Zara. He wondered where they would go once they were across the bridge. Neither of them had been to Genève before but they agreed to rendezvous at St Peter's Cathedral. Everyone knew how the Calvinists had taken it over but it was a well-known landmark all the same. He calculated if it took another day to cross over, then another day might suffice before they could be reunited.

Half a mile on, Pierre stopped. He seemed to be listening.

Auguste, impatient behind, said, 'What?'

'I don't know. I thought I heard something.'

'I didn't.'

'Hush. Keep your voice down.'

Pierre indicated with his flat hand for them to get down.

Auguste heard it then. A faint sound of twigs breaking. Feet, trudging behind them. He looked around; nothing. They squatted in low scrub at the edge of the wood. Before them, a wide field faded into a faint layered mist over a raised bank and he guessed the river must bend in that direction. The sound became louder and he heard voices. The language was guttural, it was not French. Pierre in front lay flat and August pulled Monique down further. He placed his arm around her, covering her.

He could feel sweat forming beneath his collar, his mouth as arid as when he rang Brunner's doorbell. Nausea spreading from his stomach. Not far now. Only yards to go; now this. He was living and breathing the life of Job and he knew it. It was as if this was some kind of test, sent by God. He would not crack. He knew after all he went through to get here, he possessed the strength and will to come through.

They waited lying down, damp and dishevelled, expectant and tense. Nothing happened. The sound of the tramping feet faded. All became as still as Saint Sacerdos' Cathedral at night. Auguste gripped his rifle. He knelt. He sighted all around but saw nothing. Still they waited. Minutes passed.

'Auguste, they've gone I think,' Pierre said, his voice a croaking whisper.

'Are we going now?' Monique said.

'Yes my little one,' Auguste said, 'now we go together to freedom and happiness at last.'

They stood, each of them looking around for any kind of movement. There was none.

Auguste heard vehicles on the road to his right. He wondered whether they were taking soldiers away or bringing them. Inside, he knew no one would be searching for them here but he also understood how, if they were seen or questioned, they had no papers and no explanations. The sweat on his neck made the collar chafe and he ran his fingers around the rim.

Progress was slow. The ground was muddy and the bushes reached up with spiky fingers prodding and scratching as they pushed their way forward. A shout sounded to their right and they lay down again. Another shout, German voices, this time further forward. They belly-crawled for a hundred yards and then stopped by a hedge in front with a dry-stone wall to the right.

In a whisper, Pierre said, 'Auguste. You stay here. Keep her close.'

Auguste grabbed his arm.

'What are you doing?'

'I'm going to see where they are.'

'No, I'll go. You stay with Monique.'

Pierre turned towards his friend. He smiled. 'You have experience in this? No. I will go. This is what I've been doing ever since I left Monique behind. It's what I do. Get through the hedge if you can. I'll be back.'

'Papa. Don't go,' Monique whispered.

'I'll be back in a moment Bubeleh. Stay here with Uncle Auguste.'

Auguste watched Pierre's brown muddy soles disappearing in front as he crawled away. An odd thought came into his head. Since childhood, they were friends, competitors and rivals. The final curtain was now lifting. Auguste possessed no doubt about whom Pierre was or what role he played. He was a hero. He always had been. He taught him to smoke; he taught him to fish and now the lesson was one of risk and stealth. Yet there was no jealousy now, only a deep admiration for his friend. It was as if, from the moment he saw him in the square, on his bicycle, defiant and angry, Pierre continued to grow in Auguste's eyes. Perhaps he always was a hero and Auguste failed to understand it. It was always Pierre who seemed to save him, rescue him and redeem him even from the collaborationist path he once trod.

They lay still for further moments then crawled forward. A ditch lay before them, the length of the hedge. Muddy and cold, it stretched for half a mile, as far as Auguste judged. Turning to the left, with Monique in front, they searched the hedge for a gap. A shot rang out. Then another. They collapsed down, ossified for moments, both of them. Then they moved again. He could see Monique trembling as she shifted forwards, her little knees wobbling as she crawled.

Hurrying, Auguste pushed the child forward through a hole in the hedge. It was too small for him to follow. Monique turned, still lying flat, her face up to the gap. The look in her eyes told him everything. He shared her fear, as a man might wince at another's broken bone.

'Wait there,' Auguste said.

He pressed his index to his lips, hoping she would not cry. He was leaving her. There was no other choice and her distress burned him as if he was abandoning her. He had to find a way through, without being visible. And the sounds of many feet and German voices came ever closer.

3

He crawled. He prayed too. A gap must appear, there had to be a way through.

Then relief. A space appeared where he could pull out some rocks. He created enough of a gap to crawl through.

Another shot. This time he felt it too. It felt as if someone had thumped him on the backside and he flew through the hedge. There was pain from his right buttock to the back of his thigh, a searing discomfort as if some huge dog savaged him, snapping jaws biting, tearing.

Fighting the pain, he knew to stay would be his death. Frantic now, he crawled again to the right to find the little girl; to flee, hide. Ten yards, crawling. Twenty yards, stumbling and limping, keeping his head down below the hedge top. Desperation drove him on. Had he lost her? How could he explain to Pierre? She had to be there. His breath came in gasps, his heart thumped in his chest and his eyes searched for some sign. Forty yards and he could see her.

Still stooping and hobbling he took her hand as a man might scoop up a ball on the run and she needed no encouragement, no urging. She let go his hand and set off ahead.

They ran in this way for a hundred yards and came to the stone wall. He lifted her over and followed, his right leg feeling weak but useable still. Auguste felt the wound with his hand. It was superficial, the bullet must have grazed him. To him, it was a ridiculous wound. They heard more voices, distant now. They lay still.

Twenty minutes passed and they said nothing, neither Auguste nor Monique daring to move.

A sound above them made him grab his rifle.

A whispering voice said, 'Auguste? Auguste?'

It was Pierre.

'Here. I've been shot.'

Pierre clambered over the wall.

'Shot?'

'Only a graze. They shot me in the arse.'

Pierre reached out and drew his child to him.

'With your backside, how could they miss?'

They both smiled. The tension ebbed but they knew they could not move yet. Almost an hour passed in which every sound, every movement seemed filled with threat, though the pursuit seemed to have ceased.

August thought of Odette and Zara. Were they safe? Would his God not guide them? He prayed in silence but the Hail Marys seemed stale in his mind somehow. Nothing could reassure him except the sight of his two loved ones, his two reasons for living.

They stayed there for another hour. Time passed. Pierre looked over the wall and reassured no one could see them, they tramped on through the muddy ditch and then back into a field.

They plodded on, hampered by the dense bushes, and came to a wide expanse of brown, untilled fields. Keeping to the hedgerows, they climbed a steep bank and to Auguste's relief he saw the river flowing fast below. It was forty meters wide here and the strength of the current made it impossible to swim. They needed the boat.

'Auguste, you wait here with Monique and I'll find the boat.'

They waited. Auguste and Monique sat beneath a hedge but they were silent. They had nothing to say to each other and the absence of conversation seemed comfortable. Within minutes, Pierre returned. He sat with them.

'I found it. I've dragged it to the bank. A little push and we are away.'

He was smiling and for once, Auguste smiled too. He could feel the sway of the current on the boat already. They stood and Auguste looked over his shoulder. Something attracted his attention; he was unsure what it had been. He reached a hand towards Pierre and held him still.

'I saw something,' he said.

'What? We have only a hundred yards to freedom. Come.'

He strained against Auguste's hand and then they climbed the few yards up the bank. Auguste heard the shot before he felt it. It was like someone kicking him hard in the back. The violence of the impact pitched him forward and he lay face down, immobile. No pain came at first, then a dull ache began to gnaw him. Pierre lay on his stomach, the sten-gun cracked its staccato tune. Auguste heard more rifle fire. He tried to get up. His legs would not respond. He felt nothing below the waist. Confusion struck him. What was happening? He felt pain below his ribs on the left side. He reached down. It was as if a huge hole opened up to his groping fingers and he knew. No flesh wound. No bandages and hot soup.

'I think they are being more careful. I may have hit one. The field is crawling with them. They must have seen me with the boat. Here, let me help you up Auguste. Monique, come.'

Monique sat, her face in her hands, higher up the bank. She did not move. Auguste said, 'Pierre. My legs, they don't move. I can't feel them. Leave me.'

'Hah, you goys are all the same. Give up at the least discouragement. Here.'

'No. Look.'

Auguste lifted the edge of Brunner's coat. The hole gaped, though Auguste could not see it. He could see Pierre's face though. He knew without looking, he was losing blood. His breath came in ever increasing gasps as if hunger for the very air surrounding him became a priority. Dizziness came too and a cold sweat.

'Tie your scarf around me, tight. It may staunch it a little. Then get me to the top there.'

'What? I'll carry you.'

'No, it's no use. Do it. There is no time. Leave me the sten-gun and a rifle. Hurry man.'

With trembling fingers, Pierre took off his long woollen scarf. He tied it over the wound and watched the blood trickling through. It mixed with the tears dripping from his face onto the green wool.

He placed his hands under Auguste's armpits and dragged him the few yards up the slope, next to a rock and a bush providing some cover at least, to the right. He rolled his friend over in silence. Auguste groaned. It took no more than a minute.

Auguste looked up at him.

'Pierre...'

'Don't say it. You know I will look after them.'

'I know. Now go while I can still focus to shoot. Hurry. I won't be long.'

He tried to smile his encouragement but all he managed was a grimace.

'Monique. We must go. Hurry.'

He took the child's hand. She turned.

'Uncle Auguste,' she said. She was not crying. 'I will never forget you.'

'Say kaddish for me sometime, Monique.'

This time he managed a smile and he turned away from her as best he could. He did not look back for them again. Focussing his attention on the field below, he saw a man stand and run stooping, towards him. The German had a brown uniform and carried a rifle. It was a distance of a hundred yards and Auguste aimed the rifle. He took carful aim. He fired. A spray of mud flew up in front of the advancing soldier. The man dived. Auguste lost sight of him.

A darkness began to impinge on his peripheral vision. He shook his head. He had to buy time. He saw nothing ahead. No movement in the early morning light. He had difficulty holding his head up. A thirst such as he had never felt before raged in his mouth and throat. He managed to reach to his breast-pocket. He found his cigarettes. It took a superhuman effort, but leaning on his elbows, he extracted a Gitanes and lit it. He realised with chagrin, he had used his last match.

The aromatic smoke hit the back of his throat. His head did not spin as it always had done before. His vision sharpened instead.

A stray thought appeared. He was going to see St Peter. The angel would judge him. Had the Maquis priest lied to him or had he received absolution? Did it count?

Another soldier to his right stood up and ran, crouching, towards him. Auguste's vision was clouding over. He stuck the cigarette in the corner of his mouth and took aim. He did not care where the bullet landed, as long as it kept their heads down. The recoil against his shoulder jerked his upper body and made him grunt with pain.

'Odette, where are you?'

'Ma fleur, will you remember me?'

Sounds and pictures. Voices from the past. His mother, her arms open, taking him in her arms. His father, pipe stuck in his mouth, scolding.

Auguste shook his head. He fired the gun. It could have sent the bullet anywhere. He ceased to care. His eyes began to close. The heat of the cigarette-end woke him. It burned his lip. He thought five minutes must have passed. Was it long enough? Could he leave now?

He groped at his side for the sten-gun. He had never fired one before and he fiddled with the safety catch. By mistake, he set it to 'on'. He realised the mistake in his confusion and flicked it up. He fired a burst. The recoil made his hand judder and the spray of bullets flew in a random pattern.

His eyes darkened but he could still hear. It felt as if he was there but also somewhere else.

He felt a pressure on his shoulder. All remained black.

A deep voice said in German, 'He's dead.'

'No,' said a second, 'still breathing a little.'

'He was a rotten shot. If he'd been a professional, he could have got me twice at least.'

Auguste wanted to open his eyes. He wanted to tell them he had no wish to kill them.

A girl's voice in his head whispered, so soft he strained to hear it, '*Te absolvo.*'

Then Auguste heard the girl's faint laugh, like tinkling silver bells and he understood.

It was the gentle voice of an angel.

EPILOGUE

The camera crew stood silent in the gloaming. The darkening room seemed smaller to all of them and the interviewer realised he still sat forward in his chair. He leaned back and a wave of exhaustion flowed over him. His back ached.

Zara looked up as if expecting comment. The interviewer stood up. For once, he had nothing to say. He glanced at his watch. Six-thirty. No lunch today. He noticed how his stomach rumbled and became aware of the hypnotic quality in the old woman's story.

'I… I…'

'Yes?' she said.

'It's late. We had another inter…'

His voice faded as if anything he had to say became meaningless. It was his first time. He was a virgin in the arms of a gigolo. He realised how when he walked into the room he was confident, smug. Those feelings now departed. They were replaced by the kind of humility he never imagined he could feel before an old lady, a woman whose life was, after all, spent.

He wanted to tell her how he felt, but this time, no words came.

'You liked my father's story?'

'I… I…'

She smiled a wan smile and stood. 'Can I go to the WC now? Doesn't time fly?'

When she returned, the men had packed up. It took time for them to load the van. The media man, the man in charge, the boss, stood in the sitting room. He felt embarrassed but he had no idea why he felt like this.

Zara said, 'I hated them all you know.'

'What?'

'Not my father. To him I was his little flower. The rest of them I mean.'

'You hated them?'

'Monique took my father from me. He died to save her. He died to save Pierre too. My mother allowed it to happen. She must take the blame as well. My papa was a wonderful man. If those Jews hadn't come along he would still be alive. Monique ruined my life.'

'But... but don't you care how he felt about it? He gave his life for them because he was a good man.'

'You think that helped me? Do you think I care about that? I lost the only person who loved me unreservedly.'

She picked up the cap-badge from the low table by the chair.

'See this?' she said, 'This piece of metal is all I have left of him. He loved me and I will never forgive them for letting him die.'

Her face was different now. Not old and wrinkled. The interviewer wondered if the half-light played tricks on him but it was almost as if she was a young woman, animated and furious.

'Right-ho. Well, we'll have to be off then.'

His exit was swift.

Zara stood looking at the closed door and she could hear a voice in her head.

'Never forget your Papa loves you, never forget.'

A slow smile came to her furrowed face as she returned to the chair in the sitting room, where she sat staring out of the window at the gathering dark.

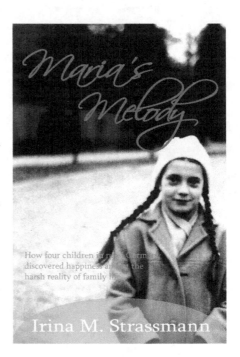